"AND THE 'PROFESSOR' IS YOUR LOVER?" SAM DEMANDED TO KNOW.

"That's none of your business."

"I'm only asking out of concern for your welfare."

"Please, Sam, don't patronize me."

"I'm not. I mean it."

Maryanne's eyes narrowed as she retorted, "Sam, we've had this conversation—or a version of it—at least twice before. I suppose it's just typical of your gender to simply ignore what I said."

"Excuse me if I don't follow you."

"You're not excused. I'll repeat what I hoped I'd made clear before. I don't need any man's concern for my welfare. *I* know what I want. *I* make up the rules for what goes on in my life. Including the man I choose to date . . . or to be my lover."

Sam's gaze held for a long, silent moment. When he spoke, his voice was low and direct. "Then perhaps you'll consider me a candidate for that honor."

CANDLELIGHT ECSTASY SUPREMES ®

ALL IN GOOD TIME

Samantha Scott

A CANDLELIGHT ECSTASY SUPREME

Published by
Dell Publishing Co., Inc.
1 Dag Hammarskjold Plaza
New York, New York 10017

With love to Jeffrey, John, and Sam.

Dell ® TM 681510, Dell Publishing Co., Inc.
Candlelight Ecstasy Supreme is a trademark of
Dell Publishing Co., Inc.
Candlelight Ecstasy Romance®, 1,203,540, is a registered
trademark of Dell Publishing Co., Inc.

ISBN: 0-440-10099-2

Printed in the United States of America
First printing—April 1984

To Our Readers:

Candlelight Ecstasy is delighted to announce the start of a brand-new series—Ecstasy Supremes! Now you can enjoy a romance series unlike all the others—longer and more exciting, filled with more passion, adventure, and intrigue—the stories you've been waiting for.

In months to come we look forward to presenting books by many of your favorite authors and the very finest work from new authors of romantic fiction as well. As always, we are striving to present the unique, absorbing love stories that you enjoy most—the very best love has to offer.

Breathtaking and unforgettable, Ecstasy Supremes will follow in the great romantic tradition you've come to expect *only* from Candlelight Ecstasy.

Your suggestions and comments are always welcome. Please let us hear from you.

Sincerely,

The Editors
Candlelight Romances
1 Dag Hammarskjold Plaza
New York, New York 10017

CHAPTER ONE

The peach-colored chiffon dress swayed gently against her ankles as Maryanne waited in the dimly lit corridor. She smiled cheerfully up at her husband, an unsuccessful attempt to veil the nervous anticipation playing havoc with her insides, and watched intently as he checked the door to make sure it was shut, then turned back to her once more.

"All set?" His dark eyebrows lifted briefly for a moment, then settled back into place above his deep, jet-black eyes.

"Mmmm." Maryanne raised a hand to push back a nonexistent stray tendril of softly curling honey-blond hair.

Elliot Douglass winked conspiratorially at his wife. "You're gonna knock 'em dead, honey."

Maryanne drew in a small breath and let it out in a whoosh. "I doubt that, but thanks anyway."

They walked down the corridor together, reaching the elevator just as it arrived. Well, here goes, Maryanne thought as the elevator made its slow descent, and a fresh battery of butterflies flitted around inside her stomach. With any luck at all, the evening would race by and all this would be behind them soon. Strange how different they were, she and Elliot, about parties of this sort. He'd been looking forward to this reunion for the past six months and was as eager to get downstairs right now as she was reluctant. Oh, well, there was nothing she could do at this point but grin and bear it. She'd certainly had enough experience in faking her way through these sorts of gatherings over the years. The bad part was that she just didn't seem to feel any better about them.

The elevator jolted to a gentle stop, the door opening to a hum of voices and music. Elliot's hand rested lightly on the small of Maryanne's back, guiding her from the elevator into the hotel lobby, then down a green and gold carpeted corridor to the banquet room.

"You okay?" Elliot asked, his dark eyes narrowing slightly as they noticed the strained expression on her face.

"Elliot, really, I'm fine. Would you quit worrying about me?" Maryanne laughed lightly, her green eyes widening in feigned annoyance. "You're going to drive me nuts if you keep asking me that."

"All right, but—"

"Elliot Douglass! I can't believe it! My God I would never have thought the likes of you would ever show up for this." They both turned to see a slightly plump, short woman hurrying to catch up, and an equally short, husky man trotting along at her side.

"My Lord, he's even more handsome than he was in

high school." The woman's round face was wreathed in smiles; her eyes lit in obvious admiration.

The man smiled and extended a hand to Elliot. "I'll plead the Fifth on that one, if you don't mind. How's it been going, old man?"

"Fine. Just fine. Great to see you two. You look as though life's treated you all right over the years." Elliot turned, cupped his hand around Maryanne's elbow, and said, "Honey, I want you to meet Judith and Roscoe Mosely. My wife, Maryanne."

"Nice to meet you." Maryanne smiled graciously and extended her hand to each of them.

Roscoe shook his head slowly. "Elliot, you always did know how to pick 'em."

Maryanne smiled dutifully and stood listening to the conversation among the other three, but her gaze wandered and she noticed the line forming at the opposite end of the corridor. A table was set up just outside the entrance to the banquet room, and one by one the reunion attendees and their spouses were placing their signatures in a large white album before going inside.

"We've been living in Dallas for the past ten years," Judith was saying. "We'd like to get a piece of property in the country somewhere, sometime." She spread her hand outward and shrugged. "But that's pretty far in the future. When the kids are out of school."

"How about you guys?" Roscoe chimed in, his round eyes darting rapidly from Maryanne to Elliot. "You got any kids?"

Elliot placed an arm around his wife's shoulders and smiled affectionately. "No. That somehow hasn't been in the cards for us."

Maryanne flushed slightly as the couple looked expectantly at her, obviously waiting for her comment. "Well, not yet, anyway," she said.

"Hey, you sometimes get more than you bargain for when you go that route," Roscoe added wryly. "There's certainly something to be said for not having 'em at all."

Maryanne's smile remained fixed, but the corners of her lips tightened slightly. As Roscoe asked Elliot about the field of work he was involved in, Judith drew up a bit closer to Maryanne, turning her shoulders as if to exclude the men. She spoke in a low, confidential tone. "You know, they're doing such extraordinary things now—artificial insemination, test-tube babies." She shook her head from side to side. "I tell you, it just absolutely amazes me. There doesn't seem to be any reason at all you can't have children nowadays."

"That's true," Maryanne replied, absolutely amazed at the woman's audacity. Was she wrong or had she just met the woman? God, the night was going to be a long one. Too long.

"Well, I just wouldn't worry about it if I were you," Judith continued. She hesitated, then wrinkled her nose and sniffed shortly through one nostril. "I've had *three* girl friends"—she held up three fingers—"who didn't get pregnant until after thirty years of age. Oh! I didn't mean that—"

"I'm thirty-three," Maryanne inserted smoothly.

"Oh, but you could pass for twenty-nine easy. Really. I didn't mean . . ."

Again Maryanne smiled. "It's all right. I know what you meant."

"Well, anyway, all I meant was, it seems *no* one is even

12

thinking of having children these days until they're in their thirties. I tell you, there are times when Roscoe and I—" Judith's eyes suddenly widened as she looked over Maryanne's shoulder, her mouth opening into a wide O before she clapped one hand over it. Then in a high-pitched, girlish voice she squealed, "Oh, my *Lord*! I don't believe it. I just don't believe it for one minute. Marge Magensky, is that you?"

Maryanne turned around to see the object of Judith Mosely's apparent excitement. A tall redheaded woman in a crimson off-the-shoulder gown was standing right behind her, her heavily made-up eyes batting dramatically.

"Judith Watson, if you don't look like you just graduated," the redhead gushed, stepping around Maryanne to slide an arm around the shorter woman's shoulders. Maryanne stepped back out of the way.

"Get outa here, Marge, you're lyin' through your teeth." Judith laughed delightedly, obviously enthralled by the surprise meeting with Marge, her thoughts completely diverted now from her conversation with Maryanne. Another man had come up to join Roscoe and Elliot, and for the moment it looked as though Maryanne had been completely forgotten by everyone.

She had no objections, however. Indeed, she was grateful for the rescue. She glanced around, noting that the line waiting to sign the guest book was becoming longer, and she turned back to say something to Elliot about it. But just then he broke off his conversation and turned around to face her. "Honey, I'm gonna walk over there with Roscoe and Joe for a sec. I'll be back in—"

Maryanne shook her head slightly. "Sure. I'll get in line to sign in. It's pretty long already."

"Good idea. See you in a little bit."

But by the time Maryanne reached the front of the line to enter the ballroom, Elliot still hadn't returned. He was probably off with one of the swarm of old school friends he was getting reacquainted with.

Well, that was okay. She didn't mind. In fact, she'd much rather stand here observing everything and everyone around her than tag along, being pulled into conversations she had no interest in. And if they were anything like that ridiculous one with Judith Mosely, she'd be better off just holing up in a corner somewhere and biding her time until the evening was over.

Maryanne drew a deep breath and expelled it slowly, almost wistfully. Absently, she stroked a palm across the smooth satin of her evening bag, her fingers snapping and unsnapping the gold-plated clasp. There was one advantage to being here; it was a heck of a lot prettier and certainly more cheerful than their dimly lit hotel room. A glimpse into the banquet room beyond the corridor revealed a bright, decorative scheme of the school colors commemorating the class of '63. Red and white streamers extended in pinwheel fashion from the center chandelier; baskets of red-and-white carnations graced tables covered in alternating patterns of red and white linens; clusters of scarlet balloons floated from the ends of each table; and on one wall of the room hung a life-size poster of a leaping cougar—the school mascot.

It was rather interesting just standing here, anonymous for the time being, watching all these people who had graduated from high school with her husband twenty years ago. They'd missed his tenth reunion, and except for a few people here whom they'd kept up with over the years, she didn't recognize anyone. Elliot was five years older than her, and she hadn't met him until she was in her senior year at Nacogdoches High, which meant that most of these people had been in college when she was still in high school. But it was interesting to watch them—the women dressed in all their finery, wearing long gowns and jewelry—and Maryanne suspected that this was one of the few events of the year that offered most of them the opportunity to do so. The men were in suits, of course, middle-age paunches strategically concealed by three-piece suits. They didn't look bad, though, as a whole. Maryanne could only speculate as to how much the years had changed them, in physical as well as in emotional ways.

The couple in front of her bent to add their names to the enormous white book and Maryanne took a step out of line, scanning the anteroom and the corridor behind it for any sign of her husband. He was nowhere in sight. Oh well. . . .

"Ma'am?"

She turned around to see the petite blond woman in charge of the sign-in procedure grinning up at her, holding out a pen. "Would you please sign in?"

"Oh . . . Yes, of course. Is it okay if I sign for both of us? My husband and myself?"

"Sure."

Maryanne took the pen and neatly wrote their names— Mr. and Mrs. Elliot J. Douglass. She straightened and smiled once more before moving away from the table toward the entrance to the banquet room. Then she stopped and stood for a moment, her eyes slowly scanning the large, gaily decorated room. It was filling up quickly with reunion attendees, most of them standing around in

15

small clusters, drinks in hand, their voices becoming louder and more raucous by the minute.

Where was Elliot? Her gaze swept the room once more, but she didn't see him. Her shoulders lifted slightly, then fell as she sighed in resignation. She supposed she'd see little, if anything, of him the rest of the evening, or for that matter the entire weekend. Wistfully, she thought of what she'd rather be doing with Elliot—visiting with her father, perhaps going on an outing to Lake Nacogdoches—having a quiet, peaceful weekend, which they both sorely needed. A wave of homesickness washed over her. How ironic that she should feel this way in her own hometown! If only Elliot shared her feelings about being here. Under these conditions she'd almost rather not have come; it was too much like dangling candy in front of a baby. She was here where she wanted to be, yet she really wasn't. But it wouldn't do a bit of good to hash it over like this; resignedly, she turned her thoughts elsewhere.

There was another room extending off the far corner of the banquet room, and Maryanne glimpsed a long, heavily laden buffet table in the center of it, a line of people already gathered around. The gentle rumbles in her stomach, which had been ignored, for the most part, all day long, clamored rebelliously now as seductive aromas wafted through the air. She couldn't wait around all night for Elliot and she might as well enjoy *something* while she was here. As Maryanne started out across the room toward the buffet, making her way slowly through the unfamiliar crowd, she was completely unaware of a pair of dark-brown eyes that had been watching her intently for the past several minutes and that now grew suddenly alert and tense as she moved out of sight.

* * *

Sam Lancaster stood with his back to the wall, both literally and figuratively. He lifted the clear plastic cocktail glass with gin and tonic to his lips and took a healthy swallow, draining it completely. The fact that he'd gotten himself suckered into coming here tonight was still eating away at him like an acid-drenched ulcer in the pit of his stomach. He'd managed to miss the first one of these shindigs, and now here he was for the second one. All because of Sissy, naturally. She loved this sort of thing, even if it was a far cry from what she considered socially advantageous. She'd always considered his hometown of Nacogdoches a hick town and nothing more. The more he'd grown to yearn for it, to long to come back and settle down after all these years away, the more adamant Sissy had become in her resistance. It was not unthinkable, however, for her to approve of flying down for this reunion. As a matter of fact, although it wasn't even *her* reunion, she'd jumped right in when they'd been contacted, offering her services as a member of the planning committee. She'd talked about it—hell, been absorbed by it—for the past six months.

Was he ever sick and tired of hearing about this reunion. A twinge of guilt tugged at him on rare occasions for feeling that way—especially now, seeing how successful her efforts had turned out—but, damn it, he couldn't help it. He just wasn't in the mood for a high school reunion. Not in the least. There were a thousand other things he'd rather be doing than standing around in an uncomfortable stiff collar and a three-piece suit, already on the way to pickling his brain in the hope of lifting his spirits. He'd already been accosted tonight by an assort-

17

ment of former acquaintances and friends he hadn't seen for at least ten years, and it was all he could manage to appear even remotely interested in anything they had to say. It wasn't just a matter of greetings; they expected you to talk about yourself, too. He'd repeated himself so often the words ran through his head like a broken record. "Yeah, been doing pretty good. . . . No, haven't had too much problem with the recession. We're selling almost as much property now as this time last year. . . . Yes, she's fine; staying with her grandmother till we get back. . . . Just for the weekend, right, flying back on Monday. . . . Thank you. Yes, Dad was very sick, especially at the end. I don't think he would ever have been any better."

God, he was sick of it. You don't see people for five, ten, *twenty* years, yet they act as if they have some indisputable right to know every deep dark secret of your life. Sam lifted the glass to his lips and remembered suddenly that there was nothing left. He glanced toward each of the two bars set up at opposite ends of the ballroom and noted which had the shorter, more accessible line. He took a few steps, heading for the one nearest him, then stopped dead in his tracks, his attention arrested by a flash of peach chiffon that had flickered into his line of vision.

From where he stood, he could see only the woman's back, but Sam Lancaster knew her identity with absolute certainty. No one but Maryanne would wear such an unpretentious yet devastatingly alluring gown and probably have no idea of its true appeal. The sight of her literally took his breath away. He hadn't seen her for four years, and he suddenly realized how much he'd missed her. Unconsciously, he rubbed the palm of one hand along his jaw, watching as she slowly turned, absorbing every detail—

18

face, hair, the smooth column of her throat, her tawny shoulders and slender arms—and the delicate hands clutching tensely, too tensely, at the satin evening bag. Even from here he could sense her discomfort as she stood alone in the doorway.

Where was Elliot? he wondered. Sissy had told him the Douglasses were coming, but he hadn't seen either one until now. Suddenly he felt a familiar prickle of nervousness in his stomach, and he realized he was in dire need of that extra gin and tonic. Just exactly how he was going to make it to the bar, however, was another thing altogether. At the moment it seemed a virtual impossibility.

He knew instinctively there was nothing rational he could tell himself that would prevent him from doing what he was about to do, yet he made himself wait, his hands busily rearranging the collar of his off-white shirt, his neck stretching and straining to be free of the constraining material. All the while his gaze remained fixed on Maryanne, who was still standing just inside the doorway, a vision of pure, uncluttered beauty and poise among all the dressed-to-kill, ostentatious people. She turned again, slowly, her white, partially bare shoulders rising and falling as she took a deep breath and reached up to smooth back a strand of honey-blond hair.

The gesture was achingly familiar, and suddenly, without conscious warning, his feet began moving, but when he was just a few inches behind her, she started to move away.

"Hey, good-lookin'," he called quickly, "can I buy you a drink?"

Maryanne turned around, eyes wide, obviously unsure if she was being addressed. Then all at once her features relaxed completely and her entire face awoke in a delighted smile. "Sam! How nice to see you!" And she meant it, from the bottom of her heart. The tall dark-haired man standing there smiling down at her was exactly what she needed at this moment.

"Nice to see you, too, Maryanne." Sam's intense gaze swept over her, first downward, then back up again, followed by a low, dramatic wolf whistle. "Damn, woman, but you look better every year."

"You look pretty good yourself, Sam Lancaster." He did indeed. The years had been good to him, filling out the lanky frame, carving maturity and handsomeness into the boyish face she recalled from their younger years.

She continued to smile up at him, and Sam felt his body take warmth from the lovely glow in her green eyes. If it was true that a man was punished for breaking the eighth commandment, Sam Lancaster was sure he would burn in hell for the rest of eternity. He'd coveted the wife of another man for the past thirteen years, and never so much as at this very moment. But he'd become an expert long ago at disguising those feelings; after all, he'd had almost fourteen years of experience.

"Well, where's your old man?" Sam glanced around, emphasizing Elliot's absence.

"That's something I would like to know myself. He disappeared with some friends in the corridor and I seem to have lost him." She paused, then asked, "Is Sissy here?"

Sam raised his eyebrows in a wry expression. "Oh, yeah. Hell, she's on the organizing committee."

Maryanne's look of surprise was tainted with amusement. "It was nice of her to give her time. Especially—"

"Especially when it's not even her own reunion," Sam finished. He shrugged and added, "But she loves this sort of thing. Thrives on it would be a better description."

Reunion attendees were pouring in now, forcing Maryanne and Sam to step to the side and out of the way. Sam suddenly took a step forward as a large hand landed roughly on his right shoulder. The voice that followed was as resounding as the slap. "Sam Lancaster, you old devil, where you been hidin'? Sissy told me you were around somewhere, and I've been lookin' for you for the past twenty minutes."

"Hello, Don." Maryanne caught the flicker of irritation in Sam's eyes as he extended his hand to greet the stout, partially bald man. "I've been milling around, having a drink while Sissy is off running things." He turned pointedly and said, "Don Milson, this is Maryanne Douglass, Elliot Douglass's wife."

"Well, hello there," Don bellowed, shaking his head from side to side dramatically. "I always did say Elliot had good taste in women."

The smile on Maryanne's face remained in place, but the barest flicker of her gaze toward Sam told him she had heard enough already. So had he.

"Hey, well, I'm glad you found me, Don. But listen, we've got some people waiting for us over there." He nodded toward the center of the banquet room. "Say, listen, stop by when you get a chance and we'll talk."

"Yeah, sure. See you later."

The man moved away, and Sam stepped closer to Maryanne and said to her in a whisper, "C'mon. Follow me."

She went willingly, lifting the hem of her skirt and

21

walking behind him as he threaded his way through the crowd. Miraculously, he found a table in a dim, temporarily empty section of the room. The five-piece band, which had finally finished testing their assortment of instruments and sound equipment, began their first number, and the noise level in the banquet room instantly increased to deafening proportions. Maryanne was grateful to Sam for locating a corner where they wouldn't have to scream at each other.

He pulled a chair out for her, then went around to the opposite side of the table and sat down. They looked at each other for a silent moment. Then Maryanne put a hand over her mouth to stifle a chuckle.

"What is it? What are you laughing about?" But he was smiling too, entranced by the miracle of her nearness.

Maryanne removed her hand and said, "I was just thinking how good you are at that sort of thing. I was worried we were going to be stuck with Don for the next half hour."

Sam leaned an elbow on the table and propped his chin between thumb and forefinger. "I've been known to be a fool on a few occasions in my life, but tonight is definitely not one of them. A man who would prefer to stand around talking to Don Milson when he has the opportunity to spend at least a few minutes in your lovely company is nothing short of a lunatic."

Maryanne cast him a wry glance. "Now you're starting to sound like him."

"Maybe so. Only *I* mean it." And he did, more than she'd ever know.

"Well, Sam Lancaster, I don't care if you mean it or

not—thanks for the rescue."

"My pleasure, ma'am, my pleasure."

Maryanne smiled at him once more, an affectionate, loving smile for a dear friend, a smile that in its very innocence pierced Sam Lancaster's soul with a bittersweet pang of regret.

CHAPTER TWO

"You look like you're enjoying this whole thing about as much as I am," Sam said. He sat back and crossed both arms over his chest, casting a cursory glance around the crowded dance floor and then looking back at Maryanne. "Well?"

"What, well?"

But her pretense of incomprehension didn't fool Sam. "You know exactly what I'm talking about, Maryanne. Parties never were your sort of thing. And this"—he gestured with one hand—"is more than your ordinary party."

Maryanne pressed her lips together and smiled in the utterly natural way that always pulled the same heartstrings in Sam. "All right, I'll confess." She laughed. "I really didn't want to come tonight. But it's not for me, anyway, so it doesn't matter if I'm having a terrific time or not."

Sam looked at her for a moment, then shook his head from side to side. "You never change, do you?"

Some of the smile faded from Maryanne's eyes and her brows drew together slightly. "That doesn't sound too much like a compliment."

"It's not. I always did think you were too much of a fool over Elliot."

Her expression deepened into a frown of displeasure at his impertinent remark, and the transformation of her lovely features indicated clearly enough to Sam that he'd gone too far. He and Maryanne had always enjoyed a refreshing candidness with each other—but four years was four years. He unfolded his arms and suddenly bent forward. "Hey, I didn't mean it like that."

Maryanne regarded him steadily. "Then what did you mean?"

Sam tugged at an earlobe and looked away for a moment. Why the intense reaction? he wondered. He wouldn't have expected it, but then, she'd always had a too-serious side. And how well he knew her vulnerability. He chuckled, making light of it. "I just meant the guy's always had a way of getting you to do what he wanted." He threw up a hand and added, "But listen, that makes us two of a kind. Hell, it's *my* reunion and look how Sissy had to drag me here."

When it was put that way, Maryanne did see the humor in the situation. Neither one of them wanted be here, but here they were, sitting on the sidelines, hoping everyone would leave them alone until it was over. She smiled and smoothed the white linen tablecloth. "Yeah, we are a couple of fools. But at least this only happens every ten years."

25

"And even that's too often. Listen, would you like a drink?" Sam offered, hoping she wouldn't. He didn't want to get up and leave her, not for one minute.

"No. Thanks anyway." Maryanne leaned back in her chair, her shoulders relaxing visibly. They were in a very dim corner of the banquet room, seated at the end of the heavily decorated table, apparently the only ones who wanted to be left alone. By now Maryanne had stopped wondering where Elliot was; once they arrived, he normally didn't need her at functions of this sort. In fact, he probably got along just as well or better without her. His extroverted personality contrasted sharply with her introverted one, and she'd long ago learned to tolerate that difference in their natures—among others.

"So how's Chicago?" she asked.

"I was just going to ask you the same thing about L.A." Sam grinned.

"Nope, I asked first."

Sam sighed resignedly. "What can I say? Chicago is Chicago. Sissy loves it."

Maryanne tilted her head to one side. "And how about Sam? Does he love it too?"

Sam chuckled soundlessly and sighed again. "Not really. The business is good. Despite the rotten economy, believe it or not, good commercial property is still as valuable and sought after as ever." He paused, then said, "In that respect, everything is going great."

"What about all the other respects? If I remember correctly, four years ago you said you wanted nothing more than to buy some land in the country and retire from city life."

Sam scratched the side of his nose thoughtfully. "Did I say that?"

"Come on, Sam, you know darn well you did. And that wasn't the only time. Ever since I've known you, you've been telling me how much you wanted to get away from the crowds."

Sam was surprised. So she remembered things about him, too, did she? Somehow, knowing that was tremendously important to him, enormously flattering to an ego sorely in need of nourishment. "It's one thing to express a desire, and another to realize it."

His words sounded so forlorn, so full of regret, that Maryanne could see he hadn't abandoned the wish in the least. "Well, I guess it just takes us more time than we expect to make our dreams come true." The double entendre in her words was obvious to Sam, but he refrained from remarking on it. For the moment, at least. Although Maryanne was open about the subject of her own unrealized dreams of having a family, Sam had always been an unwilling participant in such conversations, had always been more than a little uncomfortable—and with excellent reason.

"Oh, well, it's not so bad," Sam amended. "Like I said, Sissy loves it there and Melissa is starting first grade this fall. Even if I had some concrete reason to move—a solid business opportunity—I wouldn't want to force Sissy to leave. She likes everything just the way it is."

The band's medley shifted into a slow, early seventies number, and the bittersweet ballad suddenly awoke in Maryanne an acute sense of nostalgia. How swiftly the years had flown by. How incredibly different their lives were—she married for almost fourteen years; Sam married and the father of a seven-year-old daughter. It just didn't seem possible that they really *were* grown-ups now —adults in every sense of the word—assuming the roles they had seen their parents in only a short time ago.

Maryanne had felt this aching, profound awareness of the passage of time often of late. Yet there was an emptiness within the ache, a longing for something other than what she and Elliot shared. If only he would settle down in some business, some profession he could *really* get involved in. Maybe then they could finally establish roots, settle down in one place for longer than the two years they had averaged. How much she identified with Sam, she thought, suddenly longing to share her feelings with him. Sam had always been able to get her to open up; she could have used a few more friends like him over the years. But confiding in someone who used to be one's husband's best friend, someone she saw only every four or five years at best, had its limitations. And over the past few years she had rarely met anyone else she trusted enough to share her deepest feelings with; she'd never been in one place long enough.

But now here was Sam, good old Sam, as eager to see her as she was to see him. As he talked, she watched his face, noting the changes the years had wrought—a few more lines, a deepening of the grooves alongside his mouth, a swarthiness in the formerly fresh-faced complexion. He'd always been good-looking, and time had actually improved those looks, as it had for Elliot. But whereas Elliot possessed a carefree, go-for-broke sort of character, Sam had become quieter, more serious. It wasn't hard to read between the lines and see that his marriage hadn't fared too well. It was a shame; Sam was such a wonderful person, such a caring, sensitive man. Maryanne had often wondered about his reasons for marrying Sissy, had even discussed them with Elliot on occasion. But Elliot wasn't the sort to get involved in such "gossipy" discussions. Nevertheless she wondered if Sam was happy; somehow she doubted it. He did seem to perk up, though, whenever he talked of his daughter. How sad, Maryanne reflected. So many marriages seemed to turn out that way, with the child the only thread holding together the fragile, tearing fabric of the relationship.

"I guess I'll have a chance to talk to Elliot later," Sam said, switching subjects, "but tell me, what's he up to nowadays?"

Maryanne's eyes closed briefly, and a tiny sardonic laugh escaped her lips. Then she looked up into Sam's eyes and shook her head slowly.

"What's so funny?" Sam asked innocently.

Maryanne clucked. "Oh, Sam, you know more than anyone else what a loaded question *that* is."

Sam lifted a shoulder and cocked his head to one side in silent admission.

Linking her fingers together, Maryanne stared at them for a moment, her expression now serious. "What can I say? He's still a sales rep for Lombard Industries. We've lived in L.A. for the past year and a half. I guess that's as good an indication as any that we might stay for a while. I hope."

"You've never liked all the moving around, have you?"

"No. Oh, it's had its good points, I guess, but . . . I don't know, I suppose I'm just not cut out for it." She grinned ruefully. "After almost fourteen years, you'd think I'd be used to it."

"But you're not."

Maryanne shook her head and sighed. "No. It . . . it wouldn't have been so bad if . . ."

"If what?" He knew what was coming, of course. God, how he hated to hear her say it.

She stared out toward the crowded dance floor as if looking for someone or something. "Oh . . . I've always thought having kids would have helped, you know. Not just for me—for Elliot, too. It might have helped him settle down and make up his mind about what he really wanted to do. Be steadier, really stick with one job for longer than two years." She looked back at Sam, and the depth of emotion in the deep green eyes was almost more than he could bear. He shifted in his chair, wondering which tack to use to divert the conversation. But she went on before he could say anything.

"Maybe someday things will work out for us." She smiled and raised her eyebrows. "I'm not totally over the hill yet."

God, no, Sam mused. "I would say you haven't even begun the climb."

Maryanne smiled broadly, and at that moment Sam was sorely tempted to stand, take her by the hand, and lead her to the dance floor. What better excuse to hold her in his arms, to feel the soft sun-kissed flesh of her shoulders beneath his fingertips, to smell the sweet rose-scented fragrance of her hair. But he wouldn't, of course. He would never even attempt such a thing. To secretly covet, to love, another man's wife was sin enough; to act upon those feelings was a course for fools.

"I can't believe how many showed up tonight," he said,

eager to divert his thoughts from the uncomfortable turn they'd taken.

"It looks like everyone in your class is here."

"Mmmm."

"Don't you want to circulate and see all the faces you haven't seen for ten or twenty years?"

"And have lived without very well," Sam added.

Maryanne chuckled at his almost painful reluctance to mingle. It was so much like her own. "Really, though, Sam, people might start talking if we stay here much longer." She grinned playfully. "You know how people are. They might assume something was going on."

There was no ambiguity in her comment, a fact Sam understood with more than a small degree of sadness. But he returned the smile and stood, then walked around the table to help pull her chair back. He felt a certain awkwardness standing so near her just then, and it was a wrenching effort to step back, to pretend that he was willing now to leave her, when his entire being, his very soul, ached for this beautiful, extraordinary woman he had no right to and loved in vain.

"Elliot, there you are," Maryanne called softly, and Sam turned to see Elliot walking toward the table. How sweetly she spoke, Sam thought, how lovingly. And how much he would have given to be addressed himself in that warm tone. He scratched the back of his neck and watched as his longtime friend and old army buddy leaned down to plant a chaste peck on his wife's cheek. Then Elliot straightened and extended his hand. The two men shook hands briskly and clapped each other on the shoulder in an old familiar gesture.

"Sam Lancaster, you old devil. You're lookin' fit."

Sam smiled knowingly. "What you really mean is I've put on weight."

"Well . . . true," Elliot conceded. "But it's about time you finally caught up with the rest of us. You don't look like a skinny kid anymore. Listen, I saw Sissy a few minutes ago. She said to tell you she's tied up with Rhonda something or other. She'll see you later."

"Thanks," Sam commented dryly. The message was unnecessary; he hadn't expected to see his wife for the remainder of the evening anyway.

"So"—Elliot looked from Maryanne to Sam—"what have you two been doing stuck back here in a dark corner? Come on out and join everyone. A lot of people have been asking about you, Sam."

"We were just about to start mingling," Maryanne said, sliding her arm around her husband's waist. "But first, how about a dance for old times' sake? That always was one of our favorites." The band was now playing a slow, sixties Motown tune.

A flash of pure, agonizing jealousy surged through Sam at the adoring look on Maryanne's face, and he turned his head, pretending to scan the crowded dance floor. How glorious it would have been to hear those words directed at him. Damn, he felt every inch an immature, lovesick teen-ager. Reluctantly he returned his gaze to the happy couple standing next to him.

"Honey, do you mind if I pass on this one?" Elliot was saying. He looked suddenly preoccupied by something or someone on the opposite side of the roomful of undulating bodies. He jerked his chin upward in that direction as he said, "There's Scott Jergenson. I want to catch him for a sec."

Sam noticed a flicker of disappointment flash across Maryanne's face, smoothly replaced by an understanding, wifely smile. "Sure, honey, go ahead. But find me later and we can make it up."

Elliot smiled briefly, planted another peck on his wife's cheek, and turned to thread his way back through the crowd. Then, as if on second thought, he stopped and said, "Hey, Sambo, do me a favor. Make my wife happy and take her for a spin on this one. That way I won't feel so guilty."

Sam shook his head. "You should feel guilty anyway. But don't worry, I'll be happy to do it."

Maryanne rolled her green eyes heavenward as she smiled. "It's all right, Sam, you don't have to bother. The song's almost over anyway."

But Sam wanted to bother, very much so. God knew how many years it would be before he saw her again, let alone had the opportunity—the *offer*—to hold her in his arms. "Then we'll hang on till the next one," he insisted, grinning and taking her by the hand. "C'mon. You know you want to dance."

She did. The melody was one she would never forget, a wonderfully romantic song that evoked memories of a sweet, uncomplicated time in her life. But the fact that it was Sam, not her husband, who wanted to dance with her did bother her; after all, it was Elliot she shared those memories with, not Sam. But as he led her onto the crowded dance floor, miraculously locating a spot among all the jabbing elbows and moving feet, Maryanne felt strangely pleased. At least Sam wanted to dance with her—unlike Elliot—and in many ways he, too, was a part of those same memories. The music was much too loud to talk

33

over, so as they danced, Maryanne just let the memories wash over her; the crazy spur-of-the-moment dates whenever Elliot had had time off from school, weekend outings to the lake, the whole group of them lazily sprawled out on blankets, reveling in that once-in-a-lifetime period of few responsibilities and many dreams.

Maryanne supposed that those memories were what made this sort of function so appealing; it was a time for recapturing the sense of what it had been like before all the children, the work, the humdrum grind of everyday life. And really, this wasn't so bad, she thought, feeling somehow completely at ease within Sam's arms. For the first time that evening she was a part of it all. She was actually enjoying herself!

She moved her right hand a little, and slid it across Sam's hard, broad shoulder. How different it was to dance with a man other than one's husband. Quite interesting, as a matter of fact. Where her hand would have already begun to slip down Elliot's arm, here, with Sam, it remained still on his shoulder. He smelled different, too, a clean, wholly natural scent, undisguised by any of the colognes Elliot never ever forgot to wear. And Sam could dance! That, too, was completely unlike Elliot, who always did it only for her and was so impatient, so eager to get it over with.

The music ended, and immediately the band launched into another slow number. "One more time?" Sam asked, still holding her hand in his own. He felt intoxicated, drugged by her nearness. He ignored the inner warning to stop now, while he could, to prevent the yearning within him from becoming even more agonizing later on.

Maryanne smiled eagerly, ready to say yes, when suddenly her attention was drawn to a voice at the entrance to the banquet room. Its deep tone boomed above the din of music and laughter. Maryanne and Sam glanced in the direction of the voice, but they both would have recognized it blindfolded. Indeed, Joe Bob Simmons usually made an indelible impression on everyone he came into contact with, and Sam and Maryanne's relationship with him had certainly exceeded brief contact. Only his head was visible now, towering above the circle of friends who soon surrounded him.

Maryanne swallowed unconsciously, and some long-forgotten anxiety rippled through her. She stared straight across the room, her gaze fixed on the huge former University of Texas football star. Finally, after several moments, her gaze shifted slightly and she caught a glimpse of Elliot, his face crinkling into laughter as he responded to something Joe Bob was saying. She frowned; Elliot had said he was pretty sure Joe Bob wasn't going to make it tonight. The two men had corresponded ever since the end of their tour of duty in Vietnam, and Joe Bob's latest letter had said he doubted seriously he could make the reunion. Secretly, Maryanne had been immensely relieved by the news. She'd never liked the man and had never understood her husband's close friendship with him. But that was another story, and she certainly didn't want to start thinking about it now. There was nothing she could do about Joe Bob's presence now anyway—except to retreat to a far corner of the room once more. Undoubtedly she'd seen the last of Elliot for the evening.

"Maryanne?" Sam touched her elbow, and as she looked back up at him he saw her swallow uncomfortably. He'd watched her reaction when she saw Joe Bob with

Elliot, and he'd needed no explanation of the play of emotions on her face. "We should dance or get out of the way," he said, hoping his smile would break through the somberness that had suddenly overshadowed her gaiety.

"No, I really don't like that particular song," Maryanne said softly, and she started to move ahead of him off the dance floor. Sam followed as she headed for the table they had just left, but Maryanne turned, smiled very briefly, and said, "Listen, I'm going to visit the ladies' room. I'll see you later. You need to 'mingle' anyway, remember?"

Sam grinned wryly and said, "I suppose you're right. Don't disappear now, okay?"

Maryanne nodded and turned to make her way toward one of the side exits. Sam remained where he was, his gaze following her intently as she slowly moved across the crowded dance floor. Then he glanced back at the entrance where Joe Bob still held court—Elliot was in ever-loyal attendance. Sam's jaw tightened as he watched Elliot clap a hand on the big man's shoulder. It was no less affectionate a gesture than the kiss he'd bestowed on Maryanne. Sam turned away from the scene in disgust, unable to stomach any more of Elliot's behavior. *What a complete ass the man is,* Sam thought heatedly. *And he doesn't even have the brains to realize it!*

CHAPTER THREE

The rest room nearest the ballroom was overflowing with women laughing, talking, and primping in front of the row of mirrors lining the wall-length vanity. Maryanne took one look at the crowd and decided to go elsewhere. She remembered another rest room near the hotel's restaurant, and when she reached it, she was gratified to see only one other woman inside, a hotel employee. She placed her purse on the vanity and fumbled inside for her tube of lipstick. But as she raised it to her lips, her hand was shaking visibly and she lowered it again.

Her insides were trembling too, yet there was nothing she could do about it. Why hadn't she let Sam get her a drink? She needed one now, she really did. God, why did Joe Bob have to show up? Elliot had practically assured her that he wouldn't come; otherwise she might have refused to attend the reunion altogether.

The mere mention of Joe Bob Simmons's name could

turn her into a quivering mass of nerves. She had never—at least so she told herself—hated any human being in her entire life. Joe Bob, however, came closer than anyone to filling her with that black emotion. From the very first time she'd met him—when Elliot returned from Vietnam—she'd been inexplicably uneasy around him. And later, much later, she had learned there was reason enough for that intuitive response.

It had happened at one of the many parties she had gone to with Elliot in the two years following his return to the States, parties she attended out of duty alone. Elliot had needed that sort of function at the time, she'd told herself, so she'd quietly gone along with him, even though she'd dreaded each and every one of them. She hadn't ever been the partying type, anyway, and had been rather intimidated by the sheer numbers of people at these gatherings. She didn't fit in and didn't think she ever would, but she couldn't quite figure out why she was so extremely uncomfortable.

Then one night at a party at someone's house—she'd long since forgotten whose—she'd understood the reason why. Returning from the bathroom, she had quite innocently overheard a conversation among several of the men gathered in the kitchen. Words like "hash," "coke," and "Mary Jane" kept popping up in the conversation led by Joe Bob. Maryanne, although naive in many respects, realized the meaning of the words, and she was greatly troubled at the casualness with which they were spoken. It had taken weeks of badgering and downright nagging to get Elliot to explain what that conversation was all about. Joe Bob, it turned out, had been into drugs the entire time he was in Vietnam, had even managed to function as a minor supplier while there. But he'd merely been making reference to the drugs he'd dealt with overseas, Elliot explained, and no, he didn't do them anymore. He was clean now.

Maryanne had left the subject alone, but she wasn't convinced—not by a long shot. It was behavior she would have expected from Joe Bob, and she doubted seriously that he was as "clean" now as Elliot claimed. What concerned her even more, however, was her husband's enduring friendship with the man. She knew how close the two of them had been in Vietnam and suspected that Elliot hadn't remained untainted during the war himself. How could he have stayed clean when his best friend was so involved with all those drugs?

Still, the two men had rarely seen each other during those first two years following their return, a fact that Maryanne considered a blessing. She didn't trust Joe Bob and didn't want him around her husband. The fact that she and Elliot had such different opinions of the same man had never ceased to trouble her.

Now here he was again! And, as always, his presence brought that familiar niggling apprehension. No matter that it might be an irrational, even immature, feeling. She still felt that way even after all these years. God, look at her now, hiding in the rest room just to pull herself together.

She took a deep breath, put the tube of lipstick to her lips again, and applied a touch of color. She brushed out her hair and fluffed it a bit more with her fingers. Then, standing directly in front of the mirror, she studied her reflection in one of those rare, totally honest moments of personal assessment. For a woman of thirty-three she

39

looked pretty good. To heck with pretending she still looked like a girl in her twenties—she didn't. But maturity did have certain benefits, even in the face of the aging process, and though she didn't like it, she'd nevertheless become more accepting of the slow but progressive changes. Her complexion was as fair as ever, but the feathery lines at the corners of her eyes were etched deeper and had become more noticeable as the years went by. Fortunately, Maryanne thought, what one lost in physical ways could be compensated for in spiritual ways.

For the first time in her life Maryanne felt as if she were *truly* an adult, though admittedly many would say there were areas in her life in which she was far too dependent for a modern woman of the eighties. She herself now thought that perhaps she should have paid attention to those areas a long time ago, but the fact of the matter was she hadn't. Not until very recently had she discovered a more intrinsic sense of her own self-worth.

She snapped the delicate clasp of her evening bag and stepped back from the vanity. Well, if she felt so much like an adult, then the thing to do was to get back inside the banquet room and act like one. Joe Bob was here. There was nothing she could do about it, and she *had* to stop feeling so threatened whenever he happened into their lives. *So get on out there, Maryanne, and at least try to have a good time,* she told herself. She indulged in one last sigh, pushed open the door, and stepped out into the corridor, determined, whatever the cost, to see the evening through in a better frame of mind and spirit.

Sam turned away from the bar and took a healthy swig of the gin and tonic, almost draining the small plastic cup.

Damn, why did they pour them into such small cups? He might as well turn around and order another one. He was just about to do so when a hand plopped down heavily on his shoulder.

"Sambo, hey, where ya' been?" came a slightly slurred enthusiastic greeting. It was Clifford Jennings, yet another "old friend" Sam barely recognized.

"Hi, Cliff, how's it going?" He prayed he'd gotten the name right. Sam extended his hand and reluctantly admitted to himself that his so-far-successful avoidance of these people was just about over.

"Listen, I want you to meet my wife, Wendy"—Cliff looked around—"that is, if I can find her."

"Yeah, sure, I'd like—"

"Hey, Joe Bob Simmons is here," Cliff interrupted, giving up quickly on the subject of his wife. "He was askin' about you."

"Uh . . . really?"

Cliff's gaze swept the banquet room, then stopped as he found the subject of his interest. He slapped a thick hand down once more on Sam's shoulders. "C'mon, there he is."

Any hesitation on Sam's part went completely unnoticed by Cliff, who was striding unevenly across the room, keeping a guiding hand on Sam's shoulder as if they were inseparable pals. Might as well get it over with, Sam thought, wishing he'd gotten that extra gin and tonic first.

Joe Bob Simmons was holding court within a small circle of men—ex-classmates, old army buddies—all of them paying rapt attention to the huge hulk of a man as he rattled off another of his famous raunchy jokes. The whole group exploded into laughter at the end of it. Sam

41

nodded and returned the greeting as Joe Bob spoke to him briefly, admitting him into the circle before continuing his monologue.

To say Sam was uncomfortable would be a gross understatement; he wondered how long he had to stay before he could withdraw from the group gracefully. Certainly none of these men held any interest for him, other than old, better-forgotten school yard memories. But Joe Bob was the worst. Just hearing his voice from the other end of the room had grated on his nerves. Why in the world was he standing here pretending even a semblance of interest in the one-sided conversation? He'd heard these same old yarns about Joe Bob's famous college football stints at least a thousand times before. Joe Bob had been a University of Texas star linebacker for two years, during which time his grades had slipped to barely passing, just the level at which Uncle Sam could draft him for the war in Vietnam. Sam, still single, had seen the handwriting on the wall and had enlisted, as had Elliot. How in the world the three of them had ended up in the same headquarters in Saigon for two and a half years was a mystery none of them had ever figured out.

Elliot had formed a hard and fast friendship with Joe Bob immediately, a relationship Sam had found disconcerting, to say the least. Sam and Elliot had been best friends during their college years at Stephen F. Austin, and at first he'd been somewhat piqued by Elliot's waning loyalty. But the friendship between the other two men had brought out a side of Elliot that Sam had never observed before, and for the first time he began to rethink his entire relationship with Elliot—and in a far from positive light. Sam had disapproved of the things Joe Bob was getting involved in and had made his misgivings quite clear to Elliot. But Elliot didn't see any harm in occasional "indulgences," as he so delicately put it. Sam had understood the term well enough—drugs and women. He had been sick with disappointment at the change in his old friend, but not just for himself. He felt bad for Maryanne, really bad; her loving, patriotic, "loyal" husband didn't exactly fit the description—not by a long shot. And he hoped to God she would never *ever* find out about that last caper Elliot had pulled off. . . .

Sam had finally been assigned to frontline duty and hadn't met up with Elliot again for another year. By then they were all back in the States. Maryanne and Elliot were back together, and not too long after, Sam had taken the leap and married Sissy. The two couples had visited each other sporadically over the years and, like tonight, each visit found Sam thinking how vastly different he and Elliot really were. He himself had changed in many, many ways. Yet Elliot was still exactly the same, stuck in the past, his head full of fantasies about some elusive fortune that was going to make him rich overnight. His fawning over Joe Bob even now was just another indication of how immature he still was.

"Joe Bob, tell the one about your first Oklahoma-U.T. game in Dallas," Charles Fordham piped up. "That was the weirdest damn second quarter I think I've ever watched."

As Joe Bob launched into yet another chapter of his illustrious football career, Sam rubbed the bridge of his nose with his thumb and forefinger. Apparently some of the other men in the group had heard this one before too, and began talking among themselves. Bored to tears with

Joe Bob, Sam turned his attention to the other conversation.

"Damn, Snyder, when you gonna give up?" Jamie Stilton tilted his head way back and gulped down another swig of beer.

"It ain't my fault. She just loves kids. Tricked me again." Fred Snyder had grown stout over the years, Sam noticed. A former dedicated bodybuilder, he had apparently given up on it, and impressive inches of muscles had turned to bulges of flab. He now sported a "nine month" paunch and had lost most of the thick blond hair he had once been so vain over. Altogether an uncomfortable, worried-looking man.

Stilton snorted. "Get outa here, Snyder. She couldn't trick you if you didn't let her. So what's the difference if you got one more mouth to feed? You been doin' pretty good from the sound of it."

Fred jerked his head sharply to the side a couple of times, a disconcerting, nervous tic. Despite Stilton's comment about his prosperity, he looked worried. The two men talked in the same vein for several minutes. Apparently this conversation was more interesting than Joe Bob's because most of the men were now listening to a recount of Fred's problem. Finally even Joe Bob got in on it, willing and eager to give advice in his other field of expertise—women. Sam, however, was itching to make his exit; he just didn't like these men, that was the plain and simple truth. He noticed Elliot say something to Joe Bob, then take his empty glass and walk away, most likely to freshen their drinks. Excellent idea, Sam thought, eager to do the same. He was about to take a step, but stopped suddenly, his gaze captured once again by the peach-colored gown.

Maryanne was standing exactly where he had first seen her this evening, just inside the entrance to the banquet room, and now, as then, his reaction was equally intense. She was, and always would be, the most beautiful woman in the world to him. Sam was relieved to see that she was once more composed, obviously having dealt with the initial shock of Joe Bob's presence. Sam paid only scant attention to the conversations evolving out of Snyder's revelation of yet another coming child. He watched Maryanne covertly, gratified to see Anne Martin approach her, take her by the arm, and lead her off somewhere. Well, at least that would get her attention off what was happening over here. Momentarily forgetting his drink, Sam turned back to the conversation and listened for a minute to what Fred and Jamie were saying, completely unaware that Anne had led Maryanne to the table directly next to the one where Joe Bob stood.

The men's conversation remained focused on Snyder's predicament—much of it consisting of rather crude joking —and Sam started to walk off again when he suddenly noticed Maryanne standing close by with three other women. He could see she wasn't listening to them; her attention had been captured by the ruckus within the group of men.

"Hot damn, Snyder, you really are a live one," Joe Bob chuckled. "Poor little inexperienced thing like you used to be! Who would ever have dreamed you'd turn into such a regular baby-maker?"

"All right, Joe Bob, knock it off," Snyder said, fending

off the round of guffaws and snickers. "There isn't much I can do about it anyway."

"Maybe not now. But you oughta take care it doesn't happen again."

"Sure thing. I thought it *was* taken care of."

Joe Bob snorted loudly. "Man, you can't trust women! Am I right or am I right?" Several heads nodded in agreement.

"You gotta take care of things yourself," Joe Bob went on. "Hot damn, you oughta take care of it the way Elliot did."

Suddenly, Sam's entire body went rigid. He anxiously glanced at the chatting group of women; Maryanne was still there.

"What d'ya mean?" Snyder inquired.

Joe Bob lowered his voice only slightly; his words were clearly audible to all in the vicinity who chose to listen.

"Hell," Joe Bob continued, "after he knocked up that gook in 'Nam, it cost him so much to get rid of it that he went out and made sure it wouldn't happen again. Checked in one afternoon at the clinic and got it all sewed up for good. He was out in thirty minutes. Didn't feel a thing. That's a fact. I picked him up myself and he looked like he could've handled a fifty-yard dash and a few good lays that same afternoon."

Rockets exploding before his very eyes could not have made Sam Lancaster more furious than Joe Bob's unbelievable monologue had. With a sickening sensation that bordered on downright nausea, he watched Maryanne's face as she took in every single word of what Joe Bob said. Even in the muted light he could see her face blanch and her eyes narrow. Then she turned her head sharply to one side, as if she'd been struck full across the cheek. Anne was still talking to her, but it was obvious that Maryanne wasn't listening. Joe Bob had moved on to yet another subject, but not a word registered in Sam's brain. Cold, piercing fury ripped through his insides, and in one lightening move he stepped directly in front of the taller man and hissed sharply, "Shut it up, Joe Bob."

Joe Bob's head jerked back in surprise, and everyone in the group was suddenly silent. From the corner of his eye Sam saw Maryanne turn and hurry away from the women. The son of a bitch!

Joe Bob frowned in confusion. He opened his mouth to speak, but Sam interrupted furiously. "You *stupid* ass. You and your damn big mouth—"

"What the hell—" Joe Bob was clearly amazed at the unexpected attack.

"You're so damn thick-headed you don't even know what you just did." Sam's dark gaze was livid and it bored into the man, but it was obvious Joe Bob had no idea what it was he'd said or done wrong. Sam glanced across the room again and saw Maryanne forcing her way through the crowd toward the exit. Suddenly he reached out and pushed hard against Joe Bob's arm, causing the man to step awkwardly to the side. The fact that Joe Bob stood four inches taller than Sam and sported an extra sixty-five pounds of flesh and muscle presented no obstacle. "Get out of my way, you stupid ape," Sam snarled as he rushed past him and cleared a path toward the fleeing woman.

Maryanne wasn't sure she could make it across the room; her lungs felt compressed and every breath came in painful burning gasps. Her heart was pounding so hard and erratically that she felt its hammering in her ears. Claustrophobia gripped her, then a seizing, squeezing panic, urging her on faster and faster. She had to get out of here! But it was too crowded; people kept getting in her way. And voices, shrill and crude, clamored incessantly in her brain until she thought she would scream. ". . . and Cindy's in the third grade now. She scored so high on her achievement test that . . . *after he knocked up that gook* . . . but she and Bobby fight constantly. I swear I don't know what . . . *cost him so much to get rid of it* . . . I tell you I thought no twins were closer than my two . . . *got it all sewed up for good . . .*"

She was going to be sick. She had to hurry up and get out of there. *Oh, God,* she thought, *I can't breathe, I have to. . . .* Something pulled at her arm. She pushed it away but it wouldn't go, and suddenly it gripped harder so that she spun around. It was several seconds before she recognized Sam holding on to her arm, gazing down at her with such piercing concern that her trancelike state was momentarily broken.

"Maryanne, wait."

Her gaze shifted to the hand that held her by the arm, and she recoiled so visibly and dramatically that Sam instantly dropped his hand.

"Where are you going?" he asked, anxiously noting the glaze over her enormous green eyes. It was every bit as bad as he had feared.

Maryanne did not utter a word, but as she looked into Sam's face, the question faded from her eyes and comprehension flooded every fiber of her being. Sam's expression spoke clearly enough. His extreme concern, the *guilt* written all over his features, affirmed beyond a shadow of a doubt that the story Joe Bob had told was not merely another of his famous white lies. No, he'd spoken the truth.

The conversation she and Sam had had earlier suddenly came back to her, and something sharp and ugly gripped her. She who had never felt an ounce of malice toward anyone in her life was overwhelmed with a sickening disgust for this man who had been a cherished, valued friend. He had *known* all those years that she was just wasting her time, that her dream would never come true, that she would never become pregnant.

The twisted look on Maryanne's face hit Sam with the impact of a blow to the stomach. He recoiled, unconsciously stepping back and away from her. She turned and left, but he stood rooted to the spot, watching her go, guilt and remorse surging through him in agonizing waves. He was seized with a humiliation and shame he'd never imagined possible.

Joe Bob's voice penetrated the blare of music and competing voices, bringing Sam suddenly to his senses. He spun around, his gaze scanning the banquet hall searching for the one person who was responsible for all this—Elliot —the man who had once been his closest friend.

CHAPTER FOUR

The room was dark except for a few bands of corridor light that slipped beneath the doorsill and across the carpet. Maryanne sat on the edge of the bed, hands cupping her elbows as she hugged her arms tightly against her chest. She was shivering, though the unairconditioned room was almost stifling, and she stared blankly into the darkness through chalk-dry eyes. Except for the shaking, her body was rigid, completely incapable of movement.

She was in a state of emotional numbness, the brain's protective reaction against the severity of the shock she had suffered. She had no memory of making her way to the elevator, of stepping inside and pushing the button for the fifth floor, or of getting off and letting herself inside the room. She was barely aware of where she was even now; time was an incomprehensible concept.

But as the minutes ticked away, recognizable thoughts began to filter into her consciousness. And as they did, she

50

became aware of physical sensation too—the ache in her stomach and chest like some heavy, suspended weight; the claustrophobic pressure on her lungs making it very hard to breathe. Then, suddenly, with the clarity of a taped recording, Joe Bob's words came back to her, their cruel brashness crushing any shred of hope she might have had that they were lies. *He hadn't been lying.* Without the slightest, remotest doubt, she now knew this was true. Elliot was the one who had lied to her, withheld the truth from her, deceived her from almost the very beginning of their marriage.

A memory came back to her—Elliot was leaving for his appointment with the doctor. It was already two forty-five in the afternoon and the doctor's appointment was for three o'clock. It took at least thirty to forty-five minutes to get there, which meant he would be late. No problem, Elliot had assured her; he'd called earlier to change the appointment to three thirty. Maryanne wondered when he'd called; he'd been at home all day and she hadn't heard him use the telephone. Well, she couldn't keep up with his every move; she'd never been the type to demand an accounting of every second of his life and she wasn't going to start. She trusted him.

But now she knew it had been a lie, just like all the other appointments he'd supposedly made when they had decided to investigate seriously the reasons for their apparent infertility. Where *had* he gone? What *had* he done?

Her own physician had suggested, quite firmly at times, that she and Elliot explore the problem together, and Maryanne had agreed that mutual cooperation would probably be more productive in attaining accurate results. But Elliot never had enough time, was always too busy with some hot new business deal, so he'd insisted on seeing his own doctor on his own time. He'd had all the tests, he told her, gone through all the rigamarole—his term for what Maryanne considered one of the most significant problems in their marriage—and nothing had been found wrong with him. He hadn't been particularly interested in the results of the innumerable examinations and tests Maryanne had undergone, none of which revealed any abnormality or deficiency.

It all made sense now—perfect sense. There was only one reason for their infertility—Elliot's vasectomy, performed while he was in Vietnam.

"Oh, God," Maryanne moaned aloud. Unconsciously she began to rock slowly back and forth. A dull pain throbbed deep, deep inside. And it hurt so bad. Yet she couldn't cry; her eyes were completely dry, as dry and desolate as the ache within.

Other fragmented scenes of their married life began to flit across the screen of her mind with piercing lucidity: Elliot's frequent out-of-town trips that almost always lasted a day or two longer than he'd planned on; his still-unrealized dreams of imminent fortune; her own total, unquestioning trust in him.

Had she really been so naive and immature as to believe completely and never question him about anything? Yes. There was no other answer. Yet, somehow, beneath the shock of humiliation and hurt, Maryanne was cognizant of another factor, some little-understood part of her character that had allowed all this to happen. It was only a subtle awareness, but overwhelming in its deeper meaning, and she pushed it aside as she slowly and agonizingly came to her senses.

She stood, still shivering perversely in the warm, airless room, then walked around the bed to the nightstand and switched on the lamp. With only the briefest moment of hesitation, she picked up the telephone receiver and began dialing her father's number.

It took Sam exactly two minutes to locate Elliot. Maryanne's husband was standing in line at the long buffet table, a plate of food in one hand, a drink in the other, chatting amiably with another of his old school chums.

Sam walked up behind him, tapped him once on the shoulder, and said, "Douglass. I think you'd better step outside for a minute."

Elliot turned and smiled cheerfully. "Hey there, Sambo, did you give my wife a turn around the floor?" He turned and stepped sideways and said, "You remember Frank Mitchelson, don't you?"

Sam nodded curtly to the other man. "How's it going?" he muttered. "Elliot, I'll see you in the corridor. Now."

Elliot frowned as Sam suddenly turned on his heel and strode from the room. Then he turned back to his friend and shrugged helplessly. "Looks like something's up. See you later, okay?"

Sam was pacing up and down in the corridor, one hand nervously jingling the coins in his pocket. Elliot grinned cockily as he approached.

"Hey, what's up? Is there a fire or something?"

Sam stopped dead in his tracks. "Where is your wife, Elliot?" he asked sharply.

Elliot looked somewhat annoyed. "I don't know. And I don't particularly care for your tone of voice."

53

"The hell with my tone of voice. You've got a lot more than that to worry about."

Elliot's jaw worked impatiently for a moment, then he said, "What are you gettin' at, Sam? I don't have to follow my wife around like a puppy dog the whole night."

"No." Sam snorted derisively. "You'd never give her the satisfaction of that much attention, there's no doubt about that."

Elliot's eyes narrowed angrily. "Damn it, Lancaster, quit beatin' around the bush. Are you gonna—"

"While you were busy socializing inside, old buddy, your wife just happened to overhear something you've done one unbelievable job covering up all these years."

Elliot's black eyes narrowed even more as he took a step closer toward Sam. He said nothing, but fixed his eyes on Sam's flushed features and waited for him to go on.

"Joe Bob opened his big mouth once too often," Sam said caustically. "About Vietnam. More specifically, about what you did over there."

Elliot's head moved to one side, his chin tilting slightly upward. "What do you mean, what I did over there."

"About your vasectomy, man. He told it all. And Maryanne heard it all."

In an instant the perpetually confident expression on Elliot's face vanished completely; his handsome features sagged, and he looked as though someone's fist had just dealt him a vicious blow to the solar plexus. Then his jaw began working furiously, his gaze searching Sam's face disbelievingly, incredulously. His eyes held the fear of a criminal who knows he is trapped.

"The son of a bitch," he muttered, swallowing deeply and looking past Sam's shoulder down the corridor.

"Yeah. It took this for you to wake up to that fact."

But Elliot ignored the jibe against Joe Bob. "Where is she?"

"I have no idea. She just took off. I tried to stop her, but—" He recalled the look on Maryanne's face and cringed involuntarily.

"All right. I'll see you later." Elliot turned away sharply and headed down the corridor toward the elevators.

Don't count on it, Sam thought to himself. *In fact, buddy, don't count on ever seeing me again.* How in heaven's name had he allowed even the guise of friendship to exist between them all this time? Elliot Douglass was nothing but a liar and a cheat—of the worst sort. And tonight he had shattered the dreams—the life—of the most beautiful, loving creature on the face of the earth.

The band was now responding to the inebriated crowd, switching to a series of rock numbers, amps and speakers blasting away and invading the formerly quiet corridor. Sam couldn't stand another second of it. He had to get away, go for a walk, anything. "To hell with it all," he muttered, completely oblivious of the weaving, clinging couple he almost collided with on his way toward the lobby.

Maryanne looped a lock of hair behind one ear, drew a deep, shaky breath, then bent to close her suitcase. She was about to snap the clasps shut, then remembered she'd left her hairbrush in the bathroom and went back inside to retrieve it. As she came out, there was a knock on the door. She stopped, looked blankly at the doorknob, then walked on toward the bed. The hardwood floor beneath the carpet creaked noisily, revealing her presence.

"Maryanne? Maryanne, let me in. I don't have a key."

Elliot's voice sliced through her like a knife. Chills raced up and down her spine at the mere sound of it, and she was shocked at the depth of fear the sound of his voice provoked. He was a stranger—a total stranger.

"Maryanne," he called out more insistently. "Come on, open the door. I'd rather not have to go down to the desk and ask for another key."

Quelling her emotional turmoil as much as possible, she threw her brush into the suitcase, snapped it shut, and swung it onto the floor. Then she drew another shuddering breath, crossed the room slowly, and unlocked the door. Maryanne did not look at Elliot. She turned and walked back to the vanity and began to switch the contents of one purse to another, performing the task mechanically and forcing herself to block out, as much as possible, the sight of him, which was almost too much to bear.

It was worse than Elliot had imagined. Tears, a scene, but not this—not Maryanne standing there in slacks and blouse, her suitcase packed and propped up next to the chest of drawers, her back turned to him as if she had no idea he was even there. A sinking sensation welled up in Elliot's stomach. *Damn Joe Bob Simmons,* he thought bitterly.

He cleared his throat a couple of times and said, "Honey . . . Listen, I talked to Sam." He walked up behind her and placed a hand on her shoulder, but she jerked away so fast it literally stunned him. Still she would not look at him; she simply picked up her large purse and slid the smaller one into her tote bag.

Elliot cleared his throat nervously again. "What . . . what are you doing?"

56

For the first time since he'd entered the room, Maryanne looked at him. "What does it look like I'm doing?" Her tone was flat, her green eyes darkened with emotion, and there was something else in her voice—a determination and a willfulness he'd never before seen, and he had no earthly idea how to deal with it.

He glanced at her suitcase and tote bag, then back at her face. Suddenly he realized what was happening. "Where are you going?"

"Dad's coming to pick me up." She glanced perfunctorily at her watch. "I need to get downstairs. He'll be here any minute."

Elliot's voice now took on a near-frantic note. "Maryanne, what's this all about? I—"

Maryanne interrupted brusquely, her voice emotionless, hard as steel. "Let's not play games, Elliot. My God, not *now*."

Elliot ran his palm slowly down the side of his face to his chin, a familiar nervous mannerism. He glanced down at the floor and back up at her. He had the look of a snared rabbit, Maryanne thought, one caught in a trap of his own making. Again he cleared his throat, and the noise grated on Maryanne's nerves like fingernails scraping across a blackboard.

"Listen, Maryanne, we have to talk—"

"About what?"

Elliot swallowed hard and stared at her, his eyes pleading with her to be the old familiar, understanding Maryanne.

"About what, Elliot?" she repeated. "About what Sam told you I overheard? About what your good *friend* revealed about you this evening? Is that what we have to talk about?"

She watched her husband run a shaky hand through his hair. She'd never seen him like this. Another day, another time she might even have found it humorous—unflappable Elliot, behaving like a petrified teen-ager, unable to open his mouth. But now she only felt sick, horribly sick, at the sight of him. Words were not necessary; she saw with absolute certainty that it *was* all true.

There was really no reason to watch him cower this way. Still, she had to hear it from him, had to allow him that one last chance to deny it all.

"I . . . There's so much that you don't know," he said finally. "So much I need to explain."

"Really, Elliot? After all these years . . . almost *fourteen* . . ." Her voice broke, and when she found it again it was barely more than a whisper. "After all these years of marriage, you have to *explain* something to me. What would that be? That you had a vasectomy in Vietnam but decided never to tell me?" His image blurred suddenly, but she blinked hard and it reappeared clearly. His handsome face had crumpled, and she could see the guilt written all over it. He obviously felt very bad. But bad for whom—for himself or for her? A rush of sadness plummeted through her as she realized she had absolutely no idea. How could she? She didn't know this man.

"It's true, then, isn't it?" she whispered. "What Joe Bob said was true."

But Elliot didn't answer. He stood motionless in the middle of the room, watching her sling the strap of her purse over her shoulder, watching her pick up the suitcase and tote bag. But when she reached the door, he made one last attempt. "Maryanne, don't do this."

She opened the door and stepped out into the hallway. She hesitated, then turned and said in a surprisingly level voice, "Good-bye, Elliot. Enjoy your reunion."

And then she was gone, the thickly carpeted hallway muffling her footsteps.

A mild breeze sifted through the dense evening air, and Sam listened as it rustled the leaves of the enormous oak tree that shaded the hotel's courtyard. He had long since discarded his jacket and vest and loosened the collar of his shirt. Now he sat leaning against the tree trunk. Only in the past couple of minutes had he begun to cool off, both physically and emotionally. He honestly could not recall a single occurrence in his life that had shaken him as intensely as this incident tonight. He still felt helplessly weak and miserable, and he hoped to God that Elliot felt worse.

Going back inside to rejoin the reunion was unthinkable; Sam was too worried about what was going on upstairs in their room. God help Elliot if he wasn't able to set things straight with Maryanne. But how could he? There was no way on earth Elliot could make up for what he had done to her. Sam shifted his position, unaware of the sharp prickle of the bark through his shirt. *If I were a smoker, I'd have devoured an entire pack of cigarettes by now,* he thought. He bent his head and slowly ran a finger up and down the bridge of his nose. He'd been thinking random, unconnected thoughts like that for the past twenty minutes. All of them were useless diversions, his brain's desperate effort to circumvent the real issue, the one that was eating him up. That look on her face! God, he'd never forget it as long as he lived.

Guilt must have been written all over him. It had to have been, because that's what he was—guilty like all the rest who had known Elliot's secret all these years and had pretended not to know. It was none of his business, he'd told himself many times. But of course it had been his business, simply because he'd known and she hadn't. *It's my curse to love her,* he thought sadly, *to love her and to have seen utter contempt for me on her face.* That he could never get over.

Suddenly he pushed away from the tree. He had to move, get away from these thoughts that were driving him crazy. There was not a damn thing he could do about it. *It's none of your business,* he reminded himself. *Yeah, give me a thousand years and then I might believe it.*

He stepped onto the sidewalk and started toward the front of the hotel, hands crammed down into his pockets, head bowed, eyes studying the cracks in the concrete as if to decipher some meaningful pattern. Cracks in the concrete, holes in his life—one gaping hole now.

He reached the circular drive fronting the hotel just as a brown and beige four-door sedan pulled up. A man got out and Sam recognized him at once, although it had been several years since he had spoken to him. It was Maryanne's father, Jonas Anderson. Sam stopped where he was, out of sight, as Mr. Anderson got out, went up to the hotel, and opened the door to the lobby. He returned seconds later, Maryanne beside him, each of them carrying a piece of luggage. Mr. Anderson opened the trunk to the sedan, placed both pieces inside, and then opened the passenger door for Maryanne before getting back in himself. The engine churned smoothly to life, and the car slowly pulled out into the street.

Sam watched it go, the embers of his anger now stoked into a raging fire. That fool Elliot! That total, stupid fool!

For the first time since Vietnam an enormous lump rose up in Sam Lancaster's throat, one he could not force back down. He squinted and tightened his jaw, then drew in a deep, shuddering breath. The sedan rounded the corner, but Sam had already lost sight of it. Its image had disappeared along with everything else in the world behind a blinding, heartbreaking blur of tears.

CHAPTER FIVE

The business buildings and houses along North Street went unnoticed by Maryanne. Her gaze remained focused on the tops of distant towering pines, dark silhouettes against the velvet black of the night.

Jonas Anderson said nothing as he drove the sedan toward home. He glanced at his daughter a couple of times and started to speak, but she seemed so distant, so completely lost to her surroundings, that he thought it best to keep his silence. He was startled when she suddenly spoke.

"Dad . . . I'm sorry for . . . for this." Her voice was small, remote.

"For what, Maryanne? For asking me to come and pick you up?" He laughed softly. "I'm just glad you changed your mind. I thought you and Elliot were going to spend the entire weekend in town."

"We were," Maryanne stated tonelessly. She stared out the window a moment longer, then slowly turned to face her father. His tired features were carefully arranged into a blank mask.

Then she spoke again, but this time in a calm, level tone, experiencing the strange sensation of listening from outside herself to words she would never have dreamed she would say. "I'm leaving Elliot, Dad. I . . . I hope you don't mind if I stay with you. For now at least."

Jonas was shocked. But despite a deep concern about what was going on, he kept his eyes glued to the highway. "Honey, you know you can stay with me anytime. Forever, if you want. But . . . are you sure about this? It's a pretty serious business, what you're saying." He glanced at her rigid profile. "I don't want to interfere, you know that, but . . ."

"I understand, Dad. It's a shock to me, too. But I *am* sure. More sure than I've ever been about anything in my life." As she said the words, they were matched by an inner conviction, an absolute understanding that from this moment on her life would be different, vastly different. The ache, the hurt, and the humiliation racking her insides were worse than any dread disease, yet through it all Maryanne was vaguely aware of a reserve of untapped strength. She would need every ounce of it now. For fourteen years she had lived with a man she thought she knew. She had been a faithful, loving, patient, and, most of all, *understanding* wife. But everyone has a limit. And tonight hers had been reached. What she had learned tonight about Elliot could never be forgiven and smoothed over. *Not ever.*

That last pleading look on Elliot's face had filled her with unexpected emotion—beneath her own agony she had felt a deep shame for him, and an embarrassment at having been married to him.

Strange, how cold she still was; the temperature outside was in the mid-eighties; the humidity, oppressive. The car air conditioner was at its lowest setting, but she felt as if she were freezing. Instinctively she hugged her arms around her chest, shivering uncontrollably.

Jonas saw the gesture and reached over to switch off the air conditioner completely. "Sweetheart, are you all right?"

"Sure. I'm fine."

But she wasn't, and they both knew it. Jonas pressed down a bit harder on the accelerator, anxious to get her home as fast as possible. At that moment he was acutely aware of his wife's absence and felt terribly inadequate. He'd always been close to his only child, but things of this nature—personal matters—had always been Miriam's department. They had filtered down to him eventually, but by then the problem had usually been all worked out.

Now it was just him, alone, and he had no idea how to deal with this bombshell Maryanne had dropped on him. As he slowed the car down and turned into the gravel drive leading up to the house, he could see that she didn't have any idea they were home. And she was still shivering —in this humid, sultry weather! It wasn't right, not at all. The thought crossed his mind that he had better call Dr. Sanders, the physician who had treated the Anderson family since Maryanne's birth. But as soon as he stopped the car in front of the garage, Maryanne suddenly snapped out of the trance she'd been in.

"We're here," she said in a muffled tone, blinking her eyes rapidly as she began to notice her surroundings.

"Mmmm." Jonas opened the car door and went around to help his daughter out. Maryanne turned slowly, taking in the moonlit details of her father's house and grounds. There had been changes; obviously he'd been working hard over the past year. But it was the sort of thing he loved most—working with his hands, building, rebuilding, refurbishing—using his creative talents. The house was pretty much the same, a one-story bungalow, but now sporting a dark-brown siding to complement the brown and beige brick. How her mother had loved this house, Maryanne remembered. What a shame she had only been able to enjoy it for the last year and a half of her life. There were other changes she knew of from her father's letters, but it was hard to see in the darkness and she was tired, so very, very tired.

She followed her father as he crossed the narrow concrete front porch, set her suitcase down, and unlocked the door. The clean scent of lemon oil greeted her and brought on a wave of nostalgia. Why had she waited so long to come back and visit? The answer was simple—Elliot. But, no, she would not think about that, not now.

"I'll just put this in the guest bedroom," Jonas said, hesitating before moving down the hallway toward the three bedrooms on the east side of the house.

Maryanne remained for a moment in the foyer and then walked slowly into the living room. Traces of her mother's touch were everywhere—brightly patterned afghans she had knitted; cross-stitched throw pillows; pots of ivy in colorful macramé holders hanging in the bay window that looked out onto the backyard. And lots of family pictures —the life story of the Anderson couple and their only child from the time she was an infant until her wedding day. A chill traveled down Maryanne's spine as her gaze came to rest on a portrait of herself in a white satin and lace wedding gown. She stared at it, unable to pull her eyes away as a confusing rush of emotion washed over her and a lump rose in her throat. Then, hearing her father's returning footsteps, she turned around quickly to face him.

But Jonas had seen her absorption in the wedding picture, and the raw pain in her beautiful deep-green eyes was almost too much to bear. He managed to conceal his own feelings, though, and walked directly across the beige-carpeted den to the bar in one corner.

"What'll it be?" he asked, opening the double doors in the back and taking a couple of glasses off the shelf.

Maryanne shook her head, then sat down at one end of the couch, a cushiony Early American sofa she remembered from her earliest years. "Nothing. Thanks anyway."

Jonas studied her for a moment, then said hesitantly, "Maryanne, I know very little of what has happened here" —he cleared his throat, then went on—"between you and Elliot, that is. But I can recognize a situation that calls for a stiff one when I see one."

Maryanne laughed mirthlessly. "True. All right, then. B and B straight up. If you have it."

"As always. Comin' up."

After pouring them both a little from the same bottle, Jonas walked over to the couch and set the glasses on the coffee table. Then he sat down in his favorite oversize leather lounger, picked up his drink and sipped at it. Maryanne was apparently lost in thought again; she was completely ignoring her drink. Jonas was about to remind her of it, but decided it might be better to hold off for a moment and let her get her bearings. He leaned back and studied his daughter's preoccupied face. She was still exquisitely beautiful to him—hell, she'd always be beautiful to *him*. But Jonas knew it was more than paternal prejudice; a woman with Maryanne's looks and personality would have no trouble holding on to any man she chose. And any man who would let her go was nothing short of a fool. She was very much his beloved late wife's daughter, graceful, charming in a very soft-spoken way, giving—perhaps too giving at times, he had often thought. But most of all, loving.

He hated to press, wanted to give her time, but it was going to be hard. Damned hard. A marriage of thirteen-plus years didn't just go up in smoke in one day; and that's what seemed to be the case here. When Maryanne had telephoned from the hotel yesterday, she'd sounded fine. He'd been disappointed that she hadn't persuaded Elliot to stay with him, but he'd understood and hadn't made a fuss over it. Whatever had happened, it must have been something sudden and traumatic. He was concerned, really concerned, for her.

"Dad?" Her voice was small, remote, and for a moment Jonas wasn't even sure she had spoken.

"Hmmm?"

"I know I should say something . . . give you some explanation. And you deserve one, especially with me barging in on you like this."

Jonas's tone was brusque. "Now, I don't want to hear you say that again, Maryanne. You're my daughter, my own flesh and blood, and I'll be damned if I'm gonna let you sit there and imply you're barging in on me. This place is your home too, and if you want to stay for the rest of your *life,* that suits me fine. Just fine indeed."

The corners of Maryanne's mouth quivered upward and her father's face became a blurry image. Suddenly, Maryanne's breath caught in her throat and she pressed the palm of her hand over her mouth. "Oh, Daddy," she gasped, overcome by all the emotion she had been trying to keep under control. But there was no need to keep it all in now, and she knew she couldn't have anyway. Her shoulders shook and her entire body trembled with the force of the grief and sadness and pain that finally erupted. She felt her father's arms slide gently around her; it seemed a lifetime since she had felt them, so comforting and reassuring and loving.

"It's okay, sweetheart," Jonas muttered thickly, rocking her back and forth. The sound of her weeping ripped through him, giving rise to an instinctive, protective anger at her terrible pain.

She cried for a long time before her sobs gradually subsided. Taking shallow, shaky breaths, Maryanne felt her father's old faded work shirt dampen beneath her cheek. They sat still now, silent, both with their own private thoughts. Finally, Maryanne lifted her face from her father's shoulder and sat up straight, wiping her swollen eyes with her thumbs.

"Sorry about your shirt," she said with a wan smile. Her mascara had smeared his shirt with jagged, black streaks. "I'll wash it out later." But Jonas just shrugged and said, "Forget my shirt. Here." He reached over to pick up her glass. "Drink this now," he urged gently.

And she did, swallowing the dark-gold spirits gratefully. The warm sting of it soothed, and after several seconds she felt its fiery potency churning inside her stomach. She set the glass back down on the coffee table and directed her puffy gaze at her father.

"Thank you," she said softly, her eyes conveying her deep gratitude. She looked down at her lap, her fingers gently twisting the cotton-blend material of her slacks. She was tired, very tired, but she felt an obligation to level with her father. He needed to know what had happened; he deserved to know.

"Dad," she began, "I . . . I think it best you understand just why I'm leaving Elliot. I found out something about him tonight that came as quite a shock—a terrible shock." She swallowed and went on in a taut, strained voice. "Elliot had a vasectomy while he was in Vietnam . . . That's why we've never been able to have children. He never told me about it."

Jonas frowned in obvious confusion, as though Maryanne's words hadn't registered, let alone made any sense. "What do you mean? I thought—"

"That we were trying to have a child," Maryanne finished for him. "We were." She reached up and rubbed her middle finger distractedly against her jaw. "*I* was trying. He . . . he was just lying to me about . . . about everything." The words sounded hollow. *This is a dream,* she thought. *Surely I'm not saying this.*

Jonas shot up off the couch so abruptly that Maryanne was startled. She was stunned by her father's flushed, angry features. "What exactly are you saying?" he asked gruffly. "Surely you're not telling me he . . . Are you saying he *knew* all these years that he could never get you pregnant?"

Maryanne nodded slowly, her father's disbelief intensifying her own sense of unreality. Suddenly she realized the

69

consequences of Elliot's deception; they went far beyond her own disappointment and betrayal. Her father had wanted grandchildren—as had her mother—for so long. She was their only child, and they had really believed that someday Maryanne and Elliot would have children.

Jonas began pacing up and down the length of the den, an old habit denoting his extreme agitation, something Maryanne hadn't seen in years. She was thinking it would probably have been better not to have told him everything, when he stopped, swung around, and faced her. He ran a hand through his thinning gray-flecked brown hair. "I can't believe he would do something like that. Why couldn't he have told you? It's . . . it's unforgivable. I would never have dreamed . . ." His voice trailed off and he sighed lengthily, painfully. Jonas Anderson had come to like his son-in-law, but it had been a long, sometimes trying process of struggling to understand what exactly made Elliot tick. And, if the truth be told, he never really had figured it out. But Elliot had loved his daughter and taken care of her reasonably well—or so Jonas had believed.

"Dad, I'm really sorry,"

"For what?" Jonas shot back angrily. "I don't want to hear you say those two words again, do you hear me? You have nothing in this world to apologize for."

Maryanne studied the carpet at her feet and chewed one corner of her mouth. "All right," she said quietly. "You know something, Dad, I'm really tired. I don't think I can sit here very much longer." And she *was* tired, all over— her body, her mind, her soul.

"Sure you are. I've put your things in the guest room. Why don't you see if you can get some rest," he suggested.

"Thanks," she said, grateful for the soothing pressure of her father's hand on her shoulder as they walked toward the back of the house. Maryanne entered the bedroom and turned around, smiling feebly at her father. "Dad . . . I've hardly spoken to Elliot about this at all. I just couldn't. He more or less admitted it and . . . that was about all I could take. I don't feel like talking to him at all right now." She paused, then went on, "So, I'd appreciate it if you'd give him the message if and when he calls."

"Sure, honey. You don't worry about a thing. Just try to get some rest, if you can."

Maryanne nodded and attempted another smile. Then she closed the door gently as her father left. She walked back across the room, picked up her suitcase, and placed it on her old bed, one she and Elliot had shared occasionally over the years. Wearily she opened the lone piece of luggage and searched until she found a nightgown.

Maryanne undressed and slipped into the nightgown in the adjoining bathroom. Then she returned to the bedroom and removed the suitcase before pulling back the covers. She moved as if in a trance, and when she finally sat down on the edge of the bed, she wondered how in the world she had gotten there. Her mind was befuddled, almost numb from the emotional turmoil of the past few hours. It still didn't seem real, nothing did, and finally she lay back on the bed, forgetting to switch off the bedside lamp.

When morning came, its gray-gold light slipping through the slits of the amber blinds, the lamp was still burning, as was the unfamiliar, unbearable pain in her heart.

* * *

Cumulus clouds completely engulfed the Boeing 727, giving the impression, if one cared to stare out into the billowing mass, that the airplane wasn't moving at all. It was an uncomfortable, disorienting sensation, but Sam Lancaster's gaze remained fixed as he stared out the window, an empty glass in one hand, an unopened magazine on his lap. They'd left a day early, and Sissy was really upset about it. For once she'd wanted to stay in Nacogdoches; in addition to the dance, there was a barbecue being held the following day. But Sam had insisted on leaving. After last night he had no desire whatsoever to remain there. He had to get out, to escape the memories.

"May I take your glass, sir?"

Sam felt a nudge on his forearm, and he turned to find the flight attendant looking at him with a pleasant, expectant look, his wife with a surly, disgruntled one.

"Are you sleeping or what? Hand her your glass." Sissy spoke through taut, perfectly lined and glossed lips; Sam could see she welcomed the opportunity to snipe at him again.

But he said nothing. He merely handed the plastic cup to the flight attendant and said, "Thank you." Then he returned to staring out into the grayish-white mass of clouds, only too willing to hole up once more inside his own thoughts.

Sissy, however, had had enough of his silence, and as she slapped shut the magazine she had been riffling through agitatedly, she snapped, "Are you going to sit like that the entire trip?"

Sam sighed and turned his head slowly to look at his wife. "Do you mind if I just rest a little?"

"No, of course not, why should I? We have to do everything you want anyway, so what difference do my objections make?"

"Damn it, Sissy, would you just drop it? We're already on the airplane. It's not doing any good to groan about not being back in Nacogdoches. Since when have you become a fan of that dippy place anyway?" he added as an extra dig, knowing exactly where it would get him.

True to form, Sissy shot back, "You know damn well why I'm angry, Sam Lancaster. We were supposed to attend the barbecue this afternoon. I was on the organizing committee. I'm not in the habit of reneging on my social obligations."

"We'll do it next time," Sam said tiredly. He wished now he'd just ignored her.

"Next time! When? Ten years from now?"

Sam leaned his head back and spoke with his eyes closed. "What do you want from me, Sissy?"

"I want to know exactly why you insisted on leaving early."

"I told you—"

"And that was a lie if I ever heard one. I know damn well you don't have any 'important' work that has to be taken care of immediately. At least nothing that can't wait another day."

Sam was silent, hoping she would just shut up on her own. She didn't.

"So tell me, Sam. Damn it, it wasn't fair to pull me away from something you know I was enjoying."

There was a shred of truth in what she said, and after thinking it over a moment longer, Sam decided she probably did deserve an explanation.

"All right," he said, opening his eyes and looking directly at his wife. "Something happened last night at the dance that ruined everything, as far as I'm concerned. Joe Bob Simmons pulled one hell of a big one."

"What?" Sissy's momentary curiosity overcame some of the anger in her tone.

"He told everyone around him, in a voice loud enough to be heard over a freight train, all about Elliot's 'operation' in Vietnam."

"So?"

"So, Maryanne was standing a few feet away. She heard all of it."

Sissy drew an exasperated breath and clucked her tongue. "*That's* what had you so worked up?"

Sissy had struck a nerve and Sam suddenly sat up straighter. "You're damn right it upset me. It should upset *you*, too."

"Why, for heaven's sake?"

Sam's eyes narrowed as he said, "Doesn't it bother you the least little bit that you knew about something Maryanne had no idea of all these years? Something as important as that?"

"Why should it?" Sissy responded defensively. "*I* had nothing to do with it. And you didn't either."

"You should have seen her," Sam said, his constricted tone drawing his wife's attention. "She was devastated." He looked away as if the memory were too much to bear.

Sissy watched the play of emotion cross her husband's face. Then she stated in that condescending tone he despised, "Well, it was bound to happen one day. It was wrong of Elliot to keep it from her, I'll admit, but let's face it, Sam, Maryanne always was a little on the flaky side. Any other woman would have had the intuition to at least suspect what was going on. I mean, from the way she explained things, she and Elliot went to separate doctors to find out what the problem was—which was ridiculous, if you ask me. And another thing . . ."

As Sissy chatted on, oblivious to the explosive expression on Sam's face, something snapped inside him. Some deep, long-ignored hostility toward this woman beside him finally surfaced. He sat stonily, listening in silence until Sissy wound down. Here she was, giving her unsolicited opinion about a woman she could never measure up to in any way, a woman whose inherent integrity would never have allowed her even to think anything as derogatory as Sissy's denigrating barbs.

Having finished her monologue on the basic weaknesses of Maryanne's personality, Sissy sipped delicately at her bourbon and Coke, a smug, self-satisfied expression on her face. Sam remained quiet for a few moments longer. Then he turned slowly in his seat so that he was sitting sideways and forward. When he spoke, his voice was ice-cold, matching so precisely the frozen severity of his features that Sissy drew back reflexively.

"Now I'm going to tell you something," Sam began, "and I want you to listen *very* carefully." He paused, and his dark-brown eyes narrowed, then opened wide. "You will *never*, and I *mean never*, open that acid mouth of yours to speak about Maryanne in my presence. I can't stop you from shooting off your mouth to that insipid bunch of socialite groupies you hang around with, but I damn well can see to it that you keep it shut in front of me. You haven't got a sensitive bone in your body, and I doubt you ever will. It probably is asking a lot more than you're capable of, but you *will* do as I say." He moved his

75

head slowly from side to side, his eyes wandering desultorily over the lean lines of her body, then back up to meet her gaze. *You're so damn shallow,* he thought, *you'd never even suspect that Maryanne is ten times the lady you profess to be.*

Sissy gasped and her eyes widened, but the expression only made Sam wince in disgust. "Oh, cut the offended act, will you? I'm not impressed in the least." Sissy tossed down the rest of her drink and smirked hatefully at him. Then she smiled as if to indicate she wasn't in the least put off by anything he'd said.

Sam's expression darkened and he growled in a low, threatening tone. "You can cut the games, too, Sissy, because, believe me, I meant *everything* I just said. *Do* you understand?"

"Yes," Sissy spit out, then added with another smirk, "Perfectly."

"Good. Very good."

Sam leaned back in his seat again, turning his head to stare out the window once more. Sissy infuriated him, but he could handle her when he had to. What he was seriously beginning to wonder—and not for the first time—was just how much longer he could stand to live this way. When he had met Sissy and asked her to marry him, perhaps he had been more in love with the idea of love than Sissy herself. Though he would not willingly admit to being a romantic, in his heart he had always cherished the ideal of a woman he could truly share his life with, his happiness as well as his pain. A partnership based on caring, trust, mutual support. Hardly what he had with Sissy. As the years swept by, they had grown farther and farther apart. His dream of a loving partnership had remained just that—only a dream. Any love he once might have felt for Sissy was certainly not there anymore and hadn't been for a very long time. Her superficial values and shallow emotions had long since killed his feelings for her. But at least there was Melissa, his darling little girl. *She* was the reason he went on, and Sam admitted resignedly that he would sacrifice just about anything for her.

Oh, God, how tired he was. He closed his eyes and tried to let his mind drift to other, inconsequential matters, to attain, if only for a few precious minutes, the solace of sleep.

Sissy threw a resentful glance at her husband, then opened another of the fashion magazines she'd brought on board. Angrily she flipped the pages, hoping the noise was interfering with Sam's efforts to fall asleep. *Damn him,* she thought resentfully, *giving me a lecture about that woman.* He'd been angrier than she'd seen him in a very long time, and frankly she'd almost welcomed the display of emotion from him. He was usually so stolid, so everlastingly unflappable, that it had almost astonished her to see him get so worked up.

Of course she'd kept her mouth shut, no way would she have created any sort of scene on this crowded airplane. So, she'd let him spout off. Fine. Great. She knew exactly where Sam Lancaster was coming from, had suspected years ago that he still nursed a crush on Elliot's wimpy wife. It wasn't so unusual; she of all people should realize that. God, look how she'd responded when she'd met Richard in Chicago after all those years. And to think

77

she'd believed getting married would exorcise him from her system.

Well, to give credit where it was due, it had to a certain extent. Sam was a good, reliable man, and the three of them made a handsome, admirable family. After some time she'd managed to convince herself that this really was all she wanted, needed, in life. Until two years ago—and Richard. She shivered inside just thinking about what he could still do to her. Actually, she hadn't been all *that* upset to leave Nacogdoches a day early. There were things waiting for her at home that could make her forget real fast about the barbecue they'd missed.

She cast a glance at Sam and decided to slow down on the page-turning. To hell with it, maybe he did need a little sleep. It might put him in a better frame of mind. The roar of the jet engines was powerful and reassuring, and Sissy imagined the miles and miles of country they were rapidly leaving behind. All for the best, she mused. The farther they were from Maryanne, the faster Sam would forget what had happened and the faster his mood would improve.

She pressed the button on the armrest and pushed her seat back to the reclining position. Sighing deeply, she let the magazine fall onto her lap. Then, closing her eyes, she slowly began to relax. This would all be forgotten soon enough, she assured herself, probably by the time they landed. Lord, it wasn't as if it was *that* big a deal.

CHAPTER SIX

Maryanne was able to think more clearly now, though vestiges of pain and suffering and hurt too deep to be fully dealt with hovered precariously close to the fringes of this state of calmness. Walking carefully along the pebble-strewn narrow beach leading down to the lake, Maryanne thought that this must be the way a boxer felt the morning after losing a fight. In this case the wounds were emotional, of course, but they ached every bit as much as physical wounds.

She ventured closer to the water and decided to leave her tennis shoes on; they were going to get wet anyway. The water squished between her toes as she slowly walked along the eastern shore of Lake Nacogdoches. It was a small man-made lake, only a few miles outside of the city, and its deep, blue-gray waters sparkled invitingly, soothingly. Maryanne had awakened from a half-sleep just as the sun began to rise, knowing immediately she wouldn't get any more rest. She'd risen, dressed in jeans, T-shirt, and sneakers, and gone into the kitchen to make a cup of coffee. But after only one sip she had thrown the rest away and impulsively decided that she needed to get away, to be completely alone for a few hours.

She'd scribbled a hasty note to her father, telling him where she was going and that she'd return in a little while. He wouldn't wake for another hour or two, so she had plenty of time. She'd driven carefully and slowly around the lake, and had finally parked in an area that had no visitors or overnight campers. Then she'd come down to the water's edge, stopping for a moment to roll up her jeans before setting out on her walk.

The day would be another hot, humid, sultry one, but an early-morning breeze cut through the dampness now, and as Maryanne waded through the shallow water, carefully picking her way among the pebbles and rocks at the bottom, there was a gentle waning of her misery; nature was providing, at least for a while, a sorely needed diversion from her terrible thoughts.

Maryanne let her gaze roam slowly around the lake, appreciating its clean, fresh beauty. She needed to be alone, and this glorious setting was just the place in which to consider more rationally the events of last night.

As she stared blankly into the distance, a question suddenly echoed from the back of her mind. *Why? Why had he done it?* There were, of course, answers enough; it really depended on what she wanted to believe. But deep in her heart she knew the one true reason for Elliot's deception—his total and fundamental selfishness. In a sense, one might call it a basic defect in his personality, a selfishness she had suspected all along yet had chosen not only to tolerate, but to ignore.

It was strange that she could recognize such a trait in others, had even marveled at the extremes to which certain individuals would go to satisfy their own self-centered desires. Yet for some reason she had chosen not to see the same characteristic in her own husband. She was aware that in a childless marriage one partner often assumed the attention-grabbing role of a child and pressed upon the other partner his need for an all-forgiving, all-tolerant unconditional love. Undeniably, in their marriage Elliot had been the one to demand, and receive, most of the attention—and Maryanne had willingly provided it. And although she had done so unquestioningly, for the most part, there had been times when resentment had crept into her complacent attitude. Certain memories, incidents, came back to her now with haunting clarity, and she wondered seriously for the first time how she could have been so naive, so gullible? Still, she would have gone on that way, she knew that much about herself, for she believed in commitment wholeheartedly—and she *had* been committed to her marriage and to Elliot. It was a dedication that blinded her to the fact that Elliot did not share this same sense of commitment on his end of their union. But his small acts of selfishness, even his secret vasectomy in Vietnam, were not the heart of this crisis. What hurt more painfully than anything else was the knowledge that he *had* sired a child, his own child. She would have given the world to have had one, yet all he'd thought of was getting rid of it and finding the most expedient way to prevent a recurrence.

Maryanne shook her head, but the motion failed to

bring together the double image of the man she had married. Who *was* that man? She'd been an innocent teen-ager when she and Elliot had married, she knew that, but now, for the first time, she was beginning to question her reasons for remaining so complacent, so completely unassertive about her own unhappiness and confusion. Had she been afraid to admit that there were certain things about Elliot she didn't like, or was it merely youth and inexperience that had locked her into the stagnant pattern of accepting a life-style she didn't want. Was it a fear of disturbing the familiar pattern of their life together that had kept her from voicing her unhappiness? Or had life with Elliot brainwashed her so thoroughly that she didn't truly believe she had a right to real happiness, to complete expression of the person she was or might have become. All those needs had been effectively suppressed, all her energies directed to the task of making Elliot happy, soothing his discomforts and cheering him on in his efforts to succeed in the world outside of their marriage.

And that, of course, could be nothing more than a simple rationalization for her actions—or lack of them— over the years. God, he'd been so clever, so charmingly persuasive, and he'd made it so difficult for her to see behind the facade of his carefully constructed personality.

Elliot's face suddenly loomed before her, looking the way he had looked last night, riddled with guilt and regret. But what did he regret? Only that she had found him out. Then the awful scenario at the dance replayed itself once more across the unwilling screen of her mind, and she shuddered as the emotions of those horrifying few minutes possessed her anew. She recalled the men surrounding Joe

Bob, and could still see clearly the face of each man as he heard the facts that had been kept from her all these years.

But one face in particular was far more disconcerting than all the others—Sam's. His face had been a study in guilt and embarrassment and, worst of all, pity. Damn him if he thought she wanted his pity. She didn't, and she despised him for it.

All that time he'd known—he and Elliot and Joe Bob— and who else? The humiliating thought kept running through her brain in a nagging chant, and suddenly she reached up and clapped her hands over her ears.

Stop it, she told herself firmly. It made no difference what anyone else knew about her relationship with Elliot. Not anymore. She would never see any of them again. The determination of that gut-felt resolution provided a much-needed source of calm and purpose. She *knew* where she was going now. She had reached a decision that was totally her own. Instinctively her back straightened and she vigorously kicked at the surface of the blue-gray water, spraying glinting droplets across the smooth surface.

Placing her hands in the back pockets of her jeans, Maryanne slowly began to walk back toward the parking area. She'd told her father she didn't want to see Elliot and she'd meant it. She'd recognized the necessity to be alone, to get her own thoughts straightened out before she was subjected to whatever excuses or effusive confessions he no doubt had in ready supply. She'd lived with Elliot Douglass far too long not to anticipate the tactics he would try in order to gain her sympathy and forgiveness. How many times had he gotten around her by using that undeniably effective charm she had succumbed to in the beginning. But never again would it work, for though he was still the same man, her perception of him had altered irrevocably.

As she made her way up the rocky bank, water squishing noisily out of her sneakers, Maryanne suddenly made up her mind to go ahead and see Elliot. The sooner they talked, the sooner she could do what should have been done years ago.

She didn't have long to wait; the rented dark-blue Caprice was parked in the driveway of her father's house when she got back. Instinctively, Maryanne's foot eased up on the pedal, her heart suddenly tripping erratically in her throat. What was he doing here so early? She prayed that Elliot had had the good sense to keep his mouth shut with her father; she didn't want her dad involved, not at this point, anyway.

Deciding she'd better hurry inside and see what was going on, Maryanne put the car in park and got out, her feet moving swiftly along the porch toward the front door. But there were no sounds coming from inside, and as she rushed past the front door toward the den, something, some movement in the periphery of her vision, suddenly made her stop in her tracks. She turned and saw Elliot, alone, sitting tensely at the edge of the couch in the living room, a magazine clutched in his hands.

Seeing her, he stood up, threw the magazine on the coffee table, and took a few steps toward her. The morning light streaming through the curtains was not flattering; his face, which had been so handsome, so full of life last night, looked older, Maryanne thought, much older. His eyes were puffy from drinking; she'd seen that effect before. His chin and jaw were shadowed with a night's growth of beard, and his hair was oily and uncombed. He wore jeans and a plain cotton shirt half tucked in. Though she'd seen his casual side often enough over the years, Maryanne was nevertheless surprised at his disheveled state. In light of the thinking she'd done, it was almost as if she were seeing him for the first time.

He spoke first, his voice hoarse and full of irritation. "Where in hell were you?"

Maryanne didn't move from the foyer, and the look she gave him was like none he'd ever gotten from her before. "You will *not* speak to me like that, Elliot. I mean it. Especially not in my father's house. And if you plan to continue in that tone, you may as well leave."

Elliot's eyes narrowed briefly. He shoved one hand into his back pocket and wiped his pale face with the other several times. His eyes scanned the room, then came back to Maryanne. "Sorry. Your father's gone to the hardware store."

"I see. What did he say to you?"

"Not much."

Maryanne regarded him steadily. Then she said in a level tone, "It's understandable. I told him everything."

Elliot blinked and shifted his weight. "Yeah, well, I figured that much," he said uneasily. He cleared his throat, and Maryanne cringed inwardly at the annoying sound. "Damn it, Maryanne, can't you come on in here? Your just standing there really bugs me."

"Gosh, Elliot, I'm really sorry to *bug* you." She couldn't resist the sarcastic retort.

Elliot closed his eyes and drew a deep patience-summoning breath. "I didn't mean it that way. Listen, can't we just sit down and talk? Could you . . . would you please come inside?"

Maryanne clenched her jaw tightly and moved into the living room, taking a chair opposite the couch. When Elliot sat down again in silence, she prompted him with a lift of her shoulder. "All right. I'm here."

Elliot shifted nervously, and Maryanne was struck by the strangeness of the situation. The two of them were sitting alone in her father's house, about to discuss the most devastating thing that had ever happened to her. And she felt nothing, no emotion whatsoever except this haunting sensation, as if she were left only with the memory of something she had once cherished but which was now gone forever.

Suddenly Elliot plunged in. "God, Maryanne, I never intended for you to find out like this . . ." His voice faltered and there was silence for several seconds.

"I think the truth is, you didn't intend for me to find out at all. Isn't that right, Elliot?"

Elliot's pale complexion darkened visibly. He began digging one thumb repeatedly into the palm of the opposite hand, then suddenly he shot up off the couch and crossed the room to stand beside the window. "All right, damn it. No, I didn't intend for you to know. It . . . it would only have hurt you more to know the—"

"What? It would have only hurt me to know what?"

"To know my reason for having . . . it . . . done."

"That reason being that you didn't want to pay for another abortion? Is that what you thought would hurt more, Elliot? Or the fact that you were fooling around while you were in Vietnam?"

Elliot's jaw worked nervously, and he rubbed the palms

of his hands against the legs of his jeans. The conversation wasn't going at all as he'd planned. What he'd imagined was a heartfelt confession on his part, a begging for forgiveness, followed by a quick reconciliation. It had been bad enough last night, having to miss the rest of the dance; he'd made up his mind then he'd have her back for today's barbecue. He'd make this up to her—how or when he didn't know, but he'd come up with something. The only thing was, she wasn't reacting the way he'd planned.

"Look," he said, walking determinedly back across the room to where she sat. His black eyes looked pained and saddened, and he spoke in a somber, pleading tone. "Honey, please, try to understand. It was different over there, very different. It was another world, and it was like I was another person. I had no idea if I would ever even come back." He glanced down at the floor, then back up at her, his anguished expression reflecting the painful memory.

"And it was lonely, Maryanne. Real lonely. I was weak, I admit it. Most of the men were. Believe me, hon, there wasn't a day that went by I didn't think of you, but you were like a dream. There were times I'd dream of you and wake up not knowing if you existed only in the dream or if you were real." Elliot bent over and reached for one of Maryanne's hands, grateful when she didn't pull it away. Encouraged, he went on. "Oh, baby, you've got to understand. There was no right way to tell you what happened over there. I knew I'd have to someday, but when I got back and almost the first thing you said was that you wanted us to have a baby, well . . . I just freaked out. I didn't know how to handle it. I was wrong, totally wrong. I should have let you know, but can't you see? I didn't want to hurt you, and I knew then you wouldn't take it very well." He paused again, squeezing her hand tightly. "I just thought that someday it wouldn't matter to you anymore, that we would be enough for each other and you wouldn't mind that we didn't have children. Christ, look at all the couples who *decide* not to have kids!"

Maryanne didn't say anything for several seconds, and when she did her, tone was hollow and devoid of feeling. "I don't see what relevance that last statement has to our situation."

Elliot swallowed and gazed at her with wide eyes. "I guess it doesn't. I . . . I just . . . God, Maryanne, I don't know what else to say. I'm sorry, really sorry. But I love you. This shouldn't have that much to do with what we feel for each other. What we have is too strong, babe. We can get over this. Hell, we can even move on to something better."

Maryanne abruptly snatched her hand away and stood up. She took a few steps, then stopped and turned to Elliot, her features as frozen as ice. "Don't patronize me, Elliot. I'm not *entirely* ignorant."

"What are you talking about? I'm not patronizing you. I meant every word of what I just said."

One blond eyebrow rose sardonically. "I'm sure you did. For now. I suppose I can understand your unfaithfulness in Vietnam and I won't even bring up the casual affairs that I'm sure were a standard part of your out-of-town business trips. But just one question, Elliot. How do you justify all the lies, all the scheming to make me believe you really were being tested for infertility, the way I was?"

Elliot blanched at her words, guilt overshadowing his earnest expression. "I was confused. I felt bad and I didn't know what to do. But then I thought maybe it wouldn't hurt to pretend I was trying. I thought you would finally accept the fact that we couldn't have children."

"I see. Since I never would have found out anyway, I might as well think the problem was with me."

Elliot frowned at her accurate assessment and bumbled through a halfhearted objection. "That's . . . I don't think that's fair."

"Oh, you don't?" Maryanne snorted. "It seems, then, Elliot, that we have different opinions as to what constitutes fairness." She sighed heavily. "It doesn't really matter at this point anyway. This is all rather academic."

Elliot stared at her, waiting for her to go on. His passionate appeal had quite suddenly fizzled.

"It's no use, Elliot. I don't think there's anything more to be said." Maryanne glanced at her watch, then back at Elliot. "Your barbecue starts in just a couple of hours. If you leave now, you'll be able to dress and drive out to the lake in time."

Elliot frowned disappointedly. "I was hoping you would come with me."

Maryanne frowned and shook her head slowly, disbelievingly. "You obviously haven't gotten the picture, Elliot. This is not just a typical, run-of-the-mill marital argument. This is the end. I won't be going *anywhere* with you."

Elliot looked dumbstruck. "What are you saying?"

"I'm saying I want a divorce, Elliot. And I'm staying here with Dad until it's final."

Elliot stood, and when he spoke, it was in a brusque, irritated tone. "Look, I've admitted that I was wrong, and—"

"Elliot, it's over." Maryanne's green eyes softened somewhat with the emotion elicited by her words, words she'd never dreamed she could utter. And with those three words a blanket of sadness and regret descended over her, a sadness that all those years had come to this—nothing—and a regret that their marriage had become a statistic, another typical case of the American "divorce syndrome." Elliot gave her a dark look, completely different now. Irritation was the primary emotion in his eyes, annoyance at being put in the position of having to fight for something that was rightfully his, and anger at his normally willing, devoted wife who was now refusing to back down.

The screen door to the back porch slammed shut and they heard Jonas's boots thumping across the kitchen floor, followed by the sounds of the refrigerator door opening and closing. It was an interruption for which Maryanne was immensely grateful.

For all the courting Elliot had done of her father over the years, he was now quite uneasy about spending any more time in Jonas's presence. The cold reception he'd received earlier was message enough that he'd be better off leaving now. He crossed the living room to the entrance foyer, turned, and said gruffly, "Maybe it'll be better if you have some time alone to think things over. I'll call you later."

Maryanne said nothing, allowing him the illusion of having the last say. But her mind was made up—the decision was irreversible. She merely nodded and whispered, "Good-bye, Elliot." Then she shut the door behind him, standing there for a long moment before she turned and went back to the kitchen to greet her father.

* * *

Elliot did call, several times, but Maryanne was steadfast in her insistence that she didn't want to see him. And Elliot, unwilling to confront Mr. Anderson again, stayed away. He left on Tuesday morning; he was unable, he said, to afford any more time away from his job. He said he'd call in a couple of days when he got back home, and hopefully she would be "thinking more clearly" by then.

She was thinking very clearly, she thought—maybe for the first time in years—and she didn't change her mind. The first thing she did Tuesday afternoon was contact the lawyer her father had recommended, and as matters turned out, it was this attorney Elliot spoke to at the end of the week. Maryanne, he was informed, was filing for divorce. The papers would be served immediately, and if he wished to correspond with her, he could do so through Mr. Charles Raymondson, the attorney acting on her behalf.

There were letters—some of them dramatic, wordy pleas for her forgiveness; others, terse demands that she come to her senses and call this ridiculous thing off. But gradually they stopped. According to Mr. Raymondson, Maryanne would be a free woman within sixty days. After all his efforts, Elliot wasn't contesting the divorce and a mutual agreement as to division of property was reached between his own lawyer and Mr. Raymondson. Maryanne didn't even return to L.A. for her belongings; Mr. Raymondson arranged for that to be taken care of too. The fee was outrageous but worth it, for she had no desire to go back there. She had never liked it, and besides, she didn't want to chance seeing Elliot again.

After a few more weeks Maryanne found herself grappling with emotions more wrenching and devastating than she'd imagined possible. Yet in the course of doing so, she was able to make decisions, more significant ones than she'd ever had to make during all the years of her marriage.

Strange, she mused one afternoon, standing at the kitchen sink and washing the lunch dishes, her reaction to her present situation wasn't at all what she would have expected. She cried, of course, at unexpected times, but they were not tears of anguish or heartbreak, only of sadness and disappointment. And more and more the disappointment was directed not so much at Elliot as at herself. Elliot was what he had always been. The fault lay in herself for not having seen him clearly.

How many of the others they'd been friends with had known about his vasectomy, she wondered. It didn't matter, of course, not now, but still she couldn't overcome a sense of humiliation at the possibility that such an incredibly personal matter had been common knowledge to so many people. Again and again she remembered the look on Sam's face the night of the reunion dance—embarrassment mingled with guilt and, worst of all, pity. To think she had sat with him all that time sharing intimate details of her marriage that she never discussed with anyone else—the fact of their childlessness, how much it bothered her. And he had known the truth the whole time.

But it isn't fair, a small voice objected, to despise Sam for the fact that he knew everything, to practically implicate him as a conspirator in her husband's deceit. He couldn't have told her—it wasn't his place to do so. The entire issue just wasn't that simple. Still, it would be a very long time, if ever, before she could put all that behind.

The only relatively simple issue here was the matter of

her love for Elliot. There was no question as to how she felt; her love for him had died a painful, regretful, yet undeniable death. She thought of him quite often, but the memories were not good ones. It was as if she were forcing herself to reassess the marriage from a completely different perspective by continually drawing the bad memories to the forefront of her mind.

Indeed, as the summer days slowly expanded into weeks, Maryanne became aware of a gradually adjusted perception of *everything* in her life. She would soon be single, a state of adulthood she had never experienced since she'd gone straight from Mom and Dad to husband. She'd been dependent on other people all of her life, and even though she was living with her father again, that father-daughter relationship was completely different from the one they'd had in her childhood and teen-age years.

The knowledge of her impending single status also had another effect on her; she was filled with eagerness, almost excitement. One season of her life was over now, completely finished. What she wanted to do with her life from now on was her decision. She had no input from anyone else, not even her father, for much as he wanted her to be happy, he realized that the road she took must be chosen by her alone. His role was simply to be there for her, to support her in any endeavor she decided upon.

More and more the idea of attending college occupied Maryanne's thoughts. She'd thought of going many times over the past few years, but then she'd always had to listen to Elliot's derisive comments on the subject. It was a silly idea, he'd insisted in a condescending manner; she'd find it hard to adjust to the stress and demands of studying and having a strict schedule to adhere to after all these years of functioning primarily as a housewife. She'd be competing in classes with eighteen-year-olds. And furthermore, what in the world did she want to study anyway? Maryanne had always been stumped by that one and then come to the conclusion that perhaps he was right—unless she had some specific goal in mind, there was really no point in going to college.

Now, however, she began to look at it in a different light. Why not simply enroll in several basic courses, she asked herself. She had plenty of time to decide in which area she wanted to specialize. The idea appealed to her more and more, and she began to give it serious consideration.

Finally there came a day when that consideration solidified into a decision. She would do it; there was no reason not to.

When her mother had died, Maryanne had inherited a small piece of property outside San Antonio, where her mother was raised. At Elliot's urging they had decided to sell the land, but Maryanne had insisted on putting the money in a bank account separate from their savings. "For our children's education," she had said at the time. Elliot had raised a few objections, but finally had given in and hadn't even commented when the account was opened in Maryanne's name alone. His own guilty conscience had quieted him on the subject, she now suspected.

Though she couldn't say for sure what had prompted her to keep the money in her own name—perhaps deep in her heart she feared that Elliot would be too tempted to fritter the money away on some half-baked business scheme—she was glad now that she had followed her intuition. Now there would be no children, she thought with some bitterness. The small balance had been steadily earning interest and now she was certainly free to use the money for her own education. She could live with her father, which he very much wanted, and use her savings to pay tuition and other expenses.

Once she had decided, she was stirred by an unfamiliar sense of excitement, which was further enhanced by her father's enthusiasm.

"I think it's great, honey." Jonas smiled at his daughter, truly glad to see her taking such a step. He would have sent her to any university she wanted when she graduated from high school and had been disappointed when she'd popped the news that she was getting married. "In fact, it's a fantastic idea."

"Thanks, Dad." She smiled at him. "I thought you might say that." But with the excitement came a rush of doubts and fears that she wouldn't adjust so easily to this new life. Stephen F. Austin State University drew most of its students from other cities throughout Texas, and most of them were young, very young. Being a freshman at thirty-three years of age would most assuredly guarantee her a conspicuousness she was ill-prepared to deal with.

Yet it was a small concern in light of the greater significance of the step she had decided to take. For this would mark the most definite change in Maryanne's life ever, a change that had been long in coming but nevertheless was as necessary now as taking her next breath.

Day by day she was recovering, spending less and less time mulling over the past, analyzing what she had done wrong, and what she could have done better, and regretting how much of her life she had wasted. It just didn't matter anymore. All of that was over, behind her, and one day she would barely remember the pain and humiliation she had suffered. She would start this new life step by step, her own way, with nothing and no one to hinder her progress.

And she would do everything in her power to keep it that way.

CHAPTER SEVEN

The September afternoon sun beat down relentlessly, sending the mercury soaring to a record high on this late-summer day. Maryanne blotted a trickle of perspiration from her neck with the front of her cotton blouse, eager to be on her way home, where she could change into a pair of shorts and a T-shirt. As she walked along the narrow sidewalk toward the parking lot, however, her footsteps slowed somewhat and she absorbed the sights and sounds and smells of this new world of hers.

Stephen F. Austin State University had a beautiful, stately campus designed with the students' needs and comfort as top priorities. Bordering the meandering paths connecting various administrative and teaching buildings were colorful arrays of blooming plants and enormous swaying firs, and huge maple and oak trees provided a welcome ceiling of shade on days such as this one.

Maryanne loved it all. She had been attending classes

for two and a half weeks, and still the newness of it hadn't worn off. Indeed, she realized, she was a long, long way from being used to campus life. Adjusting to the routine of classes had been accomplished with relative ease, but the courses she'd enrolled in were already making significant demands on both her time and her energy. She was taking basic freshman-level courses, most of them prerequisites for any major she would eventually choose, and she was quickly finding the fifteen-year time gap since she'd last been a student a definite handicap. But even so, Maryanne had been pleasantly surprised to find she liked having to plan almost every minute of her day, loved the sense of purpose and direction it gave her life. There was nothing to hamper her, no one to claim her attention for other things, and so she was able to apply herself completely to her studies.

But as she walked toward the south parking lot, she reflected on the fact that sometimes her feelings toward this new life of hers were rather ambiguous. Since this was the fall semester, freshman classes were filled to capacity, and a substantial majority of the students were a good deal younger than her. Just out of high school, in fact.

They all looked like babies! She couldn't get over it. Of course, she'd been aware of the swift passage of time, especially during the last decade, but never as acutely aware as she was now. A girl passed her on the sidewalk just then, her smooth, fresh face smiling in friendly acknowledgment, and Maryanne smiled back. Had she once looked that young? Of course she had, but it was difficult to remember exactly what she had felt like at that time of her life.

No, she did remember. Married—that was how she'd

felt. Her life had been so completely different from these young women's, who were just starting their lives away from their families, striking out on their own for the first time, all of them experiencing at least some measure of independence. And now, at thirty-three, this was Maryanne's very first stab at it. When the decision to enroll had been made, she hadn't really thought about what her life would actually be like. Different, yes, she had assumed that much, but nothing could have prepared her for the onslaught of conflicting emotions that plagued her from the very first day.

She had searched her classes for someone her own age but had found no one. She was older than at least two of her professors! Oh, well, there really had been no choice in the matter, and she told herself that as time went on she would get used to the situation. Besides, going through this now made it easier for her to put the past behind, a past that had been almost too much to deal with.

Only the nights were still difficult, for she was not used to sleeping alone. Regardless of what Elliot had done, of how much he had hurt her, and despite the fact that she didn't love him anymore, she was still a creature of habit in many respects. More often than she wanted to admit, she would awaken in the middle of the night, cold terror spreading through her veins as she realized she was completely alone. It usually took a long time for her to go back to sleep and she hated nights like that.

But even these were becoming rare. College was the main cure. Afraid of falling behind in any of her subjects, she had decided on the first day to establish a schedule and stick to it. As her brain began the task of absorbing and filing away volumes of unfamiliar material—facts and figures, names and dates, theories and suppositions—more personal thoughts were shunted to another compartment of her brain. Sleep began to come more easily and more regularly.

All in all, Maryanne decided, she was adjusting very well to this new world of hers; she found enjoyment and a surprising sense of expectancy in each new day. As she reached her car in the lot, she shifted the books she was carrying under one arm and swung her shoulder bag around, balancing it on her hip. After rummaging around and finding her keys, she got into the car, switched on the engine, and turned the air conditioning to its highest setting.

Then she drove down the winding campus road to the North Street intersection, waiting in a long line as the signal light went through its changes twice. A hardware sign across the street caught her attention as she waited, and suddenly she remembered her promise to pick up a few supplies for her father. He was busy building one of his numerous projects—a tool shed behind the garage.

Maryanne turned left on North Street, deciding her chances of finding the supplies her father needed would be far better if she went to his usual hardware store. She pulled into the small parking lot of Richards' Hardware and Home Building Supplies and hopped out of the car, wincing from the heat as she hurried across the steaming asphalt into the store. Predictably, the air conditioning was out, though overhead and standing fans were running at top speed.

"Well, hello there, Maryanne," Walter Richards called out cheerily from behind his cluttered cubbyhole of an office. He was a large-boned, homely man with a quick and eager smile, always in a sunny mood. This was the slowest period of a particularly sluggish day and he was happy to see someone he knew.

As he stepped around the low wall separating an old plank desk from the register, he stubbed out a fat, smelly cigar in an overflowing ashtray. "What can I do ya for, little girl?"

Maryanne smiled and shook her head from side to side. "I'll let you get away with that 'little girl' bit, Walter, simply because I'm in a good mood."

"Well, I'm glad to hear that. How's it going up at the university?"

"Oh, fine. I feel a hundred years old, but other than that I'm adjusting like any other freshman."

"Oh, pshaw, you ain't no hundred years old, that's for sure. And you're so darn smart, I'm sure you'll just breeze right on through."

"Well, it's certainly not like a breeze right now."

"I take it Jonas sent you down here on a mission of mercy," Walter said, changing the subject.

Maryanne nodded, then opened her purse and fished around inside for a moment before coming up with a small metal bolt. "Do you have any of these? He said a seven-eighths would be all right too—whatever that means."

"Mmmm, I should have something real close to it." Maryanne handed him the bolt and Walter started off in his familiar lumbering gait toward the back of the store.

As she looked around, Maryanne noticed how little the place had changed over the years. She could remember coming here with her father when she was a small girl. But most of Nacogdoches was like that, with plenty of residents who had been around for most, if not all, of their lives—people satisfied and happy enough to stay put. That was an aspect of Nacogdoches that she liked—and had missed very much in California.

Following Walter toward the back of the store, Maryanne breathed in the old familiar smells of the place; it was a comfortable, secure feeling, as if she too belonged here. One thing was certain, whatever direction she decided to follow in her education, she would stay here in Nacogdoches, her hometown. She'd been gone far too long already.

The bell rang at the front register and Walter called out, "Be right there."

"Here we go," he said, turning to Maryanne with a fistful of bolts. "How many did Jonas say he needed?"

"Twelve."

"Okay. Four, eight, ten, eleven, twelve. There you go. Can I help you find something else?"

"No. This should do it. If he needs anything else, he'll just . . ." Maryanne's voice trailed off, her footsteps slowing to a stop as she recognized the person waiting at the register. It couldn't be . . . but it was. Sam Lancaster. What in heaven's name was he doing . . .

He was standing patiently at the counter, one hand absently jingling his ring of car keys and the other clutching a brown paper bag as he studied a do-it-yourself advertising board next to the register. He was dressed in old paint-splattered jeans, white tennis shoes, and a blue cotton-knit pullover. His hair was longer than she remembered, curling thickly down the nape of his neck, and his face and arms were tanned a toast-brown. Maryanne's initial shock at seeing Sam rapidly turned to astonishment at his appearance. Despite his disheveled look, possibly because of it, he exuded a raw virility that she had never before been aware of. Something sharp and disturbingly sensual flipped over in her stomach, and she swallowed convulsively, embarrassed and irritated at her reaction.

Sam saw Walter first, greeted him, then started to put the bag he was holding on the counter. Suddenly he froze as he saw Maryanne standing there. His smile vanished, and he seemed to be struck mute for a few moments.

Walter, who had popped back behind the register, said in his normal, good-natured tone, "Howdy, Sam. What's the matter, didn't it work?"

Although he was being spoken to, Sam's gaze never left Maryanne. Her face was flushed, and her discomfort at seeing him was obvious.

"Uh, no, it didn't," Sam answered finally. "I decided to go with the copper-plated. I have the other parts anyway."

"Well, I think that might be the best thing to do. I tell you, some of these 'kits' don't deserve the name. They don't give you enough . . ." Walter's voice droned on; he was completely unaware of the tense, wordless exchange taking place between his two customers.

Maryanne had moved closer to the counter to pay for her purchase, and when she turned finally and said, "Hello, Sam," it was all he could do to break away from the hypnotic pull of her enormous green eyes. His heart thudded in his chest as he heard himself answering, "Hello, Maryanne." He smiled and added, "I sure hadn't expected to see you here."

Maryanne accepted the change Walter handed her and said, "I had to pick up something for Dad. But I could say the same about you."

"Yeah . . . I guess that's true." As she started to move

away from the counter, Sam suddenly turned to Walter, who had returned with the proper-size copper tubing, and said, "Listen, be all right if I just make up the difference on another trip, Walter? I'm sure I'll be back tomorrow or the next day, and that'll save you the trouble of a refund."

"Sounds good enough. I don't need any more paperwork at the moment. Well, if you two don't need anything else, I'll just mosey on back to my 'office.' "

"Thanks a lot, Walter. See you later."

"Bye, Walter," Maryanne said.

"Tell your pop to take it easy."

"I will."

Maryanne walked out to the small porch that fronted the hardware store, truly at a loss for words. She was overwhelmed by a tumult of emotions. When Sam joined her on the porch, she turned to him, her tone as sharp and demanding as the expression on her face.

"What are you doing here in Nacogdoches, Sam? I didn't know you visited frequently."

Sam laughed and shook his head. "I don't. Actually, I live here now."

"You what?" Maryanne's eyes widened in disbelief.

"I live here," he repeated. He cocked his head slightly to one side and said wryly, "You sound as though that upsets you. Does it?"

"Of course not. I'm surprised, that's all," Maryanne said with forced nonchalance. Just meeting him like this had upset her terribly. But to hear that he was actually living here now! "I thought you and Sissy were pretty much stuck in Chicago," she added.

"We were. But I had an unexpected business opportunity here"—he shrugged—"so I headed down to Nacogdoches. As you know, it's what I've been wanting for years."

"What changed Sissy's mind? I thought she never wanted to leave."

"We're getting a divorce."

The bluntness of his statement, the unexpectedness of it, stunned Maryanne. Even if she had been able to talk, she wouldn't have known what to say. But it wasn't necessary—Sam spoke up first.

"It's a long, complicated story. But tell me, what are *you* doing here?" Actually he already knew she was living with her father; he'd been here for three weeks and news traveled fast in Nacogdoches. Ever since he'd learned of it Sam had been tense, wondering when and under what circumstances he'd eventually run into her. And he'd been tempted often enough to seek her out or phone her, but given her cool reaction now, he was thankful he hadn't.

"I'm living with my father," Maryanne replied. "My divorce from Elliot will be final next week."

Sam nodded once, then lifted the neck of his T-shirt away from his chest. An unruly mat of damp brown curls glistened underneath, and he blew a whoosh of air through his lips. "I keep wondering when autumn is going to get here. It's as hot as mid-July."

"It is, isn't it? Well, I've got to be going, so . . ."

She had taken one step down the old wooden stoop when Sam impulsively reached for her, grasping her by the elbow. Maryanne looked back at him in surprise, and Sam said hastily, "Listen, Maryanne . . . we . . . it would be nice, I think, if we could talk. The last time you and I saw each other it was a very ugly scene and . . . Well, I'd like to explain my part in all of—"

"There's no need to," Maryanne said crisply. "There's nothing I don't know or understand—now."

Sam released her arm and shoved his hands inside the back pockets of his jeans. "Maybe so. But . . . Well, I'd just like to give my version of the whole sorry mess."

"There's really no reason to, Sam. The 'whole sorry mess,' as you so aptly describe it, is over and done with. Elliot and I have gone our separate ways. He's a part of the past, a past that has nothing to do with my life now. And never will again."

The words were harsh, for Sam, too, was a part of that past. Yet as he studied the green eyes staring back at him obstinately, he could see that she was different now, very different. And it was he who was at a loss for words.

"So, I'll be on my way now," Maryanne cut into his thoughts, continuing on down the stoop. He followed her to her car, and as she opened the door he said, "I'd still like to give you a call sometime, Maryanne. I understand how you feel, but"—Sam hesitated and swallowed—"I'd still like to . . . talk."

"I meant what I said, Sam. There's *nothing* to talk about. And I'd rather you didn't call."

As Maryanne got inside, a blast of hot air hit her full in the face. The vinyl seat was scorching hot, burning her legs even through the cotton material of her slacks, and she switched the motor on quickly and backed the car out without a backward glance.

Sam remained where he was, and as he watched her drive away, he felt the tiny spark of hope he'd so carefully refrained from nourishing flickering dangerously low.

He'd been foolish even to consider the notion for one second. Maryanne had always belonged to another man; now that she was free, she had no feeling for him other than scorn. And he understood her reaction, but empathy didn't lessen the pain and sadness. He got into his car, turned the motor on, and headed out of the parking lot. The afternoon was far from over, and he had a lot of odd jobs to take care of before he called it a day. Which was a good thing; the best thing he could do was to set his mind on other things and try to forget his painful meeting with her.

Maryanne drove at a furious pace, her frustration and anger at seeing Sam building by the second. *Why* did he have to come back here to live? Why *now,* when her new life was just getting off to a firm, healthy start. Sam Lancaster was nothing but bad memories, an unwanted reminder of the very part of her life she never wanted to deal with or think of again. It had been three months since the reunion, and she had come a tremendously long way in dealing with the hurt and disappointment and humiliation. And all on her own. The last thing she wanted was Sam's presence reminding her of what she'd banished from her memory—a past that was over and done with forever.

Jonas walked out of the garage just as Maryanne pulled into the driveway. As usual when he was working around the house, his dress was a bit on the zany though definitely practical side. He wore an olive drab work suit, one of several he owned, and a baseball-style cap, from the back of which hung a white handkerchief to protect his neck from the sun. Dark prescription glasses completed the outfit. Maryanne smiled and shook her head. He never changed. He'd been wearing that same outfit, or some version of it, for as long as she could remember. The "Mafia-sheik" was what she'd always jokingly called him. Jonas claimed he couldn't understand her amusement; it was the most practical outfit he could wear in this sort of weather, he insisted.

As she pressed down the emergency brake and gathered her books and purse in one hand, Jonas came around to open the door for her.

"What's the big hurry? I've never seen you take the gravel road that fast."

Maryanne groaned as she pulled herself out of the car. "Was I going too fast?"

"Let's just say if you do that often enough, that shiny fender is gonna be covered with scratches." Jonas stepped back and cast a glance at the rear fender of the car.

Maryanne sighed deeply and shoved her hair back from her face. "I know. You're right. I was just in a hurry to get out of this heat. Let's go inside."

"Did you remember—"

"Yeah. Here, they're in the bag in my purse."

Jonas nodded and accepted the small bag, then walked ahead of her to open the back kitchen door. "I've got supper ready. Are you hungry?"

"Starved. What are we having?"

"Spaghetti. I hope it's not too heavy."

It was, especially for a hot day like this, but Maryanne wasn't about to voice an objection. She was much too irritated and hungry, and she needed food, any food, in her stomach. "Sounds great. Do we have any wine to go with it?"

"Sure." Jonas opened the refrigerator door and removed a bottle of California burgundy from the side door. "You go on and get into something cooler. I'll put all this on the table."

"All right." Maryanne hesitated before walking off to her bedroom. "And, Dad, how about getting a little cooler yourself?"

"Hmmm?"

"Your outfit." She glanced pointedly at his hat-hand-kerchief headgear.

"Oh, yeah," Jonas mumbled absently, lifting a hand to remove it.

Maryanne grinned. "Be back in a sec."

After changing into a pair of brief white shorts and a cotton T-shirt, Maryanne walked barefoot back to the kitchen, relishing the feel of the cool air of the house on her skin. As her father laid out the stainless and plates and put the food and wine on the table, she tidied up the den, picking up scattered newspapers, half-read copies of *Newsweek* and *Time,* and puffing up throw pillows on the sofa and love seat.

"Dad, you remember Sam Lancaster, don't you?"

"Sure. He's back in Nacogdoches, gone into real estate development here."

Maryanne straightened up and stared at her father. "How did you find that out?"

Jonas dislodged the cork from the wine bottle and said, "Something wrong with it?"

"No. Of course not. I just wondered . . ."

"Joe told me about it last week."

"Oh." Joe Lancaster was another of her father's numerous acquaintances. He was also Sam's uncle, Sam's closest relation here since his parents' deaths five years ago.

"Come on, sit down," Jonas said, taking his own seat at the dinette table in the breakfast nook. He put salad on his plate as Maryanne helped herself to a serving of spaghetti. "Why'd you ask about Sam moving back?"

Maryanne shrugged, then reached for the sauce. "I saw him today. At Walter's."

"I see. . . . Why do I get the idea it wasn't such a happy occasion? I thought you two were good friends."

Maryanne took a long sip of her wine, then said stiffly, "We *were* good friends."

Jonas said nothing for a moment. He chewed in silence, appeasing his healthy appetite. "And you're not anymore?" he finally asked.

"No."

"Sounds kind of final."

"It is."

"Mmmm." Jonas went back to eating for a few more moments. Then he said, "Well, I sure don't understand it. You and Sam have known each other for as long as . . ." His voice trailed off as he suddenly realized what he'd almost said. The subject of Maryanne's marriage had been off limits for the past several weeks. Privately, Jonas thought it would help if she talked about it; there was so much she obviously hadn't worked through. Not that he was a therapist or anything like that, but it didn't take a professional to see that the girl was only covering up, pretending to be completely over something that had hurt her a great deal. She was doing fine, there was no doubt of that, but it would help her, and him, too, to accept and understand if she'd open up on the subject. It was almost as if she were denying the whole thing. And no one knew better than he how futile *that* was.

"As long as I knew Elliot. Is that what you were going to say?" Maryanne asked bluntly.

"Look, honey, there's no need for you to put me on the defensive. I can't help but bring it up sometime or other. He was my son-in-law."

Maryanne sighed, feeling contrite about her unnecessary curtness. "I'm sorry. I just don't like to talk about it—or him—that's all."

"I know that much. And I haven't tried to make you."

"True."

"But, honey, you are my daughter and I can't ignore what I see before my very eyes. You're not the same— you've changed a lot."

Maryanne frowned and her shoulders straightened perceptibly. "I *hope* I have. I have no intention of letting the past ruin the rest of my life. I won't make that mistake."

Jonas laughed dryly and shook his head from side to side. "No, you've sure made up your mind on that one." Then he leveled his gaze at her, his tone soft yet firm. "But you can't ignore the past, either."

"I'm not."

"Yes, you are. It's what you're doing with Sam. He's a part of the past and you don't want to have anything to do with him."

His words hit home. He was exactly right. Maryanne's lips twitched, and she suddenly pushed her plate back. She wasn't hungry anymore. "There's more to it than that, Dad. Sam knew all about Elliot and what he'd done in

Vietnam. He knew about it and Sissy knew about it—*everyone* knew about it."

"How do you know that for certain?"

Maryanne threw her napkin on the table. "Oh, Dad, come on. I'm not a child. And I'm not going to be a fool anymore. Nice, sweet little Maryanne, walking around for thirteen and a half years with her head in the clouds, blind to what's going on right under her nose. It's kind of ironic that I've figured out in three months what I should have known for years. What *everyone,* not just Sam, knew all that time—that I was a stupid, gullible fool."

"First of all," Jonas said, unperturbed by her outburst, "you weren't being a fool. You were just being yourself—a trusting, loving person. It was Elliot who was the fool. He took his chances and look where it got him. He lost the most valuable thing in his life."

Maryanne got up from the table, too agitated to remain seated. "Oh, Dad, it's sweet of you to say that, and I know you probably really believe it, but that's not the point."

"Then what is?"

Maryanne poured herself another glass of wine and refilled her father's glass. Then she sat down and took a sip of the wine, which was finally beginning to calm her down. "The point is, I want to start my life over again. Without *any* reminders of what went before."

Jonas regarded his daughter silently for a moment, his gray eyes darkened with sorrow and concern. "Sweetheart, I can understand that. Lord knows, there were times I wished I could stop thinking about the past too, but it doesn't work. You have to deal with it."

"I know, Dad. And I am trying to deal with it. In my own way and in my own time. And I've been doing fine.

I just don't need Sam Lancaster stepping back into the picture to complicate things."

Jonas sipped his wine and nodded a silent response.

Maryanne spoke quietly, the look in her eyes softer now. "I'm sorry I even brought all this up. Except . . ."

"Except what?"

"Except that there is one thing I want you to do for me."

"What is that?"

"I don't want to talk to Sam. If he calls, which he very well may do, I just want you to tell him I'm not here or that I don't want to talk to him . . . or whatever. Just keep him away."

Jonas sighed and shook his head in agreement. "Honey, you know I'll do anything you want, but I see Joe pretty often. I don't know if it's entirely possible not even to mention his name on occasion."

"I don't care if *you* talk to him or see him. *I* don't want to see him, and I would appreciate it if you'd do what I ask."

"All right, then. If that's what you want."

"It is."

Later that night, as Maryanne struggled to keep her mind absorbed in the pages of *Madame Bovary*, which she was reading for a literature course, the conversation with her father kept popping into her thoughts. She'd meant what she'd said about not wanting to talk to Sam. Yet . . . she couldn't ignore the part of her that wanted just the opposite, the part that was clamoring with questions about

113

what had happened to *his* life.

She supposed it was because they'd known each other all these years that her curiosity was piqued; it was only natural that she'd wonder what in the world had happened to bring all this about—Sam living in Nacogdoches and divorcing Sissy. Though they'd never really talked openly about it, it had been obvious to Maryanne that Sam wasn't happily married; but she'd assumed he'd stayed with Sissy for the sake of their daughter. So why a divorce now at a time in the child's life when she would need her father most? Were all men that way in regard to their children? Ridiculous! One could not condemn the entire male sex because of the actions of her husband and his former best friend. Her own father was very loving and had always had her best interests at heart.

Still, there were so many single-parent households these days, most of them headed by women. A depressing realization, Maryanne mused, finally giving up and closing her book. It was useless; she wasn't going to get any more studying done tonight.

Nevertheless she gave it one more try as she curled up in bed with a biology lab manual propped against her knees, her eyes determinedly fixed on the first page of her reading assignment. Her mind, however, had no intention of cooperating, and resignedly she closed the manual, placed it on the nightstand, and turned out the light.

Moonlight filtered through the bedroom curtains, changing the pale green bedroom walls to a deep silver-gray. The languid whir of the ceiling fan was lulling and soothing and within minutes sleep claimed her weary body.

It was an active, disturbing sleep, however, filled with unwanted fragments of memories and images of the past. She was sleeping in a king-size bed, alone, for Elliot had not returned from a business meeting yet and she had been too sleepy to wait up for him. She lay half on her side, half on her stomach, her face partially buried in the plump down-filled pillow. There was a familiar sound—the front door opening, followed by footsteps across the parquet floor of the living room.

He was home—good. She smiled, still partially asleep, drifting off into a more peaceful slumber now that he was home. Odd, but there were no sounds of running water or closet doors opening and closing, none of the usual sounds he made before coming to bed. She felt the bed move as he got in, then turned expectantly, her eyes still closed, toward the arms that would soon lovingly envelop her. They did, and she sighed, giving herself up to the warmth that surrounded her. But this, too, was different, and she opened her eyes to find that it was not Elliot who lay beside her but another man.

"What—" she asked in a frightened voice, her eyes opening wide in alarm.

"Shhh, it's okay."

"You're not Elliot," she said, still unable to see him clearly.

"He knows. He asked me to tell you he couldn't come tonight."

"But who are you?"

"Shhh." He bent his head to hers, his lips warm and inviting as they pressed against her own. His hands moved under her nylon gown, sliding it upward, his fingers stroking lightly, probing, evoking an instantaneous physical response within her.

Maryanne's eyes flew open and she stared wildly at the window, the rays of moonlight gradually giving her a sense of reality. Her heart pounded, and she raised up on her elbows in an effort to calm the crazy, alarming effect of the dream. Her upper lip was moist with perspiration and she wiped it with the back of one hand.

What in heaven's name had gotten into her? What a stupid, ridiculous dream. She'd dreamed often enough of Elliot over the past several months, but most of the dreams had been angry ones, scenes that went over and over some trivial incident she had chosen to ignore when it had actually happened. Her dreams were the forum for arguments that had never taken place, accusations that should have been made, but they had never dealt with their sexual relationship. Indeed, Maryanne had felt no desire for sex in months and she was glad of it. For one thing, there was no one to satisfy those needs, so, out of necessity and circumstance, she had put them on hold; and, for another, it made life one hell of a lot simpler.

But now this . . . this *ridiculous* dream—a sexual fantasy that had no root in reality, a fantasy that was disturbing and threatening to her peace of mind. For the man in her dream had been Sam Lancaster, and she had wanted him . . . more than she had ever wanted any man. Maryanne swallowed spasmodically. She couldn't understand why her mind would play a trick like that on her. She didn't *want* to understand.

She forced herself to think about something else, and gradually she began to relax. She was tired. There were so many different things on her mind now with school and all. . . . It was almost funny, if she let herself think about it that way. She drew a deep breath and let it out slowly, then closed her eyes.

She just wouldn't think about it anymore. And in time she would forget all about a meaningless dream that had nothing at all to do with reality.

CHAPTER EIGHT

The memory of the dream, however, was never far from her conscious thoughts, insidiously slipping into her mind even at the busiest times of her day. At night she prayed that in time she would be rid of it altogether, like all the other better-forgotten memories of her past.

And as the last vestiges of Indian summer gradually subsided into autumn, it seemed as though her prayers were indeed being answered. Sunny marigolds and colorful zinnias were replaced by the browns and yellows of chrysanthemums. Ancient oaks and maples enriched the palette of fall colors with their deep gold and rich burgundy leaves.

Campus life was in full swing now, and though at times she still felt a sense of being an outsider, Maryanne was swept up in her studies with an enthusiasm that surprised her. It was a somewhat different enthusiasm from that of her younger classmates, yet every bit as compelling and infectious. For Maryanne was discovering the heady joy and excitement of really using her mind. She studied hard, applying herself with an intensity that was almost completely absorbing. These endeavors left her virtually no time for any extracurricular activities, but she did not even notice, for she was lost within her own little world, a world revolving around herself, her father, and her studies. She'd never been an outgoing person, the sort to make friends easily, for she had always believed that true friendships came only with time, a lot of time. And over the years, the life-style she and Elliot had led had not afforded them much time to devote to friendships. She had by now, however, made acquaintances in most of her classes and would occasionally join them at the student union to talk about classwork assignments over coffee. The age difference still prevented these friendships from growing into something more lasting, but she was doing quite well on her own. So she told herself.

Lake Nacogdoches had become a frequent haunt over the past couple of months, and her visits there had increased to an average of one a week. It was close, a mere fifteen-minute drive from her father's house, and the early-autumn weather made her visits there a perfect time for relaxation and quiet reflection.

The lake provided a soothing, soul-mellowing retreat, a place where she felt at peace with the world and was able really to think about the inner confusion that still troubled her at times.

Today, a Friday afternoon in early October, was ideal for the drive. She'd had a short day, her classes ending at noon, so she decided to go home first, change, then head out to the lake. By one thirty she was there. She parked her car, slipped her knapsack across her back, and set off for her favorite spot where three towering pines stood in triangular fashion just near the water's edge, the red-dirt ground between accommodatingly flat.

She set her book-laden knapsack beside a tree. Then she straightened and stretched backward, pressing her hands against the small of her back and expelling a lengthy sigh. Her gaze spanned the perimeter of the dark-blue lake, noting a few scattered visitors, two fishermen in small dinghies on the far side, and the reassuring presence of the brown and beige van of the park patrol.

Not yet ready to get down to her studies, she started off for a walk along the water's edge. Her gaze idly swept her surroundings once more, and she noticed another car pulling into the same parking lot she'd used. But it appeared as though the driver had no intention of stopping, so she turned her gaze away, mentally calculating how much of her biology reading assignment she would have to cover today. It was a lot, but it was good to know that if she had to get down to business, she couldn't have picked a better spot in which to do so.

Sam circled the asphalt parking lot slowly, his gaze taking in the small scattering of visitors at the lake. He had recognized the car as soon as he drove up; Jonas had told him where she most probably would be. He was anxious and somewhat worried for several reasons, not the least of which was the fact that Maryanne didn't want to see him, as Jonas had informed him. Sam couldn't blame her, of course, but neither could he completely extinguish that persistent flicker of hope that she might change her mind eventually. Eventually! How much time did that mean?

There was no getting around it now, though; he had to talk to her, to try to get her to the point where she would at least speak to him. Jonas had agreed wholeheartedly. He hadn't wanted to talk to Maryanne about the proposed business venture between himself and Lancaster Development because he knew far too well his daughter's feelings about its owner. But *something* had to be done, and since the problem involved Sam himself, Jonas decided Sam should be the one to take care of it.

He pressed his foot down on the emergency brake and reached for the door handle. Well, at least they could talk in private; there was no one else around. It bothered him that she was so isolated here, but according to Jonas she came here frequently, so he could only assume she knew what she was doing.

Maryanne was engrossed in a textbook when he approached, and didn't even hear the crackle of pine needles under his feet until just before he reached her. She whipped around suddenly, her complete surprise at seeing him evident in the expression on her face. "Sam! What in the world are you doing here? And how—"

"Your father told me you'd be here," Sam interrupted, coming to stand before her.

"He did?" Her features grew taut and her eyes narrowed perceptibly.

"Yes." He nodded silently, wondering how to begin. "Listen"—he scratched the side of one cheek—"I know you'd rather not see me—your father explained that some time ago. But . . . well, we both decided that considering the situation between us, it would be better if you were informed of everything. Now."

Maryanne put down the large yellow marker she was

holding. She looked puzzled. "What in the world are you talking about? And who is 'we'?"

"Jonas and me. Or Jonas and the Lancaster Development Corporation, I should say."

Maryanne stared dumbly at him. "I'm sorry, but you're not making a bit of sense."

Sam compressed his lips, then let out a whoosh of air. "No, I guess I'm not." He dropped down and sat across from her, conscious of not coming too close. "Actually, it's pretty involved."

He crossed his long legs Indian style, linked his hands together and stared at them for a long moment before looking up at Maryanne. "I suppose it would be best just to get straight to the point."

"Yes, please do." Maryanne resented this interruption of her studies, but even more disturbing was the presence of this particular visitor, one she had specifically told her father to discourage.

"Your father, me, and my uncle Joe signed a contract last week," Sam stated bluntly. "Concerning a business partnership, to be specific."

Maryanne's shoulders straightened as she leaned backward a bit. "That's preposterous. My father's retired. I can't imagine what sort of business he'd want to get into again."

"Yes, well . . . He may have told you—or perhaps you already knew—that I'm involved in real estate development here in Nacogdoches. Have been for the past few months. To make a very long story short, your father has decided to develop the twenty-five acres he owns near the Loop into one-acre single-family housing subdivisions. He's been sitting on that prime property for years and has finally decided it's about time he did something with it. I think he's made a wise decision."

Maryanne stared disbelievingly. "I don't believe what you're saying. He's never said one word about it to me."

"That's because of . . . Well, like I said, your problem with me."

Maryanne got up and walked a few steps away from the tree, agitatedly rubbing her hands up and down the sides of her arms. Suddenly she realized Sam was telling the truth; he was much too straightforward a person to be exaggerating or fabricating something like that, and besides, what would be his reason for doing so? But she was shocked by her father's apparent secrecy in the matter. They had become very close since she'd been living with him . . . or so she'd believed. Suddenly she turned and said, "Dad doesn't have the kind of money it takes to finance that kind of an operation. He owns the land, our house—but that's about it."

"Exactly. That's the reason for the partnership. My uncle Joe and I will be financing part of it, and I'll be arranging the rest. I'm the money man; as developer, it's my job to arrange the financing aspect of the operation. It shouldn't be too difficult to do through the local banks. Your father is a highly respected person in this community."

Maryanne shook her head. "I just don't believe it," she murmured.

Sam attempted a smile. "Well, you'd better. It's true, and I think you should be happy for your father. It's a project that he's really excited about, something he needs at this time in his life."

Maryanne's features grew rigid and she shot back,

"Don't you think it's just a *little* presumptuous of you to make such a personal assessment of my father's 'needs'? I must admit, though, I'm astonished that Dad decided not even to consult me about whole thing."

"It is *his* land," Sam said quietly. "There really wasn't any reason for him to consult you."

"Don't be condescending with me, Sam Lancaster. You know damn well what I'm talking about."

Sam was quiet for a moment. Then he said, "The fact that you don't want me around. Is that it?"

"Precisely."

Sam sighed heavily, his head dropping as he stared down at his hands. "Maryanne, look . . . I don't know what else to do, how to convince you how sorry I am about . . ."

Maryanne glared at him and said in a seething tone, "Sorry about what, Sam? About pretending for all those years that you knew nothing about Elliot's vasectomy? Is that it? Sorry that you talked to me—how many times—about the fact that I wanted children and that *Elliot* wanted children and told me it sure was commendable that we were going to all that trouble to find out what the problem was?" Maryanne leaped to her feet. The sudden rush of anger surging inside her had made her heart race, and an acid lump had formed in her throat; she was astonished at the intensity of her reaction.

"I'm sure you are sorry, Sam," she went on, "but let me tell you something. I don't want your sorrow or your pity. Save it." She was standing in front of him now, her green eyes glaring furiously. "And let me tell you something else. 'Sweet, innocent' Maryanne doesn't exist anymore. Unfortunately I learned it all the hard way—how people

I've thought for years were my friends and really cared about me were actually lying, laughing behind my back, feeling sorry for me. Not to mention a husband who deceived me all those years. Oh, yeah, Sam, I really should be more understanding of my father's needs, because what difference should *my* feelings make? I mean, I've been stepped on so many times—why not once more?"

Maryanne heard the self-pity in her voice and despised it. But she couldn't stop herself. "You were part of the whole scheme that kept me from knowing something very important, *crucial* to my life." Tears welled up in her eyes and Sam's face was little more than a blur. When she found her voice again, it was thick and barely audible.

"Can you even imagine how it must feel? To have *wasted* all those years loving a man who had so little respect for me that he would keep something like that from me? A man who loved no one, really, but himself. You'll never understand the humiliation that goes with realizing that everyone else knew but me. God, what a fool they must have taken me for. . . ." Her voice broke completely then and her features crumpled. She turned away, ashamed to let him see her breaking down this way and astonished at her own sudden loss of control over emotions she had so carefully kept in hand all this time.

Sam felt a powerful wrench in his gut at the sight of her slender back, her delicate shoulders heaving spasmodically under the curtain of honey-colored hair. Instinctively he came to his feet, yet he could not approach her. He felt wretched seeing her so upset. He shouldn't have come; he should have insisted that Jonas tell her everything.

The best thing to do, he reasoned, was what she had wanted in the first place—leave her alone. But he couldn't

125

do it, couldn't bear to leave her when what he wanted more than anything in the world was to hold her in his arms and see her smile again, just once. The emotions that overtook him were stronger than reason, for he found himself walking over to her and placing his hand on her shoulder until she turned halfway and looked at him uncomprehendingly.

And then his other hand found its way to her smooth, flushed cheek, its wetness moistening his fingertips. But it was the sight of her eyes that seared him to the core—deep, moss-green pools of misery and hurt and humiliation. He could stand it no longer. She was weeping openly now, great sobs punctuated by jagged gasps for air, the corners of her mouth quivering spasmodically.

Sam silently pulled her toward him, pressing her head against his chest with one hand and letting the other rest lightly against the small of her back. He closed his eyes, memorizing every detail of sensation evoked in him by this woman whom he loved so very much, breathing in her distinctive, sweet feminine scent. If only he could will away this pain she was suffering, this hurt she had tried so desperately to deal with alone.

He waited until the last of her weeping subsided, half-afraid she might realize where she was and pull away from him. But she didn't; her head continued to rest upon his chest, her back moving in and out in an erratic pattern until her breathing gradually became regular. Then he opened his eyes and very gently pushed her shoulders away from him.

She made no attempt to move, yet refused to look at him, turning her head and staring off into the distance. Suddenly, Sam could no longer ignore his need for her.

Very lightly, and with utmost care, his lips grazed the side of her face. She didn't move an inch. Then, with infinite tenderness, he turned her face toward his, though her gaze was still averted. He kissed each of her eyelids, tasting the salt of her tears and her silky lashes on his tongue. And when a deep shudder shook her body, it transmitted itself through every fiber of his being.

Slowly, tantalizingly, he eased his chin down the length of her nose, halting momentarily to gain control of his senses. But when his lips met hers at last, the exquisite sensation sent them reeling again. Yet somehow he garnered enough self-control to come to grips with the physical reality of the moment; the kiss he had dreamed of so many, many times before over the years was actually taking place. And the reality far exceeded the fantasy. For not even in his fantasy could he possibly have imagined anything to equal the sensation of her petal-soft flesh melding with his own, the thrill down his spine as her tongue shyly touched his own, exploring tentatively, then bravely, the inner recesses of his mouth. He was surprised by her response, yet supremely happy that she was finding as much pleasure as he.

Exactly how long the kiss lasted neither knew, but it was Sam who drew away first, fearful that he would lose what little remaining control he had over the fire of his passion.

Maryanne was stunned when he let go; she felt as though she had just awakened from a deep, drugged sleep; she felt disoriented and slightly off-balance. A warm flush began at the base of her neck and slowly swept upward. Distractedly she ran her fingers across the slight depressions under her eyes, keeping her gaze fixed on the ground.

She couldn't begin to look at Sam; she was confused, racked by a torrent of emotions that had begun with a desperate grief and anger and had ended with a passionate indulgence that was as incredible as it was unforgivable.

She swallowed, then turned away from him, walked back to the table, and began to gather her things. She expected him to say or do something, attempt an apology, come to her again, but he did nothing. Indeed, she finally looked up to see if perhaps he had gone. He hadn't. Curiously, he had moved a few feet away and was gazing out over the lake, hands shoved into his back pockets, his wide dark-brown eyes squinting against the descending rays of the afternoon sun. Seeing him that way, Maryanne had the strange sensation that she really didn't know him. But that was absurd. She knew him very well, too well now.

He appeared lost in thought, and she could only speculate as to what was going on in his mind. But it wasn't necessary to know that, she reminded herself. In fact, she had no desire to know it. Her own motives for what she'd allowed to happen could be examined and analyzed later, but his were none of her concern. Turning around, she crouched down and placed her books in the knapsack, then slung one strap over her shoulder and straightened up. The movement caught his attention, and as he turned around he said, "What are you doing?"

Maryanne braced herself and answered in a calm voice, "I'm going home."

"Maryanne, I—" Sam shoved a hand through his hair.

"Don't say anything, Sam. It's not necessary. I just went a little crazy. I'm sorry. It won't happen again." She paused, then said, "I don't like what you told me about your business arrangement with Dad, but if it's what he wants, I won't make any objections. But I won't be a part of it either. What I asked of you before still holds. I'm trying to start a new life for myself, Sam—a *new* life. It might not make sense to you or to Dad, but that's the way I feel and that's the way it's going to be. The past is over and done with and . . . you're very much a part of that past. So please, leave me in peace. All I ask is that you go your way and I go mine."

Sam's jaw tightened and he nodded once, saying not one word as she walked away from him—again. He turned back to look out at the lake once more, wondering what kind of fool he'd been to do something so presumptuous and stupid, but knowing at the same time that if he had a thousand chances to change what had just happened between him and Maryanne, he'd make the same choice, again and again.

CHAPTER NINE

Jonas was upset. He bustled around the house like a nervous hen, checked the wall clock in the den every five minutes, and wondered why in hell he'd done something so stupid. He should have talked to Maryanne himself, explained how and why he'd decided to go into business with Sam and his uncle. But hell, he'd never been much of a talker, just one to go and do whatever he felt needed to be done.

And so he'd made the decision to develop the parcel of land he and Miriam had purchased twenty years ago—their little country retreat, except it had never turned into that. It was still nothing but a tract of land overgrown with brush and pines, its value now lying solely in its prime location. Actually, he'd been thinking of doing something with it—at the very least selling it—for some time now, especially after Miriam's death.

Joe Lancaster, Sam's uncle, had brought up the subject

not too long ago, and the possibilities he'd mentioned had sounded truly interesting. So much so that Jonas had even begun to get a little excited about it, and for a man with few passions left in life, he'd reasoned the wisest thing would be to go with it.

The hitch, of course, and a major one at that, was Maryanne. It was ridiculous for a grown man to be so intimidated by his own daughter, but nevertheless that was the case. He loved having her here, enjoyed having someone to share things with, and after a year and a half of painful adjustment to a house full of empty rooms, that was a luxury he wouldn't trade for anything in the world. But the possibility that he was jeopardizing that luxury with this new business deal he'd gone into with Sam and Joe was keeping him on pins and needles. Maryanne had to be told, of course, but he'd had to tread so lightly where the subject of her past was concerned, that he literally hadn't known how to go about bringing it up. So he'd taken the chicken way out, and persuaded Sam to tell her.

Right now he was sincerely doubting the wisdom of that decision. She'd asked him specifically to keep Sam away from her and he'd gone and done just the opposite. He'd gambled on the possibility that Sam could get through to her, but it was entirely possible that in doing so he might destroy her trust in him, alienating him completely.

And that was something he just couldn't live with. At the sound of tires on the driveway, he set down the glass of juice he'd been sipping—he didn't really want it, he'd just needed something to do—and peered through the curtains over the kitchen sink. She was back. She got out of the car, slung purse and knapsack over opposite shoulders, and walked toward the back door, just as she always did. For an instant he wondered if perhaps Sam had not been able to find her and talk to her, but as she entered the kitchen through the utility room, her cursory glance in his direction told him that indeed Sam had.

"Hi, Dad," she said, plopping her books and purse down on the counter, then lifting the hair off the back of her neck in a familiar gesture. He could remember her doing that as a little girl.

"Hi. Are you hungry? I didn't cook anything, but there's some cheese and—"

"It's all right, I'm not that hungry. Maybe later." Maryanne sat down at the kitchen table, crossed her arms over her chest, and came straight to the point. "Sam came out to see me at the lake. He said you asked him to."

Jonas swallowed uncomfortably and scratched the stubble on his chin. "Yes . . . I did. I . . . Maryanne, I'm sorry I didn't tell you myself—"

"Why didn't you?"

"Because you've made it clear enough that you didn't even want to see Sam, let alone be around him. And . . . I knew if I went on and entered into this partnership, that very well might be the case. I knew you'd be upset."

Maryanne sighed and said, "I'm sorry you felt you couldn't talk to me. It's true, though, I *don't* want to see Sam. I feel the same way I did before. But it can be worked out. I don't see any reason why we should have to get in each other's way. I mean, it's not as if he'll be here all the time, is it?"

"No. But I sure wish you didn't feel that way, Maryanne." The stolid expression on her face warned him it would be useless to go any further, so he said, "But it's your decision and I won't say any more about it."

"Thank you." She paused and, looking down, said, "I am disappointed that you didn't discuss the development project with me, though."

"Well, I've had it on my mind for a long time and it's only been recently that I've decided to take action." Jonas picked up his unfinished glass of juice and walked over to join Maryanne at the table. "Your Mom and I always thought it would be our little country place, but"—he shrugged—"it just never materialized. I was always so busy with work and all that we just kept putting it off. Then after she died, I started thinking it might be best to go on and do something about it instead of leaving it for you to contend with when I'm gone."

"Oh, Dad, now don't start getting morbid."

Jonas finished his juice and said, "Nothing morbid about it. The fact of the matter is that it'll be worth a heck of a lot more developed into prime real estate than being left the way it is. And besides, the whole thing really does interest me. It's something I can sink my teeth into."

Maryanne smiled. "Well, I'm glad for you, then. How soon do you think it'll be before everything's finalized and you get started on it?"

"Oh, no more than a few weeks at the outside." Jonas's enthusiasm was evident as he launched into a description of the initial plans for the housing development. Maryanne listened, nodding and commenting, asking a pertinent question now and then, pretending an interest she really didn't feel. It was impossible; her mind was far too concerned with the confusion of her emotions, the acutely disturbing memory of what had happened between her and Sam. On the way home she had forced herself not to think of it and had been fairly successful. What had happened had happened, she'd reasoned; she had been upset, distraught—reason enough to allow Sam to comfort her, to provide a bit of physical contact she hadn't had in a very long time.

But that wasn't the entire picture, and she was very well aware of the fact. It didn't at all explain the depth of her response, the undeniable desire she'd felt for him. And there was still the dream, that ridiculous, totally unrealistic fantasy that perhaps revealed more about those needs and desires than she was ready to deal with. Indeed, judging by what had actually happened between her and Sam, there truly was reason for concern. But it wouldn't do—it simply wouldn't do. It was imperative that she adhere to the path she'd settled on, one that meant her life would truly begin again with absolutely no impediments from the past, no ugly reminders of what she would live without from now on—and that included Sam Lancaster.

Settling into her "new" life was accomplished with relative ease. Jonas was busy with his new business venture and respected Maryanne's wish to remain completely uninvolved. It would have been easier, of course, if Sam had never returned to Nacogdoches, but he had, and it was gratifying to see her father get so wrapped up in the new business venture. But the very nature of Jonas's association with the Lancasters precluded any hope on Maryanne's part that she could manage to avoid Sam altogether. Jonas had made himself available to the others involved in the project at all times, and more often than not Maryanne answered calls to the house for her father. Invariably the caller was Sam.

She was not necessarily rude to him, but was curt

enough to get the point across that she'd rather not be talking to him at all. There was always some message to deliver to Jonas, some reminder that required her jotting down a message and making sure it was correct, enough to keep her on the phone talking to him longer than she cared to.

Then there was the day she literally ran right into him. She'd gotten home from a long day of classes one Thursday afternoon, when Jonas telephoned. He'd forgotten some important papers at home, he said; he'd been searching all over the office for the folder they were in and finally remembered he'd left it on top of his bedroom bureau. Would she mind very much driving over to the site office and bringing it to him? He and Joe needed the information right away, and Sam would be joining them in an hour. There was no polite way to refuse, so Maryanne had agreed, telling him she'd be there in fifteen minutes. At least there was enough time that she could avoid seeing Sam.

Jonas and Joe were bent over the large gunmetal-gray desk in Joe's office, peering down at a thick stack of blueprints. Both were obviously preoccupied and gave Maryanne scant notice when she walked in with the folder.

"Is this it?" she asked Jonas.

"Hmmm?" Jonas pulled his gaze slowly away from the desk, then opened his eyes wide as he saw Maryanne standing there. "Oh, yeah! Thanks, honey." He immediately rifled through the folder and turned to Joe. "Here you go, Joe, this is what I was telling you. . . ."

Maryanne smiled slightly and shook her head. Joe hadn't even recognized her presence and her father had already forgotten it. Oh, well, she hadn't intended to chat with them anyway. She reached inside her blazer for her set of car keys and walked back down the hallway to the front office, temporarily blinded by the brilliant late afternoon sunshine pouring in through the windows and glass door. She squinted and looked down to avoid the glare, and as she pushed one hand out to reach for the doorknob, she was startled to feel something warm and woolen against her palm.

Uttering a little gasp, she jerked her head up, shocked to see that she had been pushing against Sam's sweatered chest. He had been walking in as she approached the door, and his tall form blocked the sun. Looking up at him, she noted the grin of amusement playing across his mouth.

"Sam!" she exclaimed, shoving her hand back inside her jacket pocket. She felt silly and embarrassed, and she attempted a hasty cover-up for her telltale reaction. "I . . . um, I'm sorry. I was just leaving."

"I see." Sam continued into the office, heading straight for the small kitchenette in one corner. He picked up an almost empty pot of coffee, grimaced, then set it back down on the burner. "I guess we're down to the dregs again. The usual." He paused. "I'll make some more. Would you care for a cup?"

Maryanne fiddled with the edge of her jacket, annoyed with herself for just standing there; she should be on her way out the door. "No . . . thank you. I was just leaving." She made no move to turn and walk out the door, however, and just stood and watched as Sam removed his jacket and leaned his broad back against the edge of the counter. What on earth was she waiting around for?

"Why are you here?" he asked, raising one eyebrow in curiosity.

136

She swallowed convulsively and then cursed herself immediately for the nervous reaction, which he'd definitely noticed. "I brought some papers Dad left at home. He said you were all having a meeting and he needed them right away."

Sam nodded and then came around the counter, placed a fist on his hip, and chewed one corner of his mouth, his dark eyes narrowing as if in thought. Then he smiled in his most winning fashion and asked, "You still mad at me?"

Maryanne managed a chuckle; the effort it took was obvious. "Of course not, Sam. I never was."

"Ha! Don't ask me to believe that one. Anyway, I'm sorry about . . . following you to the lake. I know how much you want to avoid me." He shrugged. "But it's bound to happen sometime or other."

"I know," Maryanne admitted in a small voice. She pushed at the hair on one side of her face, the unnecessary gesture drawing Sam's attention. He frowned, very slightly, as if concentrating on that one small movement of hers. Suddenly the walls of the small front office seemed to move inward, bringing them closer and closer to each other, and Maryanne felt a panicky sensation rise within her. It was absolutely ridiculous, this reaction to being with Sam, but reality was reality and she wasn't about to waste any more time standing here, her heart tripping all over itself, as if she were about to lose control completely.

Absurd, she thought, grasping for the keys in her pocket. She pulled them out, dangled them noisily, and said with feigned nonchalance, "Well! I'm sure you have to get into your meeting, and I need—"

"Maryanne, don't." Sam's voice was low, his gaze fixed

137

directly on hers. "Don't get so upset. I'm not coming after you, you know. You don't have to worry about that."

She stared at him for a moment, dumbfounded. He sounded so kind, so understanding. And oddly, that very fact irritated her immensely.

"I'm not worried about anything, Sam." She turned, took a couple of steps to the front door, then gave it a push. She was getting out of here—now. "I'd better get going. I'm late as it is. Good-bye."

Her hands were shaking on the steering wheel as she backed the car out of the gravel lot and onto the access road. To hell with it, this just wouldn't work. She couldn't go on freaking out every time she saw or spoke with Sam. She had to get her emotions under control. There was nothing between them, despite that unfortunate scene at the lake—there never had been and never would be. And for what had to be the hundredth time, she reminded herself that everything was all right, they were friends, old friends who just happened to be crossing the same path once more.

There were other occasions when Maryanne had to deal with Sam after that, mostly telephone calls to the house for Jonas. She took them in stride, though disconcertingly the mere sound of his voice still had a jarring effect on her. Just why she was so affected puzzled and confounded her; she could see no reason for it, because they ran into each other so seldom and the memory of that one kiss, and of the dream, hardly ever haunted her anymore.

Other aspects of her life were coming along fine, however; Maryanne was finally getting used to, indeed really enjoying, the college routine. She immersed herself in her studies, spending an equal amount of time with each subject because she still had no solid ideas about what she wanted to major in. Economics interested her a great deal, as did government and political science. Where in the world had she been all these years, she often wondered, astonished by the extent of her ignorance concerning the world and what was happening in it. She supposed this was a reaction to her intense involvement in the last years of the Vietnam war; yet long after the war was over, she had continued her indifference toward everything not specifically connected with her own small world. All she'd cared about was her life together with Elliot and her unrelenting determination to have the children she so desperately wanted.

And look at her now, she thought ironically; she had neither a husband nor children. Now there were only herself and this ferocious hunger awakening in her mind. There was no way she could nourish it enough. She struggled to make up for lost time, but found that the more she learned, the more she became aware of her own ignorance.

Another person was aware of this intensity in her, this genuine love of all things to be learned. His name was Michael Donover and he was Maryanne's twenty-nine-year-old history professor. He hadn't noticed the willowy honey-blond woman until the second week of classes, and he'd later wondered why in the world it had taken so long. Granted, the class was very large, almost a hundred students, so it was nearly impossible for him to know them all on a name basis, even by the end of the semester. But over and over again his gaze was drawn to the slender woman who usually sat in the fourth row and was by far the most attentive student in his class. She noted every word of his lectures, even when he indicated that what he was saying was just an aside and would not be included on exams. After the fifth week of class he found his concentration seriously ebbing on more than one occasion, and he could not ignore the cause of it any longer.

He ended his lecture early one Friday afternoon, much to his students' grateful surprise, since the Lumberjacks had an important game that night. Maryanne was stuffing her notebook inside her knapsack as the other students began filing out, and suddenly Michael decided the time was right to get this out of his system.

"Mmmm, excuse me, Miss . . . ?"

Maryanne looked up at him and Michael was struck full force by her lovely, intensely green eyes. Unconsciously he swallowed, then smiled rather nervously.

"Anderson. Maryanne Anderson."

"I'm sorry. I never get to know my students' names even by the end of the semester."

Maryanne smiled back at him and he noticed the light yet distinct feathering of lines around her beautiful eyes. He was surprised; it was rare indeed that he looked out upon any faces other than those of teen-agers.

"I don't see how you could," she answered. She waited, but he said nothing else, just stared at her, so she tilted her head to one side and asked, "Is there something you wanted to ask me?"

"Oh." He laughed lightly and said, "Sorry about that. I . . . well, I'm afraid you'll think this horribly presumptuous of me but . . . I'd like to take you out to dinner, Miss Anderson. Tonight, if you're free."

Maryanne was shocked but carefully hid her surprise at the totally unexpected request. "I don't know if I consider it presumptuous or not, but I am rather . . . surprised."

140

Michael shook his head slightly and gave a self-disparaging smile. "Well . . . I'm rather surprised at myself. I'm sorry if I offended you but"—he planted his forefinger just above his upper lip—"I didn't even bother to ask what your marital status is."

Maryanne laughed. "No problem. I'm divorced."

Michael nodded, then lifted a shoulder inquisitively. "Well, then, that makes this all fairly legal, seeing as how I'm unattached too. So how about it, Ms. Anderson. Would you care to accompany me to dinner tonight?"

Appropriately charmed and more than a little flattered by her professor's attention, Maryanne answered, "I would like that very much, Mr. Donover."

"Great. And Michael is more appropriate, I think." He reached inside his jacket for a pen and said, "Would you jot down directions to your house, Maryanne, and I'll—"

"Actually," she interrupted, "I was coming back to campus around six. I need to visit the library and tonight is ideal since most of the student body will be at the game. I'll have my car, so it would be better if we could just meet somewhere."

"All right, that sounds fine. Have you been to La Hacienda?"

"No. I've heard it's nice."

"It is. Why don't you meet me in the lobby there around seven thirty? Will that give you enough time at the library?"

"Sure." Maryanne held her knapsack close to her chest and smiled up at him. "I'm looking forward to it."

"Me too."

"Bye," she said, then left the arena-shaped lecture hall.

"Good-bye," Michael Donover said, very reluctantly

pulling his gaze away from the gentle sway of the skirt over her slender hips.

Maryanne glanced at her watch, surprised at how little time had passed since she'd gotten here this evening. She'd already accomplished everything she wanted to cover for the research she was doing on an English term paper. She closed the book she'd been scanning and taking notes from, then stacked it atop three others on the large oak table. She'd been right; it was very quiet here tonight, almost as if she had the entire place to herself . . . which was probably one reason she'd been able to finish so early.

The restaurant was only a short drive away down North Street, so she didn't have to hurry. She was nervous enough about the evening, and had taken a long time to decide on an outfit. The weather had been pleasantly cool of late and she'd finally decided on a "casual but classic" look, choosing a tartan wool skirt and pale green pullover sweater. She'd arranged her hair into a loose topknot and at the last minute put on a strand of pearls with matching earrings, a present from her parents many Christmases ago.

A tiny, unmistakable quiver rippled through her insides as she entered the restaurant lobby and looked around for the smiling face of Michael Donover. She chided herself inwardly for the girlish feeling. But it persisted and she was forced to admit there was ample reason for it. As pretty as she'd been in high school, Maryanne had been agonizingly shy, that particular aspect of her character causing most of those years to be rather lonely ones. She'd had only a handful of dates and found even those exceedingly difficult to deal with. She hadn't enjoyed dating at all.

Until Elliot. He'd been the only man she'd known for the past fourteen and a half years, and going out with other men now, a most natural thing for most women, was definitely an unfamiliar game to her. Yet she felt almost relieved that she was finally doing this, as if it were a task she needed to get out of the way, a vital step on the road to the independence and maturity she was determined to achieve. Not that Michael Donover was to be considered a task, of course, but nevertheless she knew nothing of him except that he presented fairly interesting lectures in her history class. And he was nice-looking too: tall, blond-haired, quite a gentleman in fact. So, all in all, she assured herself, she couldn't be getting off to a better start.

And indeed the evening did turn out to be pleasant enough. The food was delicious and afterward she and Michael settled into an easy conversation over drinks. And, as at the fateful reunion months before, Maryanne was once again unknowingly being closely scrutinized by a pair of dark-brown eyes.

Sam and Joe Lancaster were also at La Hacienda that night, entertaining prospective investors in their new development project. Though seated at a corner table on the same level as Maryanne and Michael, they were effectively obscured by a profusion of plants, a major part of the restaurant's decor. From where he sat, Sam had a perfect view of the couple while himself remaining hidden. He was strangely quiet tonight, almost to the point of being noncommunicative, and Joe made several unsuccessful attempts before finally pulling the younger man into the conversation.

Sam was infuriated by the jealousy rising up in him and it was all he could do to sit the evening out with the other men. Ever since the last meeting with Maryanne, hardly a moment had gone by without his wondering about her—where she was, what she was doing, how she was. He had to keep reminding himself over and over again that she had made it perfectly clear she didn't want to see him and that he had to respect that request. Yet he couldn't forget what had happened between them, he just couldn't.

And now there she was with another man, obviously having a great time. He couldn't see the man's face, but he agonized as he wondered who in the world could possibly think he was good enough for her. The dinner with his business associates dragged on while Sam relentlessly and surreptitiously continued to observe Maryanne and her date. It was absolutely ridiculous, but he was helpless to stop himself. When he saw the man accept his change from the waiter, Sam began to get really nervous. He reached for his own wallet, then extracted a few bills and set them down on the table.

"Gentlemen, it has been an enjoyable evening, but I'm going to have to beg off for the night." He grinned and nodded to each of the men as he stood. "Tomorrow is going to be a killer on the site. I want to make sure I get there early."

The other men nodded and uttered understanding comments, but Joe's eyes glimmered with curiosity and a shadow of irritation. Sam ignored him, said good-bye, and left. Maryanne and her date were already gone and he grew impatient when he had to thread his way through a large party being led to their table through the crowded room. Concerning what he was going to do, he had no idea; he was just reacting to his feelings, relying on instinct.

The cool night air had a nip to it, yet Sam was grateful for it tonight. He needed a little fresh air, anything to help get his head set on straight. What in the world was he doing, anyway, lurking around out here like some second-rate spy, checking up on a woman who wanted nothing more from him than to be left alone. Lord help him, but he just couldn't seem to help himself. It was hard enough living in this small town knowing she was close by, and working until he was about to drop dead, simply to get her out of his mind. He was obsessed with her, that was the plain fact—and it didn't seem to be getting any better.

He stood on the stone steps to the entrance for a moment, adjusting his tie and coat as if they needed adjusting, his gaze slowly scanning the south side of the parking lot. Suddenly he saw her walking alone toward the end of a long row of cars. Her date was nowhere in sight, which surprised him. Then, before giving himself the chance to question his actions, he was walking quickly toward her. She was unlocking the door when he caught up, and she turned around quickly at the sound of his footsteps.

Her expectant expression faded rapidly as she saw who it was. "Sam."

"Hello, Maryanne." He gave a backward nod of his head toward the restaurant and said, "I saw you leaving, so I though I'd catch you before you. . . . I wanted to ask you something." Lord, had he forgotten how to speak English? He sounded like a schoolboy asking for his first date.

"What is that?" Her nonchalant tone belied her struggle

145

to overcome her internal reaction at seeing him again so unexpectedly. Sam's attire was entirely different from the casual outdoor style he usually wore; tonight he was almost rivetingly handsome in cream-colored slacks, blue and white pinstriped shirt, and navy blazer. His dark hair was ruffled by the evening breeze and his brown eyes shone in a way she'd never noticed before. But the most compelling thing about him was the way he seemed not to notice, to be completely unaware of his own vitality, his own magnetism.

"Has your father mentioned the groundbreaking ceremony and party I'm hosting on the fourth?" he asked.

"No," Maryanne answered. "He usually doesn't clue me in on every little detail of what's happening with the business. That's the way I prefer it."

Sam ran his hand through his already tousled hair and let out his breath, which he was unaware he'd been holding. "Uh huh. Well, I just thought perhaps he might have mentioned it since it is a rather important occasion for him." He leveled his gaze at Maryanne, then said, "But since he hasn't, I will. Your father would appreciate it more than you know, Maryanne, if you were there to share the day with him. It would mean a great deal to him."

This really was the first she'd heard of any ceremony or party, and suddenly she experienced a stab of guilt that her father had felt too inhibited even to tell her about it. Much as she disliked the fact that Sam was the one to be saying so, he probably was right about it being a big occasion for her father.

"Thank you for telling me," she said quietly. "I will talk to him about it."

"Good." He tried to meet her eyes, but she seemed

totally occupied in the task of sifting through her purse for her keys. "How did you like the food? It's a nice place, isn't it?" he ventured.

"Yes, it is. The food was very good." Maryanne's hand was on the door handle of her car and unconsciously she tightened her grip. There had to be more than coincidence to this chance meeting in the parking lot, but strangely she found it difficult to summon up the resentment she should be feeling toward Sam. She should just get into the car and be on her way, but something was stopping her. In some indefinable way she felt unable to break off this meeting with Sam. The deep sound of his voice, his tall, solid presence in the darkness, the way she could feel his gaze moving over her like a gentle, soothing breeze—all of it combined to create some pull she didn't want to analyze; indeed, she had spent weeks avoiding doing just that.

Perhaps it was the disappointment she felt over an evening that had turned out to be rather flat. Michael Donover was very much the proper gentleman and she liked him in many ways, but she had tired early on of talking primarily about one subject: Michael Donover. Oh, he'd seemed interested enough about her at first, but after a few predictably polite questions he switched back to what he obviously thought was the more fascinating topic. And so the night had moved to a close at a rather boring pace, and she'd been glad she'd brought her own car. He'd asked her out for another date and she'd hesitated. Perhaps once they got to know each other a little better, Michael wouldn't feel the need to talk so much about himself. She should give him another chance, she decided; besides, she had nothing better to do. So she had agreed. But, walking back to her car, she was irritated with herself and more than a little concerned that she'd made a mistake in agreeing to see Michael again. Maybe it was natural that she wasn't objecting too much to seeing Sam here now and, in the very next second, was accepting his suggestion, which by all reason she should have refused.

"Uh, listen, I'm not really in the mood to call it a night," Sam said. "A little too much coffee, maybe. Would you care to join me for a nightcap?"

"Here?" She was surprised at her reply; she should have said no right off.

Sam sensed his advantage and immediately moved to her side, cupped her elbow, and said jauntily, "They have a really nice cocktail lounge. Did you see it?"

Maryanne was surprised but not displeased to find herself walking briskly beside him back into the restaurant she'd just left. But there were no disappointments this time. They stayed for almost two hours, the time far more interesting and enjoyable than the nearly four hours she'd been with Michael. Indeed, the entire evening with Michael was almost forgotten completely as she and Sam, on totally amicable grounds for the time being, settled into an easy, relaxed conversation. Sam asked her a million questions about her return to college. He was openly impressed with her decision to return to school and the fact that she had pulled her life together so quickly after such a devastating blow. His admiration made Maryanne feel proud of herself.

Sam was still burning with curiosity as to who Maryanne's date was, but decided against bringing the subject up. There couldn't have been that much to it; she hadn't left with him, had she? She asked him a lot about the company, and he related several amusing anecdotes about the daily office routine.

"I can't tell you what a difference the business has made to Dad," she said. She sipped at the snifter of brandy and set it back down on the table. "He bustles around as if he were at least twenty years younger."

"He's like that at the office too," Sam said.

There was a silent pause then, as if both had suddenly run out of things to say. But other matters had piqued Maryanne's curiosity, and she plunged right in about what was on her mind.

"How is Melissa, Sam?"

"She's fine. In fact I just talked to her yesterday on the phone and we agreed she could come here for Thanksgiving."

"That's great. Sissy didn't mind?"

Sam uttered a small sound of disgust. "Sissy's busy doing her own thing. Like getting married again."

Maryanne was stunned. "You're not serious."

"Quite. To the same guy she's been seeing for the past two years, as a matter of fact."

For a moment Maryanne couldn't utter a word. Then she said, "Sam . . . I had no idea . . ."

Sam grinned sardonically and raised an eyebrow. "Yeah, neither did I. Until we got back from the reunion, that is. Apparently he's some fellow she was in love with before we knew each other—which of course she never told me about. Anyway, he walked back into her life one day and presto, the spark of undying love was re-ignited."

Maryanne glanced downward at her hands cupping the brandy snifter, momentarily at a loss for words. "I didn't mean to pry, Sam. But . . . it's really hard to believe."

He was quiet for a moment. "Not really. I suppose if I'd paid a little more attention to our marriage, I would have noticed something going on. I guess I just didn't want to see. It was actually fairly typical of her, the selfishness, that is. I guess it was just a matter of time."

"Would . . . do you think she would have left eventually?"

"No. Why should she? She had everything just the way she wanted it. Husband, provider, child, the whole happy family scenario; and, of course, with her just rewards on the side: her lover—the man she really loved."

"You sound bitter, Sam."

"I suppose I am. When you find out you've been living a lie, playing a role without even knowing you were assigned the part, it tends to make you that way." He paused, then went on, "I don't know, I suppose I don't have the right to be so judgmental, play the victim, so to speak."

"What do you mean?"

Sam looked directly into Maryanne's eyes. "I didn't love Sissy. I never did. I was faithful to her and I respected her as a woman, as the mother of my child, but other than that . . ."

"You weren't happy at all with her?"

Sam shook his head slowly and then drank the rest of his drink. How could he have ever been, he thought, knowing there was only one person he'd ever loved, ever would love? "No," he answered. "But there were some good times. The most important of which was Melissa, of course."

"I assume you must have pretty good visitation rights."

"Joint custody, as a matter of fact. Sissy fought it at first, but she finally realized it was better for all of us."

They talked in that vein for a few minutes longer, and Maryanne was impressed with the extent to which Sam had gone to maintain an important role in his child's life. There were far too many men in this country, she knew, who would have simply abandoned the struggle, withdrawn altogether from the responsibilities of parenthood.

When the cocktail waitress handed Sam the tab, they looked around, surprised to see how few patrons remained. Sam walked Maryanne to her car, and after opening the door and tossing her purse onto the front seat, Maryanne turned and said, "Thanks for the drinks, Sam. And the conversation."

"My pleasure." He smiled and Maryanne felt a tug inside, the same deep, magnetic pull that increased each time she saw Sam.

"Listen," she said, "I'll think about the ceremony and the party. I'll talk to Dad about it."

"Good. I know he'd like that." It was all Sam could do to keep his hands shoved inside the pockets of his jacket. He took a step toward her. He longed to reach out to her, to pull her to him, wrap his arms around her and feel her slender, womanly body next to his. But he wouldn't risk jeopardizing the subtle yet definite edge he'd gained tonight. With his hand resting on the top of the open car door, he leaned over and smiled at her. She was staring at him, her eyes wide and questioning. Her face was so close to his—how easy it would be to lean over and cover her lips with his own, he thought. He saw her dark lashes lower, her hands stiffening on the steering wheel. Willing himself to pull back, he straightened and slammed her car door shut. "Well, good night. Take care and drive safely."

"Thanks, I will. And you too."

Maryanne locked the door and switched on the motor, and Sam watched her pull away.

She turned on the car radio and headed down North Street, her thoughts jumbled and confused; yet at the same time she felt a deep sense of satisfaction. She and Sam had had a warm, pleasant time, and despite the misgivings, the fear that she might be feeling something more for him than the friendship she insisted on, it had felt good, immensely good, to discuss things they both knew and in some respects shared. It was so much easier than starting from point A in a brand-new relationship, as had been the case with Michael.

Much as she still believed that things would be a good deal easier all around if she and Sam could keep their distance, she realized how impractical the notion really was. It was impossible to do in a small town, and it was unwise anyway, since her father and Sam were in business together. Not until now had she admitted how much she'd been bothered by the strain between her and Sam. The sheer effort involved in maintaining the position of animosity was unnerving, not to say emotionally exhausting. And she knew how much the situation troubled her father.

Well, she was glad they had finally gotten together; it would certainly make dealing with Sam a good deal easier from now on.

One thing still preyed on her mind, however: her unfailing physical response to Sam. How much simpler it would have been had certain things never occurred: the kiss that day at the lake, the haunting, erotic dream of him. Yet they had happened, and it was up to her to keep them in the proper perspective. She had reacted emotionally, at a time when she'd been acutely vulnerable. But she was better now, much better, and nothing like that would happen again. That much she was sure of.

CHAPTER TEN

Michael Donover was nothing if not persistent, Maryanne soon discovered. Her reaction to that fact, however, was somewhat confusing. She was flattered, for after all he was almost five years younger and what woman wouldn't respond to the ego boost of having a younger man chasing after her. But she couldn't ignore the other side to her feelings, a side that involved more negative than positive feelings.

She *shouldn't* feel that way at all, she told herself firmly; Michael was perfectly polite, appropriately attentive, and apparently interested enough to want to take her out almost every week. And she didn't want to refuse; she'd already decided that she needed to date and at the moment there were no other interested parties.

She'd been holed up inside herself far too long already, and it was necessary to her program of self-renewal to get out and see something of the world. She'd taken the first step—broadening her education—and was proud of herself for having done so. Dating was another form of education, and she tried hard to dispel her vague feelings of disappointment.

It was probably normal at her age anyway; one certainly couldn't expect the lightheartedness that was a natural part of one's younger years. And as time went by, she became used to having her Friday and Saturday nights planned. She enjoyed going out to dinner and a movie or driving into Lufkin for an evening out with Michael.

As the weeks rolled into early November, she became quite used to including Michael in her plans. He and her father had met and apparently liked each other, which made the situation all the more agreeable. The Thanksgiving break was just around the corner, and after talking to her father, she had decided to ask Michael to share dinner with them.

Her history class was the last one that day and she remained at her desk as the other students filed out, a few gathering around Michael to consult with him. She waited patiently, opening her textbook to note the reading assignments that Michael had assured them would be included on the midterm exam.

Finally the lecture hall was clear, and Maryanne walked up to the lectern where Michael stood gathering sheafs of paper and stuffing them back into his briefcase. He glanced up and smiled warmly at her. "I thought you were gone already."

"Nope, this is my last class, remember?"

"Uh . . . yeah, right."

"What are you today—the absentminded professor?"

Michael snapped the clasps on the briefcase and stood

it straight up on the table adjacent to the lectern. He looked up at Maryanne almost shyly and brought one hand up to smooth his upper lip.

"I'm afraid that's an appropriate description," he said, his expression turning serious.

"Oh? How come?"

"We had something planned for tonight, didn't we?"

Maryanne tilted her head to one side and shrugged slightly. "Just dinner. Why, can't you make it?"

"I'm really sorry, but I forgot about my parents. They're driving down from Dallas tonight. They'll be getting in late and I need to be there to meet them. . . ."

"I understand. You don't have to sound so apologetic."

"But I hate to mess up your plans."

"I didn't have any really, except to be with you. We can get together tomorrow—or Sunday."

"Well . . . it's a little complicated. They're staying the whole weekend."

"Oh . . . well . . ."

"I'm sorry, hon. I wish I had remembered to tell you before now."

"Really, Michael, it's all right. I understand." But she didn't—not completely. She couldn't help wondering why he was excluding her from the *entire* weekend. It would seem appropriate enough for him to introduce her to his parents. But he'd made no mention of it and she certainly wasn't going to bring it up. And something about his new term of endearment bothered her, sounded insincere. He'd never called her "hon" before and it rankled. It had been Elliot's favorite affectionate term, one he usually employed when he'd gotten on her bad side.

"I guess I'll see you on Monday, then," Michael said, his expression a picture of frustration and regret.

"Right. Oh, I almost forgot . . . Dad and I would like you to share Thanksgiving with us. We're going all out—turkey, ham, dressing, pies, the whole bit—"

She stopped suddenly as Michael winced and clucked his tongue. "What?"

"God, you're going to classify me as a first-class heel, but I'm going to have to turn you down on that, too. I've already promised Mom and Dad to be there with them."

"Oh . . ." She managed a flippant smile. "Well, one of these days we'll get it together."

Michael walked around the table and reached for her hand. "Hey, I'm really sorry, hon. Maybe if I'd have known earlier we could have worked things out differently."

She didn't like the condescending tone in his voice and pulled her arm back, clutching her books tightly to her chest. "It's not that big a deal, Michael. Really." She glanced at her watch and said, "I need to go by the bank and they close in half an hour, so I'd better get going. Have a good time with your parents."

Michael nodded and said, "I'll see you on Monday and tell you all the *exciting* things we did."

Maryanne smiled gamely. "All right. Talk to you later."

"Good-bye."

She walked out of the classroom and into the corridor, unsure of her feelings. The fact that she wouldn't be seeing him tonight didn't bother her all that much, yet there was something, some uneasy note in his voice, that she couldn't put her finger on. Oh, well, that's the way things go sometimes, she thought. They had been seeing a lot of each other lately; perhaps it would help to be apart. She'd have enjoyed having the extra company for Thanksgiving but couldn't blame him for wanting to be with his own family. It puzzled her, though, that he hadn't even suggested introducing her to his parents. Perhaps there was something in *that* relationship that was a little too difficult at the moment.

She could use the spare time anyway, to get a jump ahead on the unending backlog of reading assignments.

That evening, Jonas walked through the kitchen door as Maryanne stood at the electric range stirring a pot of chili.

"Hi, sweetheart," he greeted his daughter, planting a kiss on the top of her head as he walked on into the den. "What are you doing here? I thought you and Michael had a date tonight."

"We did. He forgot to tell me until this afternoon, however, that his parents are coming in. He'll be tied up with them all weekend. You haven't eaten, have you?"

"Nope. Been meeting with a couple of contractors this afternoon. Preliminary bids, et cetera."

"Sounds like you've been busy enough."

"You bet. How long's that going to take? I need to wash up."

"Go on. I'll have it on the table by the time you get back."

Jonas turned and Maryanne smiled as she watched him walk out of the room. His step was almost jaunty. Sam had been right about one thing, that was certain—her father was blossoming with this new business venture. Even if it didn't go well—which Maryanne seriously doubted—it was worth the investment just to observe the change in him. Just seeing him so revved up put her into a good mood. Already she'd forgotten about the scratched plans with Michael.

"This stuff tastes better than it did last night," Jonas commented as he swallowed another mouthful of chili.

"Mmmm, it does," Maryanne agreed. "The seasoning sinks in if you let it sit overnight." She picked up her fork, then said, "Oh . . . I almost forgot. Michael can't make it on Thanksgiving, either."

Jonas frowned and broke off a piece of French bread. "Why not?"

"His parents again. He promised them he'd visit for the holidays."

Jonas nodded and chewed thoughtfully. He drank some iced tea, then set the glass down, absently rubbing his fingers against the frosted glass for a few seconds. "In that case, I'd like to make a suggestion." He held up one hand. "And don't get all up in the air about it, it's just a suggestion."

"What, for heaven's sake?"

"Well . . . Joe mentioned it to me the other day. Wanted to know if you and I would be interested in sharing Thanksgiving dinner with him and Sam." Jonas cleared his throat. "He doesn't know about the . . . situation between you and Sam, so I said I'd tell you about it and see what you thought."

"Dad, there isn't any *situation* between me and Sam. I saw him not too long ago and he mentioned the ground-breaking party and asked me if I was going to attend with you. I told him I'd think about it."

"You did?" Jonas's gray eyes widened with pleasure and surprise.

"Yes. There's really no problem, Dad. I think I've come to terms with my feelings about not wanting to see or be around Sam. As you said, we've been friends for a long time, and anyway, it would be silly of me to interfere with your relationship with him simply because of my feelings."

"You don't know how glad it makes me to hear you say that," Jonas stated sincerely.

"See? I'm not such an unreasonable person after all. What the heck! It'll be just the two of us, so I see no reason not to share Thanksgiving with Sam and Joe."

"Great! I'll let Joe know about it. It'll be at Sam's house, though."

"That's all right. Just ask him what he wants me to bring."

Jonas stood up and walked around the table to plant an impulsive kiss on his daughter's cheek. It was a noisy smack and Maryanne laughed.

"Now, what was that for?"

"I'm just so happy you've decided to put all that behind you," Jonas said, picking up their plates and utensils and crossing the room to deposit them in the sink.

Maryanne sat silently, mulling over her Dad's last comment. Was that what she'd really done? Certainly things had changed between her and Sam, and for the better, but she honestly couldn't say she had put everything behind her. Time, a lot of it, would have to pass before that was possible.

Because of the holiday, Maryanne and Jonas were suddenly thrown together with Sam on an almost intimate level. Three months ago she would have sworn this could never happen. But here she was on Thanksgiving Day, racing around the kitchen, putting the finishing touches on the cornbread dressing and pies—all made from scratch—that were her contributions to the Thanksgiving feast. At this rate she was going to be exhausted by the time they got there.

But she found she really didn't mind, not at all. It was fun having the chance to sharpen her culinary skills, especially knowing there would be more than just herself and Jonas to enjoy the food. And oddly, by the time they made it to Sam's house, Maryanne was actually feeling energetic. The hard part was over; now all she had to do was enjoy herself.

She was surprised when her father turned the car down an unfamiliar street in a heavily wooded, rather new subdivision.

"Is this where Sam lives?" she asked as her father pulled into the driveway at the end of the cul-de-sac.

"Mmmm. Nice, isn't it?"

"Sure is." "Nice" was certainly an understatement; Maryanne was *most* impressed. The house was set back behind a copse of fir and oak trees, a one-story beige brick contemporary that seemed to stretch almost half a block. "God, it's so *big*!" she exclaimed. "I can't believe he would want to take all that on; it seems so much for one person."

"Do I hear a touch of envy?" Jonas cast a wry glance at his daughter as he stepped on the brake and turned off the engine.

"Come on, Dad. I don't believe you said that. You have to admit it is rather huge for just one person."

Jonas got out of the sedan and opened the back door on his side. Then he leaned in and carefully lifted a large hamper loaded down with the dishes Maryanne had cooked. "Well, wait till you see the inside. It's a real eye-opener."

Maryanne followed her father as they went up the flag-stone walk to the house. It was surrounded by colorful flowers and perfectly trimmed hedges, all of them dwarfed by huge whispering pines. *It's absolutely gorgeous,* she thought, almost wistfully. Well, all right, maybe she was a little envious. This was just the sort of place she had always imagined she would live in with Elliot someday. The thought made her uneasy. Thoughts of Elliot were not welcome today—or any day. *That's* what she had against Sam Lancaster; he still had the power to remind her of the past. But her father was ringing the doorbell, and the niggling thought was forced aside for the time being.

Both of them were surprised when the front door was opened by a beautiful dark-haired little girl whose big blue eyes stared up at them openly as she said, "Hello. Come in, please."

"Why, thank you, young lady," Jonas said, stepping past the child into the foyer. "And what is your name?"

"Melissa," she answered in a soft, melodic voice.

Maryanne was struck by the child's resemblance to her father. "The last time I saw you, you were only this high." She put her hand down close to the ground and the girl smiled shyly. Maryanne turned to her father and said, "She looks just like Sam, doesn't she?"

Jonas's gray eyes twinkled as he said, "Sure does. Only a lot prettier. I wonder if you could show me the way to the kitchen, Melissa?"

"Sure." She turned quickly and strode off with an important little strut, and Maryanne had to smile. As a baby,

Melissa had resembled both her parents—she had her mother's blue eyes—but now she was showing more of her father's physical characteristics and Maryanne was pleased for her.

She followed behind slowly, taking in the details of Sam's home. It was a truly lovely place, beautifully decorated, yet with a personal touch that gave it a lived-in look. Her expectations for the day had been somewhat uncertain, and she never would have guessed she'd be so affected by just being in Sam's home. The place revealed things about him she wasn't so sure she was ready to see. She hadn't known Melissa would be here either, and that was another adjustment she had to make, for the child, like Sam, was another, albeit innocent, part of the past.

The voices from the kitchen grew louder and Maryanne knew she should go on inside and greet everyone. But as she continued down the hallway, her attention was drawn to the wall-to-wall patio doors at the side of the living room. Captivated, she crossed the room to look outside and was totally amazed at the profusion of plants and flowers surrounding the redwood deck.

"Like the view?"

Maryanne turned around to see Sam standing several feet away, casually dressed in slacks and a V-necked pull-over sweater, with a huge apron tied around his waist.

The words "World's Greatest Chef" were printed on the apron in large block lettering and Maryanne grinned wryly as she said, "The view is fantastic. May I have your autograph later, master?"

Sam looked down at his apron and smiled broadly. "But of course. This is one of Aunt Lily's little presents. I was obligated to wear it today."

"Fits you perfectly." Maryanne turned toward the patio again. "Did you do all this yourself?"

"No." Sam walked over to where she stood. "The concept was mine but I hired someone to do it for me. Your father and I will be working with the same people on the housing development, in fact."

"Well, it's nice. Very nice."

"Thanks."

Neither one said anything else for a few moments. Finally, Sam said, "I'm glad you could make it, Maryanne."

She nodded, suddenly feeling uncomfortable in his presence. It was silly, getting flustered each time she was around Sam. She had come to terms with all that, hadn't she? Perhaps it was the surroundings, the unfamiliar setting; she'd never observed Sam on his private territory, except once, long ago, when she and Elliot had visited the Lancasters. Sam had always had the appearance of an outsider looking in—and in his own home, at that. But then there had been Sissy, and now there was only Sam, looking perfectly at ease and comfortable in his own element.

The possibility that there could be another, more compelling reason for her uneasiness was undeniable. Sam was a truly handsome, virile man—that was a reality she had begun to acknowledge. It was not an easy thing to admit, especially considering that she'd come to the conclusion they were merely friends.

"Well, I'm happy to be here," she said. "And it's nice seeing Melissa. She looks like you."

"Yes, she does, doesn't she?" He stared down at her silently for a moment. "Well, shall we join the others in the kitchen? That seems to be the most popular spot in the house right now."

"That's where all the good stuff is."

They joined the others in the kitchen, and Maryanne was introduced to Sam's uncle Joe and his wife, Lily. Both were vivacious nonstop talkers, but genuinely friendly, and Maryanne liked them immediately. Despite Lily's repeated attempts to run things in the kitchen, Sam lived up to the motto on his apron and bustled about with all the authority of a preoccupied superchef.

Aperitifs were served and the tempting aromas wafting in from the kitchen were enough to whet even the most reluctant appetites. Maryanne found she was really enjoying herself as they all gathered around the huge mahogany table in the dining room. Sam insisted on playing host to the hilt, carving the turkey in expert fashion and making sure each person had more than his share of the food and wine. The conversation was lively throughout, skipping from one topic to another. Lily, however, seemed particularly interested in Maryanne and her university experiences.

"Well, I just think it's wonderful, what you're doing," she said enthusiastically, helping herself to another spoonful of dressing. "I know it can't be easy, especially after you've been away from school all these years."

"She studies hard enough," Jonas said, winking at his daughter. "Sometimes too much, I think."

"Now that's not good, dear. You don't want to burn yourself out."

Maryanne smiled and folded her napkin. "I don't think that's going to happen anytime soon. I really love it."

"Jonas," Lily said in a motherly tone, "you should see

165

to it that she at least has an active social life. All work and no play—"

"Fortunately, she's seen to that herself lately."

"Oh?" Lily turned to Maryanne, her eyebrows raised in curiosity.

Joe glanced at his wife disapprovingly and said to Maryanne, "She's just plain nosy. Can't seem to keep herself from prying into other people's business."

Lily waved a dismissing hand at her husband and kept her full attention on Maryanne. "Well, tell us about it, Maryanne. Do you have a beau?"

Joe leaned his head way back and said dryly, "Please, Lord, spare us. Lily, for God's sake, when was the last time anyone used the term 'beau'?"

"You hush, Joe Lancaster. This is woman talk, so mind your own business."

With another shake of his head Joe turned his attention to the men, shrugging resignedly. He was far too interested in getting in some good old shoptalk, anyway, to pay any further attention to his wife. And Maryanne felt the brunt of the woman's kindly but persistent curiosity.

"Well, yes," she responded finally. "There is someone I've been seeing. One of my professors, actually."

"Mmmm. That's very interesting. What does he teach?"

"He's my history professor. We've been seeing each other for nearly two months." Maryanne wanted to steer the conversation in another direction, but it wasn't easy and she hated to offend the woman; after all, she was the wife of her father's business associate.

"Now, that sounds even more interesting. I'm sure you have lots to talk about."

"True. I happen to like the course he teaches very much." *What an inane statement,* she thought. But truly she didn't know what else to say. She'd caught a glimpse of Sam from the corner of her eye and could tell he was only giving cursory attention to the conversation between the men. She had the feeling he was *really* listening to her conversation with Lily, and she was embarrassed. Which was ridiculous, she told herself. It wouldn't hurt him to know she was seeing someone; she wasn't the fragile china doll he'd thought her all these years, and it was about time he and everyone else realized that.

Lily's interest in Maryanne was finally sated and she turned her attention to Melissa, who was behaving very much like a little lady. Maryanne insisted on cutting and serving the pies since she'd made them herself, and she was treated to a round of compliments for her efforts. Afterward everyone lingered at the table with cups of coffee, and Joe said to Maryanne, "Do you think you'll be able to make it to the groundbreaking ceremony?"

Noticing the hopeful look on her father's face, she smiled and said, "I'll be there—wouldn't miss it for anything."

"Great." Joe leaned back in his chair and patted his protruding stomach. "My stomach's telling me to go lay down, but my head's telling me a walk would be better."

"And your head's correct, Mr. Lancaster," Lily said firmly, pushing her chair back and standing up. "After we get these things cleaned up, we'll do just that."

"Sam's backyard is more like a forest," Jonas said to Maryanne.

"Oh, Maryanne, if you haven't seen it before, you should let Sam show you around," Lily urged.

"That would be nice," Maryanne said. She stood up and began to gather and stack some of the empty cake plates nearest her. "But not until all this is—"

Lily placed a restraining hand on Maryanne's arm. "No, no, none of that," she interrupted. "You and Sam did all the cooking, and Joe and I haven't done a thing but sit here and enjoy it. It's our turn to pitch in."

"But—"

"No buts, right, Joe?"

Joe raised his eyebrows and wiggled them. "That's what the woman says and that's the way it's gotta be, Maryanne. Go on and take that walk now. The weather sure is nice enough for it."

Indeed, the Thanksgiving afternoon boasted a gorgeous azure sky and the temperature was ideal. Maryanne glanced longingly through the large picture window, then turned and said, "Dad, are you game for a little walk?"

Jonas looked down at Melissa and winked. "Actually, I've already promised Melissa here that I'd have a game of checkers with her. She claims she's better than me, but I'm ready to show her a thing or two."

Melissa shook her head back and forth and jumped up from the table. "No, you won't. I'm gonna go set it up in the den." She rushed off, then stopped and turned around. "Excuse me. The dinner was delicious."

Everyone smiled and agreed, and Maryanne caught the look of approval in Sam's eyes as he nodded a dismissal to his daughter. Then his dark eyes met hers and she found herself flushing deeply.

"Would you like to see the grounds, Maryanne?" he asked softly.

She lowered her eyes for a moment, but then she said,

"All right. That sounds like a good idea." She was far from sure it was a wise thing to do, but there was no way out of it at this point. And who knew, perhaps she was being overly concerned.

Sam's house sat on four acres of heavily wooded land, and it wouldn't have been too difficult, to Maryanne's way of thinking, to get totally lost on one's own. She followed slightly behind Sam as he guided her down a winding, narrow path, their footsteps crunching and snapping the carpet of pine needles that covered the ground. The temperature was cooler in the shade of the trees, but there was a deliciously refreshing crispness in the air and the pure sweet scent of the towering pines was wonderful. Sam stopped after several hundred feet, and Maryanne was surprised to see a shallow ravine several yards off to the side.

"Does it ever have water in it?" she asked, making her way carefully to the edge.

"Whenever it rains a lot," Sam answered.

Maryanne drew a deep breath and let her head fall back. She peered at the deep-blue sky peeking through the tops of the pines above. "Sam, this is wonderful. How did you find it?"

"Actually, Joe did. I described to him what I was looking for before I came down, and he just went out and found exactly what I wanted."

Maryanne sighed and shook her head from side to side. "Well, he sure did pick a dream of a place. I can't believe Sissy wouldn't have wanted anything like this. I mean, surely it matched anything you had in Chicago."

"Not to her way of thinking. Anyway, she had quite a number of other reasons to stay there."

Maryanne chewed at one corner of her lower lip, then shifted her gaze to Sam, but made no comment.

Sam reached up and tore a small dead branch from a nearby tree, then snapped it in two. "Well, all that doesn't matter anyway. Melissa likes it here. That's the important thing."

Maryanne walked a few paces, discovered a large flat rock, and bent down to remove the needles and twigs scattered across its surface. Then she sat down on it and drew her legs up in front of her, wrapping her arms around her calves. Her slacks and sweater felt comfortable, and she was glad she'd worn something so practical. "How does Melissa feel about not having her father around on a regular basis?"

"She doesn't like it at all. In fact, it was pretty rough going at first. But I think now that I've gotten joint custody we'll have an easier time of it."

"She looks happy enough here."

Sam chuckled lightly. "She is."

"You should be proud of her, Sam. She really is a darling child."

Sam tossed the pieces of branch, one by one, into the ravine. Then he slapped his hands together briskly and walked over to an ancient oak tree near where Maryanne sat. Its weathered trunk was split and he half-sat, half-leaned between its two enormous branches.

"I'm going to ask you something," he said, looking at her directly, "and if you don't want to answer, don't."

"What?" Maryanne gave him a half-smile. "It sounds pretty important."

"I don't know if it is. That's for you to say."

"Well, I won't know unless you ask me."

"I was wondering if you ever hear from him. Elliot."

Strange how the question didn't bother her, Maryanne thought. "No, actually it's been quite a while. There's really nothing for us to talk about. Everything's long since been settled . . . since the divorce became final."

Sam scratched the side of his neck and looked away. "You sound as if you're doing all right, then."

"Why shouldn't I?" Her reply was snappish and Maryanne almost regretted it; she had no need to sound defensive.

"No reason." Sam rubbed the toe of one boot against the heel of the other, fighting down the urge to bring up another subject with her, the one that had been driving him crazy ever since dinner. But he couldn't help himself; he had to know. "Is he helping you get over all of that? This . . . person you're dating?"

He tried to sound as casual as possible, but it didn't come off that way. He was jealous, unbearably so, and he heard it in his voice, but as she replied it was obvious she hadn't even noticed. And that hurt even more than if she had.

"This *person* you're referring to happens to be a good friend. And, yes, to a certain extent he has helped. Mainly he's made me realize something I should have realized a long time ago—there are a hell of a lot of other fish in the sea. He's one of them."

Sam was taken aback by her tone; this was so unlike the Maryanne he'd known all these years. Did she really feel as cold and jaded as she sounded, or was this just some defensive reaction? "Doesn't sound like you're too involved with him, then."

Maryanne's arms dropped rigidly to her side. "I think that's a little out of line, Sam. I had no intention of bringing Michael into the discussion today. If your aunt hadn't pressed the issue, we wouldn't be talking about him now."

"Does it bother you to talk about him?"

"No, damn it! What's the big deal? He's someone I've been seeing fairly regularly. Whether I'm 'involved' with him or not has nothing to do with you. But *since* you happened to bring it up, the fact of the matter is I'm not. I don't need to be involved with anyone. I'm managing quite well on my own."

"I didn't mean to imply you weren't. But . . ." Sam hesitated, provoking an annoyed response from her.

"But what?"

"I was just going to say that you're reacting rather defensively if it's no big deal, as you say."

Maryanne uttered a short, ironic laugh. "Well, if I am, is it any wonder? Good heavens, Sam, you bring up something that's really none of your business and start to get analytical with me and then you accuse me of being defensive!"

Sam held out one hand and spoke in a low tone. "Point well taken. It's just that . . . Well, you don't sound like yourself, like the Maryanne I used to know."

"Thank God." Maryanne's eyes narrowed. "What is it, Sam? Would it make you happy to see that I hadn't learned a thing from what happened with Elliot, to see me letting people walk all over me? I've made a tremendous effort to wake up, to face the music, as they say. It hasn't been easy—it's not easy being around you, for that matter.

172

I'm sorry if you don't like the new me, but it's the best I can do." She got up and walked closer to the ravine, then bent and picked up a stone.

"Is it that hard?" Sam's voice was close behind her, and she turned around quickly, unconsciously bringing her arms up around her chest.

"Is what hard?"

"Being around me. Is it still that difficult? The last time we spoke you said it didn't matter anymore."

"I didn't say it didn't matter. I meant that I've finally realized it doesn't matter anymore that you deceived me the way—"

"I never deceived you!" he interrupted quickly. "It wasn't my business to tell you something that important. And for God's sake, I certainly didn't condone what Elliot did. I just happened to know about it. It was certainly a burden I'd rather not have carried all those years."

"Yes. . . . Well, as I said, it doesn't really matter anymore. What's done is done. And as I was going to say, I finally saw it was useless to hold a grudge against you. We more or less have to be friends, now that you and Dad and Joe are in business together."

Sam was quiet for so long, staring off at some distant point, that Maryanne wondered if he had even heard her.

"So," she said, breaking the silence and taking a step forward, "why don't you show me some more of—"

Sam's arm reached out and he placed a restraining hand on her shoulder. Maryanne looked surprised as she said, "What—"

"Is that all there is to your feelings toward me, Maryanne?"

His features were stern, almost grim, and his dark eyes

173

bored into Maryanne's; she straightened and tried to pull away, but his grip became tighter.

Her eyes searched his face for some clue to his thoughts as her brain struggled to form some sort of reply. She shook her head slightly, her honey-blond hair wispy around her cheeks. "We're friends, Sam. With whatever feelings that sort of relationship implies. I don't see—"

"No, you don't, do you? You don't see at all. Or perhaps you do and you choose to ignore it." His grip tightened, and Maryanne frowned and tried to tug her arm away.

"Sam, please, quit acting like this. Let me go, you're hurting me."

The glazed look in Sam's eyes cleared suddenly and he looked down; he seemed surprised that he was holding on to her. "I'm sorry." His lips clamped tightly and he suddenly turned away, hands shoved once more into his back pockets.

Maryanne watched him carefully, curiously. She was breathing shallowly and could see that he was too. Damn, they shouldn't have come on this walk, and she shouldn't have gotten so serious with him, should have kept it light.

"Tell me," he said in a remote voice, "was that how you felt that time at the lake?"

"That's not a fair question, Sam."

"Isn't it? You didn't seem so sorry at the time."

Maryanne placed the back of her hand over her mouth and sighed heavily. She wished they could just drop it; everything concerning Sam was just too complicated and she wasn't at all sure she wanted to straighten things out. He sounded much too serious, and it frightened her. Nevertheless she felt the need to try to reach some sort of

174

tolerable level on which they could communicate. She walked over to where he stood and spoke in a quiet, sincere tone.

"We've known each other for a long time, Sam. Probably too long. We know things about each other that it would take years for others to know."

"You sound like that's some sort of problem. People pay money to therapists to help them attain that sort of relationship."

"But we're not seeking a relationship—beyond friendship, of course." Maryanne smiled almost sadly. "Don't you see, Sam, it only hurts us."

Sam's head whipped around so fast that his dark-brown hair was flung across his forehead. "We must not know each other *that* well, then, because your reasoning makes absolutely no sense to me."

"What I'm trying to say is what I've told you before. I'm not the same person, Sam. I don't want to be. I *want* to change, I *need* my life to be different. I wasted thirteen and a half years being stupid and naive—"

"Yes, I've heard all that before."

"Well, it must not have made much of an impression on you."

"I think it's a bunch of self-analytical hogwash. I think you're trying hard to convince yourself, but I think your conclusion is wrong. You can't change the person you are, Maryanne."

"I can damn well try," she said firmly.

"And *he* is helping you do it, right?" Sam's voice was accusing.

"Who?"

"That professor you're dating. The one, I assume, you

were with at La Hacienda the night we met in the parking lot."

Maryanne's mouth opened in disbelief and she shook her head from side to side. "What were you doing? Spying on me?"

"No. You were seated not far from where I was at dinner."

"I really don't believe this conversation. . . . Look, Sam, this is getting rather out of hand, don't you think?"

"Why don't you just answer the question?" Sam insisted.

Maryanne rolled her eyes heavenward and bit down on the side of her mouth. "Yes," she answered tightly. "In his own way he is helping me learn a little more about myself."

Sam inched closer, but Maryanne was standing with her back to the ravine and couldn't have moved if she'd wanted to. Strangely, she had no wish to move at all. "I see," Sam said. "And what is it about yourself that you need to know?"

Maryanne swallowed instinctively as his gaze focused on her throat. He moved even closer, until she could feel the heat of his body through the fabric of his clothes. Maryanne looked behind her, as if to reassess her position, but in that moment Sam placed a hand on her shoulder, and as she turned back she glanced at it—large and strong, matted with thick, curling dark-brown hair. Again she swallowed, then found her voice.

"Sam . . . We should be going back to the house."

"No, I don't think so," he said thickly. "I think we both are thinking about something very different."

His words rang true; Maryanne's head was filled with

images of that day at the lake, the too realistic dream she had thought was forgotten. Suddenly she felt frightened, fearful of the overwhelming physical response welling up inside her. She couldn't understand it, couldn't remember ever having felt this way with Elliot, certainly not with Michael, for her relationship with him had never progressed beyond kisses and caresses that could best be described as insignificant. Sam's other hand was on her cheek now, his thumb rotating softly against the hollow just below her cheekbone. She refused to look at him, but she felt his nearness. His breath wafted across her eyelids, sending a swift current of desire rippling down her spine.

"Sam," she whispered, unable to speak any louder.

"Don't say anything more," he said softly, his mouth pressing gently against her ear. "Please don't."

And then, as he cupped both of his hands against the back of her head, tilting it upward, her eyes deepened into a forest green. Sam's own eyes were a rich, warm brown, and as Maryanne looked reluctantly into them she caught the spark of desperation there, a need so deep, so full of yearning, she almost panicked.

But she didn't move, just closed her eyes, unable to withstand the intensity of his gaze. Then as his lips met hers, it was as though they belonged there, and any rational objection she may have still felt was put on hold as a deeper need within her ignited a response she was helpless to ignore. She acquiesced easily to his persistence now, almost gratefully, as if in doing so she could finally dispel the torment within. But a kiss is just a kiss: the thought flitted through her head, and instinctively she knew it could never satiate the aching, unbearable void she'd struggled to deny for so long.

A shudder surged through her, a combination of fear and physical reaction, and Maryanne pushed her hands against Sam's chest. But as they met the hard, lean torso, they acted on their own, her fingers probing the woolen material of his shirt, enchanted by the sensuousness even that much contact elicited. His arms slid around her, strong and solid, and she had no memory of her feet moving until she felt her back nudged up against the trunk of a pine tree. But she was mindless of the prickle of its bark against her sweater, aware only of the pressure of Sam's torso against hers, the sweet, probing sensation of his tongue meeting hers. His hands caressed the sides of her midriff and when the palm of his hand found its way to her breast, gently rotating in small, teasing circles, she moaned breathlessly and moved into the feel of his hand, against his obviously straining physical want of her. An incredible rush of sensation shook her and all she could think of was her tremendous desire, her need for this man. But as his hands pressed against the tops of her shoulders, bidding her to slide down onto the carpet of pine needles at the base of the tree, something snapped in Maryanne and she was aware of what was actually happening and what could very easily happen, and of the reluctant knowledge that she must not allow it.

She broke away from him, and Sam seemed stunned. For he, too, was caught up in a whirlwind of passion. She could see it in his dark eyes, narrowed and filled with the desire she, too, felt, but painfully denied.

"Does he know that much about you, Maryanne?" Sam asked gruffly.

Maryanne straightened her twisted sweater, then

ooked directly at him. "Michael? He doesn't need to. There's not that much to know."

"I beg to disagree with you, Maryanne, I think there is far, far more to be learned about this *new* woman you claim to be."

Angered, Maryanne said curtly, "If there is, Sam, I don't need you to discover it for me."

He answered angrily, "You didn't seem to mind too much just now."

"Oh, I minded, Sam, very much so. I may have responded, may have even enjoyed that little kiss, but it won't happen again."

"Why not? Why do you insist on denying something we both know is there between us?"

"Sam, *please*, there is nothing between us. Nothing but a friendship that goes a long way back. That and this thing between our families."

Sam scowled. "I thought you said you had changed. Why are you still so afraid? Afraid of your own feelings?"

"I'm not afraid, damn it!" Maryanne sighed in exasperation and threw out her hands. "Look, Sam, we agreed that we could still be friends. Let's leave it at that." Her voice lowered and she spoke in an almost pleading tone, "Don't push me, okay?"

Sam said nothing, just stared into the wonderful green eyes he cherished so much, his heart pounding. He had thought—really thought—that this time somehow she would . . . No, things were never that simple.

Errol Flynn techniques worked only in the movies, and he felt a pang of regret thinking that that must have been how she considered his kiss. He *didn't* want to push her; he would wait until she was ready.

179

He zipped up the front of his jacket, for the afternoon sun was rapidly dropping in the sky and the temperature had become discernibly cooler. Then he slid a hand through his thick dark hair, nodded a couple of times, and drew his lips together tightly. "All right, don't worry about it. I won't bother you again. Come on, let's get back to the house. It's getting cold."

Maryanne felt an odd sort of relief mingled with regret, but when she spoke, her tone was dispassionate. "You lead the way. I could never find it on my own."

As they walked back to the house, she asked a few questions about his land, and Sam answered smoothly, almost easily. By the time they got back, it was as if nothing at all had happened between them; they'd simply taken a pleasant afternoon walk.

CHAPTER ELEVEN

To all outward appearances, things were back to normal again in Maryanne's life. She was busy with her studies, and Sam and Jonas and Joe were wrapped up almost constantly in their new business venture. Ground would be broken within the next two weeks, and the occasion would be commemorated with a ceremony and a party.

Maryanne was troubled inwardly, however. Sam had provoked a host of jumbled feelings in her on Thanksgiving Day that were too significant to put aside. She was confused, but had no wish to grapple with these troubling emotions just now. She'd done a good job so far in adjusting to her new life, and there was still another three and a half years to go in school. She didn't need a man to complicate matters. Her relationship with the men in her life was where it should be—Elliot was completely gone, she and Jonas got along wonderfully, and she was seeing Michael regularly—once and sometimes twice a week.

Simple and uncomplicated, just the way she wanted it, the way she *needed* it.

Michael fortunately expressed no desire to push her toward any further commitment, either psychologically or physically. The relationship remained on the light side, and though Maryanne sometimes wondered about it, she was nevertheless satisfied. To Maryanne, physical intimacy implied emotional commitment, and she was a long way from being ready for that.

At home things were going especially well, though Jonas seemed to be putting in too many hours, as far as Maryanne was concerned. She had told him often enough that she thought his enthusiasm was in danger of turning into an obsession, but her objections weren't really heartfelt. He was happy—it showed in everything he did—and she was truly pleased for him. He needed to work hard in the beginning, he claimed, until the ball got rolling. Then he could settle back and relax.

Though East Texas was experiencing its fair share of cold weather, there had been very little rain, so plans were being made to begin the initial phases of development of the land. If there were no major hitches, actual construction of the houses would begin in early spring.

The groundbreaking ceremony was scheduled for the second Saturday in December and Maryanne had agreed to accompany her father, but final exams loomed ahead and she needed every spare minute for study. They decided to take separate cars and meet at the site; that way she could use the morning to study at the campus library while her father helped with the preparations for the ceremony.

The party was to be at Sam's house that night, and

though Maryanne had seen very little of him since Thanksgiving Day, she was apprehensive about going there again. By now she had fully admitted the fact that she and Sam were physically attracted to each other. She'd have been a fool to deny it, yet she recognized it as a dangerous attraction, one best ignored. As added insurance, Maryanne had asked her father if she could bring along a date and he'd said it sounded like a great idea. Michael had agreed to go with her, though she'd been puzzled by his initial hesitation. She hated to coerce him into doing something he didn't care to do, but she really needed him this time and quickly put aside her misgivings.

On the day of the ceremony Maryanne woke early to get a head start on what promised to be a very hectic day. She wanted to get to the library as soon as possible since she knew she'd have to leave before three o'clock to drive out to the site. Michael was to pick her up at the house at six thirty and from there they'd drive on over to Sam's place. After showering and dressing in a gray-tweed woolen suit and comfortable black boots, Maryanne gathered up her books and hustled into the kitchen to prepare breakfast. Her father wasn't up yet, which surprised her a little; normally he was up by six. But just as the coffee finished brewing, her father ambled into the kitchen, still dressed in his pajamas and robe. Maryanne was swallowing the last bite of toast as she carried her plate to the kitchen sink. She opened a cupboard and reached for a mug, saying over her shoulder, "You look like you could use a cup of coffee—maybe two."

Jonas groaned as he pulled out a chair and sat down. "I sure could."

Maryanne poured the aromatic brew into a mug and

proceeded to added cream and sugar, the way he liked it. "You don't look so hot," she commented, frowning lightly as she set the mug in front of him. He stared at it blankly, and Maryanne's frown deepened as she noted the deeper-than-usual creases in his forehead, the slightly grayish cast to his skin. "In fact, you look terrible. Are you coming down with something?"

Jonas turned his head to one side and rubbed the back of his neck. Another muffled groan escaped him and he sighed tiredly. "I don't know. I've got one hell of a headache; it kept me up most of the night."

"Maybe something to eat would help."

Jonas closed his eyes and leaned backward. "The thought of food doesn't sound too great either."

Maryanne walked back across the kitchen and opened a cupboard door, searching its crowded contents as she asked, "Have you taken anything for it yet?"

"No."

"Here," she said, offering him two tablets from the bottle she'd found, "take a couple of aspirin."

Jonas dutifully swallowed the tablets and began sipping his coffee as Maryanne left the room. When she returned, he had finished only half of it, however, and had moved to his favorite leather lounge chair in the den. His eyes were closed and for a moment Maryanne thought he was asleep, but he opened them as he heard her walk in. He didn't look any better at all, she noted, and it really worried her.

"Dad, you look awful. Did you get *any* sleep last night?"

"Not much."

"Well, maybe you ought to call Dr. Sanders."

184

"I'm not going to bother the man on a Saturday morning for something as silly as a headache." He sounded cross, a side of his temperament he rarely displayed, but Maryanne ignored it.

"Well, why don't you go back to bed after I leave? It's your big day and it'll be a long one, too. You'd better get at least a few hours of rest."

"I might just do that," he agreed.

Maryanne picked up her books and purse and started for the back door. "Well, then, I'll see you this afternoon," she said.

"All right." His voice was low and scratchy, and she wondered if he was catching a cold. But Jonas had always been an astoundingly healthy man; the illnesses he'd suffered over the years were minor and of short duration. The knowledge was reassuring and she forgot all about him within a few minutes. She had a full day ahead of her, and she was soon absorbed in mentally organizing her plans for the hours to be spent at the library.

It was a productive six hours, and when Maryanne left she felt a satisfying sense of accomplishment. By the time she reached the site, she was tired and more than ready for a break.

The groundbreaking ceremony was appropriately touching and meaningful, but the temperature was chilly and as soon as possible everyone trooped back inside the office—a comfortable double-sized mobile home—for the warmth and refreshments offered. Maryanne was surprised at the number of people attending. But she knew hardly any of them and spent most of her time at her father's side until Lily latched on to her. Lily worked as a part-time secretary for the company—AndLan Enter-prises—and was more than willing to give her an earful of gossip. Finally, Joe signaled to his wife from across the room and Maryanne took the opportunity to leave a little early.

The clock in the dash of her car read five thirty, which gave her an hour to get ready. Plenty of time, she thought to herself. Rolling the window down and driving slowly, she relished the cold of the brisk wind whipping across her flushed face, as well as the day's last warming rays of sunshine. She smiled to herself, remembering how proud and pleased her father had looked. She was so happy for him, so grateful to see this wonderful change brought about by his new interest. Each day he became more like his old self, the way he'd been before her mom had died.

And he'd looked like he felt better at the ceremony. When Maryanne had asked him in a whisper if he'd gotten rid of the headache, he'd nodded, indicating he was fine. Maryanne was now in a mellow, relaxed mood, and she thought about how far both of them had come in the past six months.

Her father was finally coming out of the saddest period of his life, and she had survived the breakup of a marriage. It was ironic, she mused, that the relationship she shared with her father was more fulfilling and meaningful than her thirteen-and-a-half-year marriage had been. Indeed, she was in such a pleasant frame of mind that even the one person who could have had an jarring effect on her hadn't upset her. There was no getting around the truth—just being around Sam could still jolt her emotions. But she had handled him without any problem today. They had chatted briefly, mostly about business, and then moved on

186

in opposite directions. No hidden innuendos or uncomfortable silences, just a brief, amicable conversation that signified nothing more than proper protocol for the occasion.

Well, so far, so good, Maryanne thought. Now, if she could make it through the evening without managing to bore Michael too much, she would be satisfied. He wasn't exactly gung ho about going, she knew that, but she hoped that once he was there, he would loosen up and enjoy himself.

She heard the telephone ringing as she was parking the car in the garage, and it rang incessantly until she got inside the house.

"Hello?" she said breathlessly, picking it up on the eleventh ring.

"Hi. It's me."

"Oh, hi, Michael. Just a minute, let me shut the door." She took her purse off her shoulder and threw it on the counter. Then she shut the door and picked up the receiver again. "Okay, I'm back."

"Listen, I've been trying to get hold of you for the past couple of hours."

"I was at the groundbreaking ceremony. Remember? I told you about it."

"Oh, yeah . . . I forgot."

Michael's lapses of memory about things Maryanne considered important bothered her, and a sense of déjà vu stole over her as he mumbled something about being sorry. It was as if she knew what was coming next.

He sighed dramatically, then blurted out, "I hope you won't get upset with me for this, but I'm not going to be able to make it tonight."

"Oh? Why not?" She tried not to let the irritation show in her voice, but it was an effort.

"Well . . . I completely forgot about a general faculty meeting tonight. My secretary didn't tell me about it until late last night. It's pretty important that I attend."

"A faculty meeting on a Saturday night? That sounds rather odd."

"Well, actually it's a cocktail party at Dr. Sloan's house. Business over drinks . . . that sort of thing."

"Oh."

"I can tell you don't believe me," he said in a plaintive tone.

"I didn't say that."

"Look, don't get upset. I'm really sorry, Maryanne. I'd rather be with you tonight. You know that, don't you?"

Actually, right now she didn't know that at all, but she refrained from saying so; there was no point to it at the moment.

"I guess I'll see you on Monday, then," she said quietly.

"I'll call you tomorrow afternoon."

"There's no need to do that. I've got a pretty heavy work load before final exams and I'll probably be buried in my books."

"I'll call anyway."

"Michael, you don't have to humor me. It's not necessary."

"I know it isn't. But I want to. You are going to be there, aren't you?"

"At home? Yes."

"Then I'll talk to you in the afternoon sometime."

"Fine."

Again Michael sighed, indicating his regret over the

situation. "Hon, I'd give anything if this hadn't come up. I'll be thinking about you all night."

She wondered about that. "Well, have a good time."

"I'll try," he said in a resigned voice. "All right then, talk to you tomorrow."

"Good-bye."

"Bye."

Maryanne hung up, drew a deep breath, and let it out slowly. She stood with her back to the counter, fist on one hip, staring blankly out the kitchen window. She was trying to assess her feelings at the moment and honestly couldn't figure out what it was she felt. Much as he'd sounded sorry for having to back out on her, she didn't wholly believe his reason. She'd known all along he wasn't eager to go to the party; spending an evening with a roomful of strangers wasn't exactly his thing, he'd told her often enough. But he'd said he'd make an exception just for her. Didn't he remember saying that? And why had he gone on and on about being so sorry he had to miss it? *He doth protest too much,* she thought, her eyes narrowing suspiciously.

There was something else bothering her too; the excuse he'd made about the faculty cocktail party tonight seemed somehow . . . contrived. It had a false ring, as if he'd just then thought of it.

Oh, well, there was nothing she could do about it now. She'd just have to get ready and go to the party herself. She took her time over a lengthy shower, washing and setting her hair, and then choosing what she would wear. It was silly, she thought, to spend so much time dolling up; she was only doing it for herself. But she went ahead and did it anyway, as if to convince herself how little

Michael's desertion mattered. She chose a royal-blue silk dress, with a deep-mauve sash as an interesting contrast. A diamond pendant and tiny diamond studs in her ears completed the outfit and provided an understated elegance to the ensemble. Her hair had grown several inches in the past few months; it had been ages since she'd worn it that length. She usually trimmed it several times a year to a more manageable above-the-shoulder length, but now it reached almost halfway down her back.

She played with it for a few minutes, finally deciding to wear it up in a loosely styled version of a French twist. Then she slipped into a pair of high-heeled, open-toed pumps, threw on her fur coat, and picked up her small royal-blue satin evening bag. Leaving one light on in the living room, she walked to the back door, opened it, and locked it behind her. She wondered at the amount of time she'd spent getting ready for this party. And for whom? For herself, of course—just for herself.

The party appeared to be in full swing when she got to Sam's house. Maryanne was amazed at the number of cars lining the street on which he lived, and she had to spend several minutes driving up and down before she found a spot. The night was cold, and an icy wind whipped at her feet. Lord, but fashionable clothes were simply not designed for winter nights, she thought, her teeth chattering as she walked briskly down the dimly lit street to Sam's house. Music could be heard out in the driveway, and the enticing aromas of freshly cooked food wafted into the night air, stimulating her appetite.

After ringing the doorbell several times and getting no answer, Maryanne turned the knob and let herself in. To hell with propriety, she thought, it was freezing outside! But as soon as she stepped inside, it was obvious why no one had greeted her—the din of music and shouting voices completely drowned out everything else. She had taken a few tentative steps across the foyer when a uniformed maid walked up to her and smiled questioningly.

Maryanne smiled. "Hello, I'm Maryanne Anderson."

"Sorry you had to let yourself in," the woman apologized, "but there's so much noise no one can hear the doorbell."

Maryanne was surprised; she'd never have guessed Sam enjoyed the wild rock music blasting through the speakers in the den. Well . . . one more indication of how little she really knew him after all.

Handing her coat and purse to the maid, she made her way into the enormous den, which was jam-packed with shouting, dancing, and drinking guests. She craned her neck, trying to find her father, but he was nowhere in sight. Frowning slightly, she chewed her lower lip thoughtfully for a moment. If she didn't know better, she might have thought she was at the wrong house. Where in the world had all these people come from? They certainly didn't resemble the sort she'd imagined were going to be here tonight. But as her eyes adjusted to the dim lighting, she began to recognize a few faces from the ground-breaking ceremony this afternoon. But she really didn't know any of them very well, so she continued to scan the room, looking for her father, or Joe and Lily.

Two long buffet tables had been set up in the raised portion of the dining room, and behind them stood three waiters in black and white uniforms. They were busily filling the plates of guests lined up for helpings of the enormous spread of hot and cold hors d'oeuvres. At last Maryanne caught a glimpse of Jonas; he was hemmed into a corner of the den behind three other men, a plate in one hand and a drink in the other.

As she moved toward him, she saw him nod to each of the men in turn, not touching either the food or drink he was holding. When she reached them, Maryanne poked her head over someone's shoulder, caught her father's attention, and said, "Hi, Dad. I've been looking all over for you."

"Pretty crowded, isn't it?" Jonas said loudly, shaking his head. His expression was strained, and Maryanne could see he wasn't exactly having the time of his life. He obviously was glad she had arrived, and after introducing her to the three men, he took her by the arm and guided her out of the den and into the less crowded living room across the hall.

The music was just as loud there, however, so he mouthed the words "Come this way" and led her to another part of the house, a part she hadn't seen on Thanksgiving Day. He opened the door and they entered a beautifully decorated, obviously much-used library. "I thought I'd never find an excuse to get away," Jonas said, setting his glass on a polished butler's table and sitting down heavily in a leather wing chair.

"I'm sorry I didn't get here sooner," Maryanne said, suddenly noticing the worn-out expression on her father's face. "What in heaven's name is going on, Dad? I'd pictured a more sedate sort of affair, not a rock concert."

"It isn't exactly what I had in mind either."

"And who are all those people? I only recognize a few of them from this afternoon."

"Same here."

"I don't understand. I thought this was supposed to—"

"You'd better ask Sam about what's going on. But I suspect it has something to do with his date. She's AndLan's new public relations person, I hear."

Maryanne frowned and sat down slowly in the chair opposite him. "Oh, really? I thought this was strictly Sam and Joe's thing tonight."

Jonas leaned his head back and closed his eyes, sighing deeply. "Hon, by now I don't even *care* what's going on. I'm just glad you came along when you did."

Maryanne was silent for a moment as she studied her father more carefully. His complexion was pale, almost grayish. "Dad, you don't still have that headache, do you?"

"Yeah. Hell, I never did really get rid of it." He reached up and rubbed his forehead with the tips of his fingers. "Spending most of the afternoon in that smoke-filled trailer didn't help either. And the air here isn't much better. Not to mention the noise level out there."

"Maybe you should go on home," Maryanne suggested.

"No, no. I'll be all right. Do you think you could find me a glass of cold water?"

"Sure. Is that all? Would you like some aspirin . . . or anything else?"

"No, just water."

"All right. I'll be back in a minute."

Jonas nodded and closed his eyes again, and Maryanne glanced back at him worriedly before she shut the door quietly behind her. By the time she reached the central part of the house, the noise of the party had escalated to a roar.

193

As she threaded her way through the swelling crowd, she saw a hand waving at her above the sea of heads—it was Lily. She would have liked to stop and talk to the woman, get her opinion of what this was all about, but there was too much distance between them and all she could do was signal that she'd find her later. It struck her as rather odd that she still hadn't seen Sam, and suddenly the vague annoyance she'd been harboring for the past twenty minutes expanded to downright anger.

What in the world had he been thinking of when he'd planned such a party? It was obviously not her father's concept of what this celebration was all about. Admittedly, her irritation lay rooted in her concern for Jonas's physical condition. Granted, he'd started out the day in bad shape, but this ridiculous rock concert certainly wasn't helping matters.

And the person responsible for it was nowhere around. Great, she thought, just great! But as Maryanne finally emerged into the hallway that led to the kitchen, she just missed Sam, who was walking briskly out of the kitchen with an expression on his face that was even angrier than hers.

CHAPTER TWELVE

Sam was indeed angry as hell, and most of that anger was directed at one person—Pamela Morgan. He'd been looking for her for the past half hour and still hadn't managed to catch her. One of the maids had seen her outside on the redwood deck a few minutes ago, and that's where he was headed now.

He still couldn't believe what she'd done, turning this whole thing into one asinine, ridiculous fiasco. He'd mentioned the party to her a few weeks ago and she'd offered to help him plan and set it up. After all, she'd claimed, that sort of thing was part of her job. Sam had had his hands full at the time and had readily agreed to let her take over the arrangements. He'd given her one list of everyone presently involved in the development project, and another, even more important, with the names of several potential investors. Evidently what *he'd* had in mind for tonight's party and *her* understanding of his instructions were light years apart. He didn't know fully half the people here. And the damn music was enough to permanently damage the healthiest of eardrums. He'd seen Maryanne and Jonas retreating to the library and Jonas had looked none too happy. Sam knew he must look like the world's rudest host. He'd barely said a complete sentence to Jonas and hadn't talked to Maryanne at all. Damn, but he was furious, and all his energies were focused on finding Pamela and giving her a piece of his mind.

She was outside on the deck, where the maid had seen her, as were quite a few other guests who evidently found the cold night air a pleasant respite from the stuffiness inside. She was talking in that low, breathless voice that was particularly seductive when one first met her. Yet hearing it now only fired his anger even more.

He'd met Pamela through the real estate company AndLan had been dealing with for the past couple of months. Single, twenty-eight years old, she'd been employed in a public relations capacity for the past year and a half, and Sam had decided to hire her. He'd been impressed with more than just her professional qualifications, however, and before long had asked her out.

He had begun to weary of his long, self-imposed state of isolation since his divorce. And work, no matter how time-consuming and fulfilling, simply wasn't enough to keep him happy, or even satisfied. "Happiness" was an ambiguous term anyway; he'd long since given up trying to define it. Not that he regretted having moved back to Nacogdoches, not in the least, but in all honesty, his only truly happy times were those he shared with Melissa when she flew down to visit. He'd loved having her for Thanksgiving, and wanted her again for Christmas. At present,

196

however, Sissy was choosing to act "mommyish," and things were still up in the air.

Meeting Pamela had come at a time when he was ready for a change in his life-style. He enjoyed her lively company, her wit was refreshing, and she was certainly beautiful enough to keep any man interested on a long-term basis. That wasn't his intention, however, though he suspected at times that she thought so. Yet for Sam there was a very important ingredient missing in their relationship—the sense of the magic he felt with only one other person. And that person was unattainable, always would be, he supposed. But there were other things on his mind now; he was astonished that Pamela would completely go against his wishes, which he'd made explicit enough.

He approached her from behind and tapped her on the shoulder as she stood talking to some man he'd never seen before. She turned, exhaling a stream of smoke through her half-parted lips as she smiled. "Oh, hi, Sam. I wondered where you were. Let me introduce you to—"

"Later," Sam said gruffly, ignoring the others. Taking her by the elbow, he nodded toward the house. "I want to talk to you."

Pamela frowned with displeasure, then said with forced politeness, "Why, of course." She turned and smiled at her guests. "Sorry. Minor emergency."

Sam was squeezing her elbow rather tightly, and she muttered under her breath as she hurried along beside him, "You can stop pinching my arm, for God's sake. What the hell is wrong with you, Sam?"

Sam said nothing, but he continued leading her through the house toward one of the guest bedrooms. When they

197

were both inside, he shut the door and turned to her, his eyes narrowed and his jaw rigid with anger.

"What in hell is going on out there?

Pamela's frown deepened to a scowl and her gray eyes flashed. "What in hell, *I* might ask, is the matter with *you*? You were incredibly rude out there. I don't see what —"

He flung one arm backward and cut in, "I want to know just what you call that . . . punk rock concert out there."

"Sam Lancaster, you are acting like a jerk! What has gotten into you? This is *not* a punk rock concert. It's a very carefully thought-out and painstakingly planned party. If you took the time and made the effort to find out, you'd realize you've got some of the top real estate brokers and agents in Texas in your house."

"Is that right?"

"It most definitely is. I'm amazed, absolutely amazed at you, Sam. I had no idea you had such old-fashioned tastes. For Christ's sake, I thought you were a little more with it than this."

"What I had in mind from the beginning, and what I thought you understood," Sam said in an even tone, "was that this was to be a quiet, civilized gathering of potential *investors,* an opportunity for them to meet all the others involved in the project. Real estate agents aren't exactly top priority at this moment. And from the looks of it, each one of them brought at least one or two others who don't have the slightest inkling of what AndLan Enterprises is—or even care."

"Oh, come off it, Sam. You're being unnecessarily harsh."

"I'll tell you something, Miss Morgan. The general

partner of AndLan is in the library right now, far away from your important little real estate agents. I'm sure he's about as impressed with your efforts as I am. This is not at all what I had in mind when I let you organize this thing."

"Well, what exactly did you have in mind?"

"Something a little more sane!" Sam exclaimed.

Pamela pouted prettily and said in a hurt tone, "I just wanted to create a festive atmosphere that wouldn't be boring, or—"

"Well, you blew it, babe. This whole thing has turned into one of the most ridiculous fiascos I've ever seen. Not to mention a total waste of time and money spent on a group of freeloaders, seeing how much they can eat and drink."

Pamela folded her arms against her chest and looked up at him obstinately. "You still don't see the point I'm trying to make, do you?"

"No. And I don't want to hear it either. But I'll tell you what I do want. I want you to get out there and tone it down—the music, the noise, everything. And I want you to pass the word along that this thing is not going to go on all night." He glanced at his watch. "In fact, I want everyone out of here in the next hour."

"But it's only nine thirty!"

"I don't give a damn if it's four o'clock in the afternoon. Do it!"

Pamela's gray eyes narrowed and she opened her mouth to speak, then clamped it shut. She tapped the floor with the toe of one high-heeled shoe. "All right . . . but I think you're making a mistake, Sam."

Sam didn't honor her comment with a reply. He simply

turned on his heel, opened the door, and left. When he reached the kitchen, he found Maryanne speaking to one of the maids who was busily searching through a cupboard.

"Can I help you find anything?"

Maryanne turned around, as did the maid, and despite the anger still churning within him, Sam felt himself responding to the sight of her. She was a vision, an absolute vision of loveliness and grace and poise—a natural combination of all the qualities Pamela tried so very hard to effect.

"We were looking for some aspirin," Maryanne said, smiling apologetically. "Dad has a headache and I told him I'd try to find some."

"I saw you two go into the library a while ago," Sam said, opening the cupboard next to the one in which they'd been searching. "I thought perhaps he just wanted to get away from the racket for a while."

"Well, that too," Maryanne conceded.

"Here," Sam said, turning around and handing her a small plastic bottle of aspirin. "Tell him I apologize for the way this has turned out. There was a misunderstanding, and it's certainly not what I'd planned on. I'd like to talk to him after I take care of a few things out here."

"All right. Thanks." Maryanne took the glass of water and the bottle of aspirin and started back toward the library, noticing as she went that the volume of the music had suddenly gone down drastically.

"Thanks, honey," Jonas said, pushing himself upright in the reclining chair he had moved to. He tapped out a couple of aspirin and swallowed them with the water.

"I saw Sam," Maryanne said. "He said he wanted to talk to you."

Jonas nodded and handed the glass and aspirin bottle back to Maryanne. "Sounds like the music's died down a little."

"A lot, actually. I imagine that's what he wants to talk to you about. I don't think this was his idea, you know."

"Neither do I." Jonas closed his eyes again and rubbed his temples with his fingertips. A small groan escaped his lips and Maryanne's concern grew.

"Dad, I don't think you should stay any longer."

"I'm about ready to agree with you," Jonas admitted. "I don't know, I must be coming down with something. I haven't felt this bad in I don't know how long."

"Are you feverish . . . achy?"

"Not really. Just this damned headache. I'm a little dizzy, too."

"That does it, then. You *are* going home—right now. And *I'm* driving."

To Maryanne's surprise, Jonas did not object, and that made the situation even more serious in her eyes, though she didn't let on.

"What about your car?"

Maryanne frowned and pursed her lips. "I'll just have to come back for it tomorrow." She was thinking that she'd prefer not to have to do that, when there was a sudden knock on the door. It opened, and Sam stuck his head in and said, "Good, I was hoping you'd still be here." He walked into the room, and as Jonas started to sit up straighter, Maryanne noticed the obvious effort the movement took.

"Dad isn't feeling very well."

"I'm really sorry to hear that. Can I get you something, or do anything?" Sam stood a few feet away from Maryanne, his own expression mirroring her concern.

"Actually, I'm just about to take him home," she said. "We need our coats and my purse, though. The maid took them somewhere."

"Of course. I'll tell her to get them. Jonas, I'm really sorry about the way things worked out tonight. I had—"

Jonas waved him to silence. "No apologies necessary. It's nobody's fault but mine that I'm not feeling too hot."

"Well, I don't know if it would have been worth your while even if you had been feeling well. I had other things in mind than this sorry excuse for a party. I hope you understand that."

"Don't worry about it, Sam."

Noting the disturbingly pale complexion of the older man, Sam said, "I'll have Jean bring your things right away."

"Thank you," Maryanne said gratefully, adding, "Oh, yes, I'll have to return in the morning for my car. It's parked down the street, so I'm not blocking anyone."

"You didn't come together?"

"No. I went home before coming here. Dad drove directly over from the site."

"Well, there's no point in leaving your car here," Sam said. "I can follow you in my car and bring you back. That way you can get it back home tonight."

The idea appealed to Maryanne. "Are you sure you don't mind? You shouldn't be leaving your own party."

"This isn't *my* party. And no, I don't mind in the least. I just have to talk to a couple of people and then I'll drive on over to pick you up."

"All right, then," Maryanne agreed. Sam left, and she wondered briefly what he'd meant by saying it wasn't *his* party. She supposed it had something to do with what her father had said earlier about the public relations person. But she wasn't able to speculate on it much longer, for Jean appeared with their coats and Maryanne's purse almost immediately, and the next few minutes were taken up with getting Jonas outside and into the car and headed for home.

Sam arrived just as Maryanne shut the door to her father's bedroom, having made sure he was as comfortable as possible. She'd had time to take his temperature; it was normal, but his headache had gotten worse. He'd suggested that an ice bag might feel good, so she'd gotten him one and propped it against his forehead with the help of two pillows on either side of his head. She suspected that tension had a lot to do with the way he felt and hoped that a good night's rest would help.

When the doorbell rang, Maryanne was ready to go. She locked the door behind her and followed Sam out to his car, a dark-blue Mercedes sedan.

"How's he doing?" Sam inquired, backing the car out of the driveway. He'd had a quick, no-nonsense talk with Pamela before he'd left, making sure she understood that he wanted things wound down considerably by the time he got back.

"His head is still hurting, but I think he'll be a lot better in the morning." Maryanne turned to look at Sam. "Thank you for doing this."

"Don't mention it. I'm only sorry everything turned out this way."

She hesitated, then decided to be honest with him. "Neither one of us recognized most of the people there. If you don't mind my saying so, we were a little confused by the party."

"Sorry to say, so was I," Sam replied wryly.

"What happened? Dad told me there were to be some important potential investors invited."

"That's correct. Unfortunately, our public relations person handled all the details and she had a totally different concept of what I wanted."

"I see." Maryanne said nothing more, but she was curious about this public relations person who was apparently responsible for the unexpected evening. She remembered what her father had said about the woman's being Sam's date. The thought had a disconcerting effect on Maryanne, and as much as she reminded herself how preposterous it was, she simply couldn't shake the feeling.

By the time they reached Sam's garage, most of the guests' cars were gone. Sam switched off the engine, he shook his head, and smiled wryly at Maryanne. "Some day, huh?"

"Really."

"Could you do me a favor? I'm sure you want to be on your way, but there's someone still here I'd rather not deal with at the moment. If you could stick around for a while . . . Well, I'd be very grateful."

She didn't really understand how she'd be helping him, but there was no way she could have declined, especially after all the trouble he'd gone to on her behalf. It would only be for a little while, anyway, so she agreed.

The atmosphere inside the house had altered drastically; the music was barely audible and the few remaining guests were preparing to leave. It didn't take long for Maryanne to realize just who it was Sam was trying to avoid. But she was at a loss to understand the reason behind his animosity toward Pamela Morgan.

Sam was downright rude to the woman, even suggesting in front of Maryanne that she get rid of the remaining guests immediately and have the maids finish with the cleanup as fast as possible.

"But it's only ten o'clock," Pamela protested. "They've been hired until midnight."

"Pay them anyway. But I want them out of here in exactly one half hour. I don't want to talk about it. I just want it done."

With a cool toss of her head, Pamela turned on her heel and left the room, heading toward the kitchen.

"Sam, is everything all right?" Maryanne asked quietly.

Sam nodded, but his features remained tense and impatient. "Do you mind hanging around a little longer?"

"No, of course not."

Not sure exactly what she was supposed to do, other than simply be there as Sam suggested, Maryanne removed her coat and walked back down the hallway to the library, where she'd been earlier. Its built-in mahogany shelves were well-stocked, and she enjoyed the opportunity to explore a bit.

But as she wandered around the spacious room, slowly scanning the shelves of books, her mind was restless. She just couldn't stop wondering about the relationship between Sam and Pamela. It was strange picturing Sam with someone else, although the woman was certainly lovely enough to attract most any man.

Maybe it was having known Sissy so long that made it

seem so odd; though, to be honest, Sissy had never exactly seemed Sam's type either.

Her imagination flew to other, more intimate visions of Sam and Pamela together, and suddenly Maryanne grew quite annoyed with herself. Then, in the next moment, she justified her preoccupation by telling herself she was merely curious about what was going on in Sam's life. And it was a totally natural curiosity; after all, they had known each other for so many years. Still, there existed some undeniable twinge of another, much darker emotion, a reason that drove Maryanne to vivid speculation about a matter that shouldn't have concerned her in the least. She tried once more to dismiss it completely from her thoughts. And she was almost successful.

CHAPTER THIRTEEN

There was a soft tap on the door, and Maryanne looked up quickly, almost dropping the book she'd been leafing through. Unbidden, her heartbeat quickened as Sam opened the door and looked in.

"Are you bored to tears by now?" he asked, advancing into the room. He glanced in surprise at the stack of books on the coffee table in front of her, and Maryanne smiled.

"Actually, I've been enjoying myself. You have a very interesting collection here."

Sam cocked his head to one side and said, "Well, I'm glad you found something to do while you waited."

"Is everyone gone?" It sounded that way, for she heard nothing at all from the other part of the house.

"Every last one of 'em." Sam sighed and rubbed the palms of his hands roughly against his face. "God, what a disaster." He sank heavily into the chair her father had sat in earlier, throwing his head back and closing his eyes for a moment. When he opened them again, Maryanne was looking at him with a slight frown.

"You deserve a medal for being such a good sport and staying like this," Sam said. "I'm sure you would rather be at home with your father."

"Thanks, but it hasn't been that long. Besides, I'm sure he's sound asleep by now." Maryanne paused for a moment, then said, "But I plan to make sure he sees Dr. Sanders on Monday."

"Good idea," Sam agreed.

Maryanne thought for a moment about how to frame her next words, then she said tentatively, "Sam, I know I haven't been very involved in what has been going on at AndLan. Well, that's putting it mildly, I guess. But I am curious about what happened tonight."

"The whole thing turned into one hell of a fiasco, didn't it?" He moved his head slowly from side to side, his eyes staring off as if he were lost in thought.

"Uh, does it have anything to do with Pamela?" she asked hesitantly.

"A hell of a lot." Suddenly, Sam seemed to come back to reality, and he looked directly at Maryanne as he explained further. "She volunteered to set up this whole thing and I agreed willingly, since I've been busy as hell and she *is* in charge of public relations for the company. However, I definitely overestimated her sense of what's appropriate when it comes to gatherings of this sort."

"I don't quite understand," Maryanne said, and Sam explained what the primary purpose of the party was supposed to have been and how Pamela had taken the opportunity to invite a totally different group. Finally, Maryanne nodded and said, "Why would she do something like that, so completely at odds with what you'd told her?"

"That's a hell of a good question. Ms. Morgan happens to have too high an opinion of her capabilities. I trusted her at first, but I've learned my lesson tonight."

Maryanne ran her thumb against the edge of the book she was holding and drew a deep silent breath. It was none of her business, really, yet some unsatisfied curiosity still demanded satisfaction.

"Are you . . . Have you and Pamela been seeing each other? On more than a business basis?" She felt herself blushing at her own forwardness.

Sam, who had been staring blankly at the opposite wall of bookshelves, glanced over at Maryanne in surprise. "Yes, as a matter of fact we have. What made you ask?"

Maryanne's complexion darkened as she flushed even more, and she began to slide her thumb rapidly up and down the book's binding. She tried to laugh, but the effort was pitiably unsuccessful. "Oh, Dad mentioned something about it before and . . . I don't know . . ." Her voice trailed off and she wished she'd kept her big mouth shut. There was no reason in the world she should have asked such a question; Sam's social life was certainly no concern of hers.

"What about you?" Sam asked in the momentary silence. "Are you still going with the professor?"

His emphasis on the last word gave the question a sarcastic touch, but Maryanne didn't find it offensive. "Yes. I don't think of him that way, though."

"What way do you think of him?"

The question took her aback, for she truly had no idea how to answer it. She leaned forward and placed the book on the coffee table, then stood and walked over to one of the room's beautiful multipaned windows, watching a lone Ligustrum leaf scrape back and forth against the glass in the night breeze.

"I don't know, to be honest with you," she answered softly. "He's a friend."

"Just a friend . . . nothing more?"

Sam's voice, so close behind her, startled her and she turned around quickly. His dark-brown eyes were watching her with an intensity that was penetrating and terribly disturbing. Despite her belief that she had successfully dispensed with the memory of what had happened between them before, she was instantly aware of the same powerful force that had drawn them together then. Being aware of something was one thing; doing something about it was an altogether different matter. Stubbornly her body refused to obey her brain's commands. He was standing much too close to her now, and she found it almost impossible not to respond to his nearness. The most she could do was to stand rigidly, trying desperately to muster at least a shred of control over the situation. Yet none was forthcoming and she knew deep down that she really wasn't trying.

"Well?" he prompted, his voice low, his gaze boring into her demandingly.

Maryanne swallowed and tried to look away; she couldn't. "Nothing more," she muttered feebly.

"Not lovers?"

Finally she was able to shift her gaze away from his, feeling—she didn't know how she felt—confused, perturbed, yet strangely excited. "That's none of your business," she replied.

"I'm only asking out of concern for your welfare, Maryanne."

That brought her eyes back to his and she said sharply, "Oh, please, Sam. Don't patronize me."

"I'm not. I mean it."

At last she was able to move, but as she took a step away, Sam's hand reached out and grabbed her by the arm. "I must have hit a sensitive nerve."

Maryanne's eyes narrowed as she retorted, "You haven't hit a sensitive nerve, Sam. We've had this conversation—or a version of it—at least twice before. I suppose it's just typical of your gender to simply ignore what I said."

"Excuse me if I don't follow you."

"You're not excused. But I will repeat what I hoped I'd made clear before. I don't need you—or any man's—concern for my welfare. *I* know what I want. *I* make up the rules for what goes on in my life—including the man I choose to date . . . or to be my lover."

Sam's eyes held hers for a long, silent moment. Then he spoke in a low and direct voice. "Then perhaps you will consider me a candidate for that honor."

Maryanne blushed to the roots of her hair. She was totally astonished, as much by her physical response as by the unexpectedness of his proposal. For Sam's very nearness had awakened some latent yearning within her, and his words were as erotically compelling as any physical contact. She was helpless to think of, let alone make, an appropriate response.

But what Sam did next precluded any response she might have been able to summon. He was tired of considering what was right or wrong, how far he should or shouldn't go with Maryanne. Reason had taken a backseat to a need he'd lived with for many years, a need he sensed was echoed within her.

"Come here," he said softly, taking her by the hand and leading her out of the library as he switched off the light and stepped into the hallway. Without a word he led her through the semidarkness to another part of the house. Though everything had been cleaned up by the maids and caterers, the stale smell of smoke still permeated the now quiet house. The difference between the way the house had been a few hours ago and the way it was now was striking, yet Maryanne found she was thinking of it only fuzzily. Indeed, she could hardly think at all. Her brain was numb, having acquiesced finally to the greater, more strident demands of her body.

As they rounded a corner in the opposite wing of the house, Sam stopped to open a door. Maryanne followed him into the room, her gaze automatically lifting upward to follow the smooth, angular lines of the unusually designed bedroom. The ceiling slanted dramatically from a two-story height to a mere five feet at the opposite wall, its continuous skylight allowing the pure, silvery moonlight to illuminate the darkened room.

Maryanne's gaze traveled slowly around the room and she was intrigued by its architectural ingenuity. But she didn't have time to study it long, for Sam's hand tightened on hers and she turned to look at him, her heartbeat quickening in sudden expectation. She should say *something,* she thought, yet she could not for the life of her begin to summon words.

Sam had no words either, but not for lack of them, for he would have loved to spend a lifetime talking to this exquisite woman he'd wanted for so very, very long. Yet words were unnecessary now, indeed they would have been intrusive. Instead, he pulled her close to him, letting go of her hand and placing both of his on her shoulders. Instinctively his thumbs began to rotate gently into the silk material of her dress.

Slowly and determinedly he bent his head, placing his lips gently upon hers, feeling their coolness against his own. Then, all at once, it seemed, they were kissing each other with a depth of passion that startled them with its unbridled intensity. Maryanne's breasts flattened against Sam's chest, and as he pressed her even tighter to him, she wrapped her arms around his waist, feeling him hard against her, one solid thigh boldly pushing between her own.

When his fingers pulled at the sash around her waist, she made no move to object, and when she felt him fumbling with the buttons at the back of her dress, her hands slipped beneath his woolen sweater, tugging none too gently at his shirt and releasing it from the confines of his belted slacks. They kissed, pulled feverishly apart, then kissed again, each methodically undressing the other until at last they stood completely naked before each other.

Sam was sure he could not bear to put off for another moment what he wanted more than anything, yet he forced himself to wait, his gaze finding its own reward as it traveled down the slender, curvaceous length of her. Her small, firm breasts—the nipples taut and stimulated—rose and fell rapidly as her breathing came in shallow spurts.

Suddenly, Sam could resist no longer. He rested both hands lightly on her shoulders for a moment before sliding them slowly down the sides of her arms, stopping once as his thumbs extended inward to caress the darkened tips of each breast. Maryanne shivered uncontrollably, and as Sam heard her sharp, involuntary gasp of pure, sweet pleasure, his hands continued down her arms, caressing, then lightly squeezing, her smooth, narrow waist.

Maryanne brought her hands up now, placing her palms against the light matting of hair on his chest, amazed at the broad expanse of it, wondering at his own sensation as she gently pinched his taut nipples. And as she felt his hands move farther down, caressing the rounded firmness of her buttocks, sliding around to the front of her thighs, she closed her eyes and leaned against him. When his fingers began stroking with feather lightness the sensitive inner flesh of her thighs, his caress moving upward, she moaned aloud and grasped the nape of his neck. He pressed against her even harder and she felt the full evidence of his passion; suddenly her legs felt as if they could hold her no longer.

He must have sensed her weakening, for at that instant one of his arms slid behind her knees, the other under her shoulders, and he lifted her effortlessly, kissing her repeatedly as he strode across the room toward the king-size bed. He put her down in the middle of it, then lay down next to her, pulling her onto her side and into the arc of his body.

"God, I want you, Maryanne," he whispered urgently into her ear, his hands traveling feverishly up and down her buttocks and the backs of her thighs. "Please, let me love you."

She nodded, totally unable to speak. But words, explanations, and rationalizations were no longer necessary; she needed him, wanted him more than she could have imagined possible, ached to quench this fire that suddenly burned out of control.

"Is it all right, Maryanne?" he whispered, placing one hand between her thighs and gently, very gently, pushing them apart.

"Please . . . yes." Her voice was thick and raspy and impatient.

She rolled onto her back, welcoming his weight as he balanced on top of her. She was burning with readiness for him, and with her hand guiding him, he slid partially into her. There was resistance, and Sam was surprised and had to summon even more self-control, but in a moment her body overcame it and welcomed him fully.

Their lovemaking was slow at first, but it soon quickened to an intensity that threatened to spiral out of control. Maryanne was stunned by the depth of her response, the explosion of sensation that came so easily and readily. She had never been so fulfilled, felt so complete as a woman. And instinctively she sensed the same response in Sam.

Afterward, as they lay next to each other, Maryanne listened to the rhythmic sound of Sam's breathing. She looked at him, saw that his eyes were closed, and assumed he'd fallen asleep. She looked up through the skylight, her gaze focused on the galaxy of stars that shone so clearly tonight. How strange, she thought, to feel such total, soothing relaxation. It had to be a physical thing, she decided; after all, it had been a long time since she had made love to anyone. Her body had demanded release; it was to be expected that she should react so strongly to Sam's lovemaking. Yet there was more to it, some small voice insisted. How could she explain the fact that she had *never* before experienced such fulfillment—not even when

Elliot had finally come home from Vietnam. After all that time she hadn't felt this way.

There were differences between the two men—very important ones. Sam gave where Elliot had only taken; without words Sam had communicated to her what he wanted, and he'd been willing and eager to learn what she wanted, what pleased her. Kind—he was an incredibly kind and giving man, Maryanne thought. But she had known that all along about Sam Lancaster.

The room was growing colder as the heat of their lovemaking dissipated. She noticed the shadowy outline of her clothes scattered in a heap on the floor, and then she turned to look at Sam once more.

His eyes were still closed and his breathing as even and regular as before. There was no need to wake him; there was also no reason for her to stay any longer.

With as little movement as possible Maryanne started to pull herself up and edge over to the side of the bed. But as she did so, she felt a hand on her leg and she turned around, startled to see Sam propped up on one elbow, his eyes opened wide.

"Where are you going?" he asked in a tone that indicated he hadn't been asleep at all.

"I thought you were asleep."

He uttered a half-laugh. "No. I'm not the type."

"What type?"

"The type who makes love and then rolls over and falls asleep."

Maryanne nodded and smiled vaguely, her mind filled with images of Elliot. He'd *always* fallen asleep immediately after they'd made love.

"I asked you a question," Sam reminded her in a gentle tone. "Where were you going?"

Maryanne glanced at her clothes again, suddenly shivering in the chill air. She wanted to either get up and get dressed or get back under the covers and snuggle up. . . . No, she couldn't do that.

"I'm going home." She started to push off the bed but again Sam stopped her by putting his hand on her thigh.

"Why?"

"Because it's very late and . . . and I just need to go home."

Sam looked at her intently and said, "I want you to stay here. With me."

Maryanne swallowed uncomfortably. She was shivering visibly, yet Sam still held her where she was. There was no way she was going to crawl under the covers now. "I can't do that."

"Why not? Is it because of Jonas? He'll be all right. You can call him, if you like."

"Oh, Sam, that's not the reason and you know it." Maryanne sounded distraught.

"No, I'm not so sure I do. Why don't you tell me?"

Maryanne looked straight up through the skylight, wishing that Sam would make this easier on her. She was confused and bewildered by her own lack of trust in herself, and Sam sounded far too serious. The bad thing was that he was beginning to get to her.

"Sam . . . We shouldn't have done this."

Sam flinched as if someone had thrown a bucket of cold water in his face. "What the hell does that mean?"

The gruffness of his tone startled her and she tried once

more to get off the bed. But his hand shot off her thigh and grabbed her by the wrist tightly.

"Let me go, Sam."

"Not until you give me an answer. A straight one. I'm sick and tired of talking in circles."

Maryanne winced but his hand tightened even more. "We shouldn't have . . . had sex. You and I both know that, Sam."

"Then why did we?"

"I'm sure it was something we both thought we needed. It *was* something we needed. We've both been under a certain amount of stress tonight and—"

"Stress? What gives you the right to classify making love as getting rid of stress? And who the hell are you to speak for me?"

"You don't have to raise your voice, Sam, I'm sitting right here." She tried to sound stern but her voice was shaky.

"And you don't have to act like Miss Frigid, U.S.A." He was incensed now, and Maryanne drew back as he suddenly sat up and leaned toward her, his features tightened into a snarl.

"Don't be ridiculous. I—"

"Don't *you* be ridiculous. What we just shared—having sex, as you so clinically put it—happened to mean a great deal to me." Maryanne moved slightly and Sam yanked at her wrist. "No, you stay put! You're going to listen to every bit of what I have to say, because I'm damned tired of carrying it inside and pussyfooting around every time we get near the subject." He hesitated, then spoke in a calm, direct voice. "I love you, Maryanne Anderson. I loved you the very first time I saw you." The words were

218

out and suddenly he felt as though a giant burden had been lifted from his shoulders. If only he could have told her years ago.

Maryanne stared blankly at him. Then she looked down, her hands in her lap, and she swallowed deeply, wondering how she had allowed things to come to this. How often had she told herself she and Sam were no more than friends. But now that he'd told her he loved her, she believed him. Deep inside she'd known all along that what he felt for her was more than mere friendship. Oh, God, what was she going to do now?

"I've kept those words to myself for years, Maryanne," he said, "hoping, even when I knew I was fooling myself, that I would someday be able to say them to you. I never loved Sissy. I only married her because I knew there wasn't the slightest chance of having the one person I really did love. But I'll tell you something. I would have gone to my grave without telling you if you'd been happy with Elliot. When you learned what Elliot had done in 'Nam, I wanted to kill the bastard. I was—" Suddenly Sam's voice broke and he abruptly let go of her wrist, turning his head to stare off across the room.

Maryanne made no effort to get up. She simply waited, not knowing what to do or say.

When he spoke again, Sam's voice was husky and remote, and Maryanne didn't understand what he had said. "What?" she asked softly.

"I said, did it really mean so little to you? Our making love?"

Maryanne uttered a small sigh and was surprised to feel a lump in the back of her throat. She was so confused and Sam sounded so sincerely hurt. She hadn't meant to do that to him. . . . Yet she couldn't tell him what he wanted to hear. "Of course not, Sam. It was wonderful." And she meant it, very much so. "It's just . . . Oh, Sam, this is the wrong time in my life. I'm not ready to get involved again."

"Because of what Elliot did to you?"

"No! I don't give a damn anymore about what Elliot did to me. And besides, he couldn't have done it if I hadn't let him. I'm over all that. Completely."

Sam turned to look at her directly. "Are you, Maryanne?"

She nodded slowly, then said in a firm voice, "Yes. I really am. It's just that I can't handle anything else at this point. I've started over with a new life and—"

"And you don't need any complications."

She hesitated, then said, "That's right. Can you understand that?"

Sam was quiet for a few seconds. "I suppose it makes sense," he said finally. "But I'm not sure where that leaves me. What it means in relation to what happened between us tonight."

Maryanne knew that her lovemaking with Sam had indeed meant something to her. It had been a wondrous, beautiful experience. An experience that had opened her eyes to the fact that Sam could indeed be a man with whom to share, to build a relationship based on tenderness and sincerity, which she could never have with Elliot, or even Michael. But she remained unable to admit that to him. Instead she tried to remain objective and removed. "We both have needs, Sam. What's wrong with that? We shared those needs tonight, satisfied them. Isn't that enough?"

Sam stared at her, his jaw tightening perceptibly. "For heaven's sake, I bare my soul to you and you toss back an answer that sounds like a quote from a magazine article on how to keep up with life in the fast lane. I *had* a marriage based on two people 'satisfying' their physical 'needs.' It wasn't enough then, and it will never be enough with you. I'm in love with you, Maryanne. Doesn't that mean anything to you at all?" He was a fool to ask, yet some masochistic impulse demanded that he hear from her own lips the words he knew could only twist the knife a little harder.

Maryanne looked down at the bedspread, rumpled and damp from their lovemaking. "Of course it means something to me, Sam. I . . . I just can't say what you want to hear. I . . . I'm sorry."

"No need to be sorry. No one can make another person fall in love." Sam drew a long, deep breath and expelled it tiredly as he ran a hand through his hair. "I'm sorry I stopped you from leaving."

"Sam, don't say that. I could have left if I'd wanted to."

"Do you still?"

Maryanne hesitated. "I should. Yes. I need to."

"All right, then."

She got off the bed and bent over to pick up her clothes. "I'll just be a minute in your bathroom," she said softly.

"Take your time," Sam told her.

She showered and dressed quickly, setting her mind to what she was doing, unwilling to think about what had just taken place. And when she emerged from the bathroom, the light was on and Sam wasn't in the room. She found him behind the bar in the den, dressed, and for a moment she watched him unobserved. Something pulled at her heart as she watched him pour a tumbler of bourbon and lift it to his lips, gulping down half of it. She was overwhelmed with an emotion she was afraid to define; not pity, for no one could pity Sam Lancaster. It was just that the man seemed so alone here, so dwarfed by this huge, beautiful house. A part of her wanted very much to stay the night through; but another, more insistent part was terrified that it might lead to an involvement she didn't need. No, she couldn't succumb to that. She had only just found herself, learned to function on her own—without a man. And she wasn't willing to give that up.

He sensed her presence and turned around. Setting the glass on the bar, he started toward her. "I'll walk you to your car."

"No . . . Sam, you don't have to do that."

"No problem. You're parked halfway down the road, remember? It's ridiculous to walk all that way in the dark by yourself."

"Well, all right, then."

They stepped into the cold night air, their footsteps quickening as they walked along the sidewalk toward Maryanne's car. Sam made a few casual comments about the success of the groundbreaking ceremony and Maryanne nodded, feeling confused by the complete change in his voice. It was almost as if they had stepped over some invisible line, as if their conversation a few minutes ago had never happened.

"I want to hear what the doctor says about your father," Sam said. "I'm not so sure Jonas will tell me if there's anything wrong. Not that there is, but—"

"I know what you mean." Maryanne nodded. "Don't worry, I'll let you know."

"Good."

They had reached her car, and as Maryanne slid the key into the lock, Sam said haltingly, "Listen, about tonight—"

Maryanne placed a restraining hand on his arm and interrupted. "You don't have to say anything, Sam. I understand."

But as Sam looked into her huge green eyes, desperately trying to fathom their beautiful depths, he wondered if indeed she did understand. And if she ever truly would.

CHAPTER FOURTEEN

Maryanne read the yellow-highlighted phrase in her note-book one more time, closed her eyes, and repeated it aloud. Then she scanned the next paragraph, read it slowly, and committed to memory its most significant points.

Almost finished, an encouraging voice reminded the already overloaded circuits of her brain. She was determined to have reviewed all of the semester's notes by 1:00 A.M. She was beyond tired, for she'd been glued to her desk ever since she'd gotten home at four o'clock that afternoon. Final exams began tomorrow, and fortunately Biology 101 was the only one scheduled on that particular day. She was caught up with the material in all of her subjects, but this one course was giving her the hardest time. Although it was one of her favorite subjects, she found it particularly grueling to go over and over the volumes of notes and text material without knowing for certain what was going to be on the exam.

Closing her eyes for a restful moment, Maryanne leaned back and stretched in the straight-backed chair; she didn't dare allow herself the luxury of the bed or couch, or even one of the more comfortable dinette chairs. She'd have fallen asleep in a second. Thank heaven she was already dressed for bed.

She pressed her fingers against her eyes and sighed deeply; she was too old for this. *Come on, now, no excuses.* She opened her eyes again and stared down at the next yellow-highlighted page of notes, read it over three times, then looked up and tried to repeat it mentally. She didn't remember a word. She glanced at the clock and decided it was no use. She had to get up at least by six in the morning, and if she didn't get *some* sleep, she wouldn't be worth a damn during the test tomorrow morning. She would just have to review these last two pages as she ate breakfast.

She walked down the hall and went into the bathroom for a few minutes. Then she crept quietly across the den to the other side of the house and stopped in front of her father's bedroom. She could hear his deep, even snoring. He slept a lot lately, ever since the doctor had put him on medication for high blood pressure. Jonas didn't like the fact that it made him so sleepy and slowed him down a lot, but Maryanne watched him like a hawk, making sure he took every single dose of the medicine, at least when she was around. Satisfied that he was sleeping soundly, she walked back to her bedroom, pulled back the covers on her bed, and got in. She lay staring at the ceiling for a long time. Things had changed around the house since they'd discovered the reason for Jonas's illness the day of the groundbreaking ceremony.

She'd taken him to the doctor on the following Monday and thanked her lucky stars she'd insisted on it. Saturday's illness had been, more than likely, a short-term virus, Dr. Sanders had said, but what he discovered during the examination was far more important. Jonas's blood pressure was elevated way above the acceptable limit, and the situation called for immediate attention. Maryanne's initial panicky reaction subsided when the doctor assured her that her father was in no danger of a heart attack, and in fact was otherwise in good health. But in addition to the prescribed medication that he had to take each day, there was a whole list of changes he needed to make in his present life-style. He had to take off the extra pounds he'd put on over the last several years, ease up on the high-fat, high-salt diet he'd been used to for so long, and try to eliminate any undue pressure or strain.

Maryanne had taken no chances with any of the doctor's orders. Jonas grumbled, but she firmly took matters into her own hands. She threw out the salt, saw to it that he took his medication, and, most importantly, had a long talk with Sam. She'd driven to the office site one Saturday when Jonas had said he was going to stay home and work on the shed behind the garage. It was almost finished and he wanted to complete the exterior work while the weather was still dry.

Sam was obviously surprised to see her, as were Joe and Lily, who were also there working half a day to get caught up on what had quickly turned into one of the busiest projects the company had been involved in so far. Maryanne spoke with Joe and Lily for a few minutes, then accepted Sam's invitation to join him in his office.

He indicated a chair for her to sit down in, but she shook her head. "No, thanks. I came by to tell you what Dr. Sanders said about Dad. Or has he mentioned it to you already?"

Sam shook his head. "He just told us he'd had a twenty-four-hour virus or some such."

Maryanne gave a brief sigh. "I thought as much. Well, it was more than that. He also has hypertension. Dr. Sanders was pretty alarmed when Dad saw him on Monday; he said his pressure was elevated to a dangerous level. He's put him on medication and given him strict orders to scale down any unnecessary stress. That's what I came to talk to you about."

Sam's expression was empathetic. "I'm glad you came. I share your concern, I really do. Believe me, I know enough enough about hypertension to relate to your worry over Jonas's condition. My father had the same thing." He paused, then said, "You don't have to worry about a thing, Maryanne, as far as his work load here. He's been taking on a hefty share of the load lately, but that can and will be taken care of. I promise you that."

"Thank you," Maryanne said. "This isn't something Dad can ignore or shrug off. I know he understands that, but I'm still concerned that where the development project is concerned, he might fudge a little."

Sam's eyes locked with Maryanne's and he stated very directly, "I meant what I said. You have nothing to worry about, Maryanne. Joe and Lily and I will make damned sure Jonas doesn't bite off more than he can chew. In fact,

I intend to make a few minor changes in that regard immediately."

Sam's words almost instantly relieved Maryanne, easing the tension and strain she'd been under since the visit to Dr. Sanders. She did not doubt Sam's promise, knew instinctively she had nothing further to worry about concerning Jonas's involvement with his job. She could trust Sam; above and beyond everything else she might feel about him, she knew that much. It was a gratifying, reassuring feeling, but her reaction was ambiguous. On the one hand she was strongly tempted to sit down this minute and just talk to Sam. Talk her heart out about all the frustrations she'd been dealing with alone these past few months; about how it felt to be going to college with such a different, vastly younger group of people; about the difficulty of *really* getting into the swing of things. About not just the studying and the discipline, which she actually enjoyed, but the struggle to accept the sometimes scary fact that she had taken on a challenge that was going to continue for the next three and a half years.

She wanted so much to talk to someone about all these things, and now, because of her father's problems, she needed that someone more than ever. Deep inside, Maryanne knew that Sam was the only one who could understand, who really knew her and could relate to "where she was coming from," as the kids put it nowadays. And, as she had expected, Sam had come through for her today, instantly putting her fears to rest. She and Michael had very little time to see each other now that the semester was nearing its close, but even if they had had time, Maryanne wouldn't have been inclined to confide in him. It just wasn't the same with Michael—and it never would be.

The fact remained that she couldn't dismiss the memory of what had happened between her and Sam or even try to pretend that it hadn't changed things. It had. To let Sam into her life further would require confronting feelings she simply wasn't ready to face. And so she ignored the impulse to relax now, to respond to the warmth and companionship that this man offered her so willingly and that, deep in her heart, she longed for very much. She adjusted the shoulder strap of her purse and took a few steps toward the door. "Thank you very much, Sam. I really appreciate your understanding. And your help."

"Don't even mention it. Jonas means a lot to us. We'll keep him in line. Maryanne?"

Her hand was on the doorknob and she turned slightly, shyly meeting his gaze. "Yes?"

"I'm glad you came today."

Maryanne swallowed, but could think of nothing to say in response. She nodded, then turned and walked quickly out the door, away from the man and from the memory that she found impossible to put in a less emotional perspective. She could escape the man himself; the memory, however, was an entirely different matter. That night she dreamed in vivid detail of lying next to Sam, of making love with wild, unbridled passion, only to wake up suddenly in the middle of the night, her heart pounding fiercely, a sense of panic gripping her.

She was bewildered by her awful sense of aloneness, the frightening awareness of her own solitude. It took several torturous minutes to settle down to relative calmness, to remind herself that she was all right, safe and sound and happy in her father's house.

But try as she might, it was difficult to dispel her feeling of discontent, which grew every day. Everything was just as it had been, she reminded herself; she and Michael were seeing each other as usual, her father was getting along quite well, and going back to college had turned out to be the wisest decision she'd ever made. She'd be glad, of course, when finals were over, but other than that everything was going according to schedule.

Nevertheless, deep inside she knew that happiness continued to elude her. There had been a few precious minutes of that elusive state a mere two weeks ago. She had promised herself she would never let it happen again, yet she could not forget it, just as she could never again think the same of him.

Jonas's well-being was of primary importance, however, so she forced herself to put her feelings aside at least twice over the following week. Unable to reach Sam at work, she telephoned him at home. Their conversations were encouraging; Jonas was cooperating very well at the office, no problem there, he told her. Sam was always sympathetic and very reassuring, yet just the sound of his voice was almost more than Maryanne could bear. She was grateful for Sam's politeness, his refraining from talking about other, more personal things. Yet Maryanne was strangely irritated with him. It didn't make sense; what did she want from him? Invariably, halfway through their conversation she would begin to fidget, annoyed with herself as the memory of some physical detail of the man would distract her—the way his thick, dark hair curled over the back of his collar, the short, bristling hairs bunched around his wristwatch, the slight depressions beneath his eyes.

She shouldn't give such things a second thought, yet she couldn't help it. By the time she had finished talking to him, she was ready to slam the phone down and run out the door, away from . . . from what? Her own feelings? No. She knew what her feelings were in that regard. And she was getting heartily sick of constantly analyzing the situation. So she would stop, only to be plagued night after night with recurring dreams of him. Sleep came in broken fragments, and when the alarm sounded each morning at the same ungodly hour, Maryanne felt haggard and wearier than when she'd gone to bed.

Michael wasn't much help either. He, too, was becoming busier as the semester came to a close. Yet even if he'd had the time to spend with her, she wouldn't have cared; as much as she hated to admit it, she was getting bored with their relationship. There really wasn't much more to it than friendship, or companionship. He still hadn't made any moves of a sexual nature toward her, and although there were probably all sorts of reasons for his reticence— and hers, too, for that matter—it nevertheless bothered her now, very much so.

Such thoughts would beset her well after her bedroom lights were doused, until at long last her mind became exhausted and she fell into a light, troubled sleep. The following days were difficult, yet somehow she made it through them, praying each morning she could finish that day's particular exams without falling asleep. And, miraculously, she made it.

Finals progressed better than she had hoped. The hours of study had been worth it for she did quite well on all of her exams. Her grades, for her first semester in college, were something to be truly proud of. And she was proud, very much so. Yet beyond the satisfaction and the gratifying sense of accomplishment, a discontent continued to gnaw at the edge of her consciousness. Now that classes were over, a lull came into her life, one that only strengthened the vague depression she felt.

Christmas was right around the corner, and Maryanne was seized with the melancholy that always haunted her around this time of year. Even when she'd been married, she'd felt that way, a longing for a sense of togetherness at Christmastime, and she'd always pleaded with Elliot to take her home to Nacogdoches, or even to see his own parents in Austin. But he'd always been too busy, and she'd always backed down. She could kick herself now for having done so. Just to think of all she'd missed—and all because of her misguided devotion to him—made her sick with regret.

She was glad, of course, to be able to share the holiday with her father, but she had to admit that her first Christmas as a single woman was having a sobering effect on her. And the fact that the next semester was almost four weeks away only worsened matters; suddenly the busy rhythm of her days had ground to a halt and there was a gaping hole in her life.

Trying to cast off the disturbing emotions, she had a flash of an idea after her last exam on Friday afternoon. She would stop by Michael's office and see if he was interested in making some plans with her.

As she walked down the long corridor toward his office, she became increasingly excited by the invitation she had in mind. She knocked once on his partially open door and peeked in. Michael was standing with his back to her, a batch of papers in one hand as he went through a file drawer with the other.

"Hey, don't you know school's out?" she greeted him cheerfully.

"Hmmm?" He turned and mumbled a hello through his lips, the pencil he was chewing on bobbing up and down. Then he leaned over his paper-strewn desk and opened his mouth, letting the pencil drop to the desk top. "Come in. Can you believe this mess?"

"Yes. I've been living that way at home for the past three weeks. Final exams really take a lot out of all of us, don't they?"

Michael nodded and grinned as he looked her over. "You looked pleased with yourself. You must have done pretty well."

Maryanne took a seat in the chair across from his desk and stretched her arms behind her back. "Well, I think I did. I'm eager to see grades posted. When do you think they'll be up?"

"Mmmm, probably next Tuesday or Wednesday." He shook his head. "You've got to be the most enthusiastic student I've seen in ages."

"That's probably because I'm the oldest."

"There you go again. Will you cut out that 'I'm so ancient' routine?"

"All right, all right," Maryanne agreed with a grin. "Besides, today I don't feel that way."

Michael slammed the file drawer shut and placed a sheaf of papers into his attaché case. "How come? Been remembering to take your Geritol?"

Maryanne chuckled. "I *never* forget that. It makes me more of a woman, you know."

Michael cocked an eyebrow. "My, my, we are in a good mood today."

"That's because I just had a brainstorm before I walked over here."

"What's that?" He began to shuffle through the mountain of exam notebooks stacked on one corner of his desk, his eyes glancing sporadically at Maryanne.

"Well, with all the time off we have, I thought it might be great if we could do something, you know. Go somewhere. Have you ever been skiing?"

Michael looked up briefly, then busied himself again with the exam books. "Ah, yeah. You?"

"A few times. Enough to know what I'm doing." She leaned forward and placed her forearms on Michael's desk. "What d'you think? We probably wouldn't get a very good deal pricewise since it's so late in the season, but I think Colorado would be the best place to try. Plus, it's so gorgeous there and . . ." Her voice trailed off as she realized his expression was less than receptive. "You're not exactly bowled over by the idea."

"No, no, it's not that, I just . . ." He leaned back in his chair and ran a hand through his hair. "Damn, it seems as though every time you suggest something—"

"You have something else planned," Maryanne finished for him.

Michael's brow wrinkled as he frowned apologetically. "I'm sorry, really I am. But I promised my parents I'd spend most of the holidays with them. Dad hasn't been feeling well and . . ."

Maryanne nodded and sat back in her chair, her good mood suddenly fizzling out. "I understand. Well, it was just a thought, anyway."

Michael got up and came around the desk, placing a

hand on her arm. "Don't be angry, Maryanne. I'd get out of it if I could, you know that . . ."

"Oh. Excuse me." Maryanne and Michael turned simultaneously to see a tall, slender redheaded young woman standing in the doorway, her blue eyes glaring angrily at Michael. She glanced at Maryanne as if she were nothing more than a piece of office furniture, and asked, "Are you ready to go yet, Michael?"

Her possessive tone did not escape Maryanne, and as she looked at Michael, then back at the young woman, her eyes narrowed slightly, and at the same moment she felt Michael's hand drop away from her arm. One did not need a college education to analyze the situation, she thought dryly, and as she picked up her purse and books, she produced a bright smile for both the redhead and Michael. "I was just on my way out," she said. The smile broadened and she added sweetly, "Really, professor, I *do* understand. Thank you so much for your time." *I won't be needing any more of it,* she added silently.

She nodded politely to the young woman, who had now stepped inside the office, and as she walked slowly down the hallway, she heard the door shut firmly. Her footsteps echoed loudly down the empty corridor, and suddenly a dry, perverse laugh rose in her throat.

When in heaven's name was she going to grow up and see her personal relationships as they really were? What a fool Michael must have taken her for, she thought, only to realize a second later that she really didn't care what he thought. In fact, she almost felt relieved by the scene she'd just witnessed. The redhead's eyes had glared with a telltale possessiveness that told the whole story. Obviously she was Michael's other interest and no doubt the real reason behind his commendable devotion to his parents.

By the time Maryanne had reached her car, her thinking was rational and clear. Now that she saw the situation as it really was, she knew she would never see Michael again. Their relationship had been tentative, at best; in fact, Maryanne felt almost grateful that she had an excellent excuse to call it off completely.

But a sense of disappointment drifted over her as she drove back home. She had been so excited about the spontaneous plans she'd made, and now that they had gone down the tube, there was nothing else to take their place. Once again the holidays loomed ahead—empty and depressing. Oh, there was her father, of course, and she wouldn't for the world let him know she felt this way, but she found it increasingly difficult to fight back her feelings. Well, she'd just have to think of something to do with herself. She'd catch up on the novels she'd wanted to read all semester but had had to put aside because of her studies.

There were a lot of other things she could get done around the house, too, and perhaps her father had something *he* wanted her to do. The mental pep talk continued until she reached home, and by then she wasn't even thinking of what had happened with Michael.

"Hi, Dad," she greeted her father as she walked through the back door. "How was your day?"

Jonas was standing at the kitchen sink, preparing the makings of a salad, and he turned to smile at his daughter. "Fine. Lunch will be ready in a minute. Chef's salad today."

"Compliments of the chef?" Maryanne smiled back at him.

"That's right. Are you all finished now?"

Maryanne relieved herself of coat and purse and books and opened the refrigerator door. She took out the pitcher of iced tea and said, "Yep. No more cracking the books for another three and a half weeks. I can't believe I don't have to rush back to my desk to study right after we eat."

"Well, you need the rest. It'll do you a world of good."

"What's this?" Maryanne asked, noticing a legal-size folder with the keys to Jonas's sedan on top of it. "Are you going somewhere?"

"Oh, that . . . They're just some documents from the office that I've been going over."

Maryanne's eyes narrowed suspiciously. "What's going on here? I hope you're not getting into something too involved, Dad."

Jonas waved aside her remark. "I'm not a cripple, Maryanne. Lord, there are millions of people with hypertension leading ordinary lives, and I'm hardly doing a thing as it is. Joe and Sam take care of just about everything else." He set the bowl of greens on the table and said with a small sigh, "Doesn't matter anyway. Things are progressing pretty fast now, and my part's pretty much over."

Maryanne recognized the disappointment in his voice and she wondered if he, too, was suffering from a bit of the Christmas blues. She wished she could cheer him up, but knew that it would be wrong to encourage him to get more involved in the development project. And, as he said, there really was nothing more for him to do at this point.

"Anyway," Jonas was saying, "I told Sam I'd look them over and get them back to him today."

Maryanne poured two glasses of iced tea and said, "When were you planning to go?"

"After lunch, I suppose." Jonas frowned and rubbed the corners of his mouth thoughtfully. "I just thought of something, Maryanne. Look at the wall calendar and check my appointment with Doc Sanders, would you?"

Maryanne leaned over the counter to where the calendar hung next to the telephone. "The eighteenth, at two o'clock." She glanced at her father in surprise. "That's today, Dad. You didn't tell me you'd made another appointment."

"I forgot about it. His secretary called last week to remind me I hadn't set one up, so I told her today would be fine."

"Well, you don't have much time. It's almost one forty-five."

Jonas shook his head as he took a bite of the salad. "I must be getting senile, too. I tell you, if it isn't one thing, it's another."

"Well, take your time eating," Maryanne reprimanded him lightly, noticing the way he was gobbling his food. "You're going to end up with a stomachache."

"Guess I'll just have to take that folder over to Sam after I get away from Doc Sanders's office."

"Why don't I take it over for you?" Maryanne offered. "Will Sam be at the office all day?"

"I don't really know. He's hard to catch. Would you mind doing that?"

Maryanne shook her head. "No, of course not. I don't have anything else to do."

Jonas finished his salad and got up, taking his empty

238

plate and glass to the sink. "Well, I'd sure appreciate it. I've got to get dressed now."

"Okay. I'll take it over after I finish lunch."

"Good. And thanks, Maryanne." He looked at her meaningfully; they both knew how much she had changed in regard to dealing with Sam.

Maryanne remained seated after her father left the room, slowly finishing her lunch and thinking about Sam. How little her father really knew about her feelings toward him. They were feelings she wasn't at all comfortable with; she was not sure she ever would be.

CHAPTER FIFTEEN

There was only one car parked in the small gravel lot fronting AndLan's site office and Maryanne recognized it as belonging to Joe Lancaster, but when she pushed open the door and stepped inside, no one was in sight. Then she heard Joe's voice coming from one of the back rooms, so she walked down the narrow hallway and knocked on the door. Joe was on the telephone and mouthed "hello" and waved at her to come in, so she went inside and took a seat opposite his desk.

Finishing his conversation, he hung up the receiver and greeted her with a big smile. "Well, if you aren't a sight for sore eyes. Did you come by just to see me?"

Maryanne laughed. "You know you're the main attraction around here, Joe, but sorry, not this time. Dad forgot he'd scheduled a doctor's appointment this afternoon and he was supposed to get these to Sam today." She indicated the folder she was holding. "So I volunteered to take care of it for him."

"I see. I think I know what it is . . . and Sam does need it today."

"Will he be here this afternoon?"

"There's no telling. He was here, but he's got so many irons in the fire that it's hard to know when he'll make it back." Joe scratched his jaw thoughtfully and said, "I suppose I'll just have to get in touch . . . hmmm."

"What?"

"Well, he did say something about having to drive by his house for a while. He may still be there—he just left here, about ten minutes ago."

Maryanne stood up. "Then I'll drive by," she told Joe. "And if he's not there, I'll come back and drop it off here."

"You want me to call him first and see if he's home?"

Maryanne was about to agree when the telephone rang and Joe was immediately caught up in the conversation. Maryanne waved and whispered to him that she would just go on to Sam's house, and Joe nodded.

The afternoon was cold and damp, with great heavy gray clouds moving across the sky. The weather reports were all predicting plenty of rain and Maryanne hoped it would hold off for a while longer.

Despite the foul weather, however, she felt an undeniable sense of anticipation as drove around the Loop on her way to Sam's house. It had been several weeks since she'd been there, yet in some respects it seemed like yesterday.

A tremulous thrill unexpectedly coursed down Maryanne's spine and it was impossible to ignore the fact that she had really missed him. Perhaps it was merely the Christmas season, the vague melancholy that had invaded her spirit, but she could no more deny what she felt at that moment than she could claim the sun was shining. She wanted to see him, and somehow it was a relief to admit it to herself.

The incident with Michael was insignificant by now; it didn't matter that much. She just wished she'd been able to figure out the situation earlier. Yet that, too, had taught her an invaluable lesson—she could and should trust her own instincts.

Suddenly she began to consider the possibility that her instincts were telling her something now, something she'd tried to ignore for a long time but was finally accepting as an inescapable truth—it was Sam who was worth all the time and effort she had put into her relationship with Michael. The two men were as different as night and day, and she could see now how foolish she'd been in excluding Sam from her life. It was a frightening realization, yet she had finally run out of defenses and rationalizations. Sam had been right; there *was* much more to their relationship than friendship—and it went a long, long way back.

Like a flickering ember that once again starts to expand into a beautiful glowing flame, Maryanne suddenly began to see clearly how wrong she had been to deny him, to keep him at arm's length. He deserved so much more than that. But, in all fairness, she hadn't been entirely to blame, for she had had a lot of growing and a lot of forgiving to do before reaching this point. And she had done it all on her own—that was something she wouldn't trade for anything in the world. She'd had to be true to herself first, and having accomplished all that she had during these past six months, she could finally admit that she was ready to move on.

An almost euphoric sensation swept over her as she neared the turnoff to the subdivision where Sam lived. She'd been so wrapped up in her studies, in making it through the semester in one piece, and in hanging on to her newly won state of independence, that she'd had to let the feelings she was experiencing now just simmer in the back of her mind, to be dealt with at a later time. But now that a different perspective had been reached, she recognized a readiness and willingness for something else in her life—and that included a deepening of her relationship with Sam. He'd said he loved her and that still bothered her, for she needed to take this one step at a time, needed to be completely sure of her true feelings for him, to be certain she wasn't merely reacting on the rebound. On the other hand there really hadn't been anything to rebound from. But there *was* one thing she was sure of—she felt happy, genuinely happy, for the first time in ages. And that fact alone told her all she needed to know.

A red Corvette was parked in Sam's driveway, directly behind his own Mercedes. He obviously had company, and as she pulled up behind the sports car, Maryanne let the engine idle for a moment as she debated whether or not to get out. She might be disturbing him; he was very busy, as Joe had said, and she was reluctant to interrupt or disturb anything important. On the other hand she had something important to give him, so she decided to go ahead.

She switched off the engine, buttoned up her coat, and reached for the folder that lay on the front seat. Then she got out and hurried up the flagstone sidewalk to the front door. The temperature was dropping rapidly and the frigid, damp air penetrated to the bone.

She rang the doorbell once and heard its musical chime ringing inside the house. She turned in a circle, stamping her feet as she waited, her breath forming tiny clouds of condensed air. Almost a minute went by and still no one had come to open the door, so she rang again. Still nothing. That was strange. Sam's car was in the driveway and he obviously had a visitor. Maybe he was out in back, she thought, but that would be rather odd, considering how cold it was. Nevertheless, she was just about to walk around to the back when she heard the lock click. She turned around expectantly, ready to tease Sam about his pokiness, but her smile froze, then dissipated completely as Pamela Morgan's head popped around the door, an impatient expression on her smooth, beautiful face.

"Yes?" she said, barely opening the door more than a few inches. "Can I help you?"

Maryanne could see nothing but her head, her dark hair piled loosely in a topknot. Her feet, which peeked out from between the door and the doorframe, were clad only in a pair of argyle socks. Maryanne was stunned, and her stomach did a giant, sickening flip as she swallowed convulsively. "Ah . . . Is Sam here?" she managed to say in a faltering voice.

"Yes, but he's on the telephone right now. Can I give him a message?"

"I'm Maryanne Anderson . . . Jonas Anderson's daughter." Surely Pamela knew who her father was.

But if she did, she wasn't in the least impressed, for her only reply was a muttered "Mmmm?" She could see Maryanne was shivering visibly, but that did not seem to provoke her into inviting her in either.

Finally, Maryanne said through chattering teeth, "I

244

have some papers to deliver; they're from my father." She held out her hand, indicating the folder, and Pamela's hand snaked around the door to take it from her.

"Okay. I'll give them to him."

Maryanne hesitated, stifling a crazy impulse to slap the slender, beautifully manicured hand with the folder first. But she merely handed it to her as Pamela asked, "What did you say your name was?"

"Maryanne . . . Maryanne Anderson."

"Right. I'll give him the message." And with that she simply shut the door in Maryanne's face.

Maryanne stared at it for a moment, forgetting momentarily the fact that she was almost freezing. "Of all the . . ." she muttered aloud. Then she turned abruptly and walked briskly to her car, her heart thumping furiously. When she got in and drove off, she was still shivering, and from more than just the frigid temperature.

A wave of confusion and embarrassment and disbelief almost overwhelmed her, and her eyes suddenly filmed over with a veil of tears. What in heaven's name was wrong with her? How could things like this keep happening to her? And twice in one day!

She drove ridiculously fast, having to remind herself when she reached the Loop to ease up on the accelerator. What the hell was wrong with her? She was humiliated and hurt and embarrassed for herself—all at the same time. The euphoric thoughts she'd had only minutes before had been nothing but a stupid indulgence, and all she wanted was to run away and hide. It was a childish notion, yet she had never expected to feel so hurt, so betrayed.

What a total, asinine fool she'd been again, allowing

herself to get so caught up in a fantasy. When was she ever going to grow up and face reality? She hadn't seen Sam—in how long? She couldn't even remember. Several weeks, surely. What in the world had she imagined he was doing all that time, sitting around and waiting for her to change her mind?

Spotting a highway patrolman cruising down the opposite side of the Loop, Maryanne let up on the gas pedal again; she had no idea how fast she'd been going.

When she reached her father's house, she saw his car in the garage. She'd have preferred to have the house to herself for a while; she needed a few minutes of privacy to pull herself together. On the other hand it might be better to get her mind on something else—anything else. But she found that it took an incredible effort to keep up a show of good humor when she felt so miserable. There was an edge to her voice that Jonas picked up immediately, although he said nothing.

"So, how'd it go with Dr. Sanders?"

"Oh, I've got a few more months," Jonas quipped, and Maryanne shot him a disparaging look as she hung her coat in the closet.

"A couple more centuries," she corrected. "Brrr, this place is chilly. Would you like a cup of coffee?"

"Not the real stuff," Jonas answered, changing the setting on the thermostat.

"You know me better than that, Dad. Well, what did he say?"

"Everything's great. Really. The pressure is staying where it should and the old ticker sounds terrific. I griped that I still was sleeping like Rip Van Winkle, so he made an adjustment on the dosage of one of my medications

246

And"—Jonas patted his substantially flatter stomach—"he really approved of this."

Maryanne smiled as she removed a couple of mugs from the cupboard. "You probably told him what a breeze it was to get rid of, right?"

"Of course. It wasn't any big deal. Men can always take off weight like that"—he snapped his fingers—"if they want to."

Maryanne rolled her eyes heavenward and said dryly, "Come on, Dad, spare me." She could still hear his grumbling and complaining about the new low-calorie diet she'd insisted on for him during the past few weeks. But he was only joking, and she didn't care if he wasn't, as long as he achieved the proper result.

Jonas pulled out a chair and sat down at the table, picking up the newspaper he hadn't yet had a chance to read. "Did you get that folder to Sam?"

"Mmmm. It's all taken care of." Maryanne suddenly busied herself opening the dishwasher, putting in a measure of powdered soap, and closing the door and turning it on. Jonas moved his newspaper and looked up at her when he heard the noise. He was surprised; they usually didn't turn it on until the evening. Then he watched as she opened the pantry door, removed the broom, and began sweeping the floor.

"What are you doing?" he asked. "I'll do that after a while, honey." They always shared the chores around the house, and sweeping up had always been one of his.

She barely glanced at him. "That's all right. I don't mind. There's nothing else for me to do."

Jonas looked at her a moment longer, then turned his

eyes to the newspaper again. "Well, what did he have to say?"

"Who?"

"Sam. I thought you said—"

"Oh . . . No, I didn't talk to Sam. I went by the office and Joe was there and he said I could probably catch him at home. So I drove by, but he didn't answer the door, so I gave it to . . ." She hesitated, about to say "the maid," but suddenly changed her mind. "Pamela," she finished lamely.

"Who?"

"Pamela Morgan. Isn't she still doing publicity for the company?"

Jonas lowered the newspaper and frowned slightly. "Not that I recall. I'm not up on that end of the business, but I'm pretty sure Sam fired her and hired someone else. In fact, I'm sure of it." Maryanne turned opened the door to the pantry and stepped inside to sweep it out, but Jonas caught the odd expression on her face, and suddenly it dawned on him what it was—jealousy. Interesting, he thought; surprising, but definitely interesting.

"What in the world was she doing there?" he asked.

Maryanne shrugged nonchalantly. "I have no idea," she mumbled, but the words didn't ring true and Jonas noticed that her face was flushed. There was obviously a lot going on that he'd been unaware of, and he wished once again that she felt freer about sharing her personal life with him. He hated to be in the dark like this, yet he was hesitant, as always, to probe.

She poured them both a mug of coffee, placed his on the table in front of him, and said, "I'm gonna take this back

248

to my room. I have a ton of things to straighten up and I might as well get started."

"Okay. Sure, honey."

As he watched her walk out of the room, Jonas felt a pang in his heart. He wanted so badly to know if she was really happy. She acted happy enough most of the time, but then she'd always been a good-natured child, unwilling to bother others with her problems. Still, she wasn't a child anymore. He was her father, and he wanted nothing but the best for her; she'd been through enough already.

The expression on her face when they'd talked about Sam had been obvious enough, and he wondered whether they were involved with each other, or had been. It seemed unlikely; as far as he knew, she was still seeing Michael. Suddenly he wondered what had happened in that department. It was odd, he supposed, that he knew so little about her private life when she lived right here in the same house with him. But that was the case, and neither of them had ever made a concerted effort to change things.

His thoughts returned to Sam. He'd been so furious with Pamela after that party, and a lot had happened as a result of it. Jonas had been in the office a couple of times after that when she was in Sam's office, and the words coming from that room had gotten mighty loud. After that, he didn't recall seeing or hearing from her again. As a matter of fact, Jonas remembered now, Joe had told him they'd employed another company altogether to handle the publicity for AndLan. Well, that left only one conclusion as to Pamela's presence at Sam's house today. Jonas didn't understand it. Sam just didn't seem the type to take to a woman like Pamela, good-looking as she was. But there were always other angles to a picture, he mused, and Sam surely had his reasons.

Jonas picked up his mug of coffee, suddenly remembering it was there in front of him. But he didn't drink it. He stared out the kitchen window, lost in thought, for a few more minutes. He thought of Maryanne alone in her room, feeling all . . . feeling what? Damn it, but he missed Miriam at times like these. She could have gotten it out of the girl; she always had. Then he sighed and brought the coffee mug to his lips. No use harping on it. There was one thing that would take care of whatever was troubling her—time. But he hoped it would not take too long.

Maryanne bustled around the house for the next couple of days, cleaning and turning everything upside down, and exhausting herself completely. She'd gone shopping and bought enough ingredients to keep cooking for the next year. All the while Jonas just stood back and watched her run herself ragged. He said nothing, and by the end of the week she finally wound down, for there was absolutely nothing left to do except last-minute Christmas shopping, and that she took care of in one short afternoon shopping spree, for there was only Jonas to shop for. She'd already bought and mailed presents to her aunt and uncle in San Angelo.

The holidays were really getting to her now. She'd never been alone on Christmas, except when Elliot was in Vietnam, and then she'd come home to be with her mother and father. But even at that time it had been different, for she had been married. Maryanne was plagued by thoughts of how different things were now. Michael had called and wanted to talk, but she had told him there was nothing to talk about. No, she wasn't angry, just sorry he hadn't told her he was involved with someone else; it would have made things much easier on both of them. The fact of the matter was that she simply didn't care anymore. After she'd hung up, she'd thought about the conversation for approximately two minutes and then dismissed it completely.

But she was still obsessed with thoughts of Sam and Pamela. She couldn't understand it. Sam had been so angry at Pamela the night of the party. It was just so surprising that he would continue seeing her. There must have been a compelling reason for him to do so, and Maryanne wasn't about to delude herself about what that was. Pamela was a very attractive young woman and Sam would have to have been blind not to respond to that fact. She wondered suddenly if they were sleeping together.

Don't be an idiot! Of course they are, she told herself. One couldn't expect a man like Sam to be celibate; the very thought was ridiculous. Besides, he would be a fool not to take what Pamela was obviously offering him. It was all rational and sensible, yet Maryanne was haunted that night by visions of the two of them in Sam's huge bed, making love under the skylight, with all the stars winking down on them just as they had the night *she* had shared Sam's bed.

Stop thinking about it! she told herself. But she couldn't. She was seized with an emotion that shook her to the very core and ate away at her like some terrible, dreaded cancer —jealousy, agonizing jealousy. It was like no other feeling she had experienced in her life.

It was incredible that she felt this way after all she had said about being uninvolved, and after all the strides she'd made in gaining control over her life and emotions. But she *did* feel that way—hurt and humiliated and sickened by the realization that she had waited too long and had lost the only man who'd ever really mattered to her.

CHAPTER SIXTEEN

The persistent ringing of the telephone slipped into her early morning dream, but as she was on the verge of awakening, the sound finally ceased and she relaxed again, only too willing to sink back into comfortable, trouble-free sleep. But then there came another sound, this one much louder and closer. Reluctantly, Maryanne opened her eyes, recognizing her father's knock.

"Maryanne? Are you awake?"

She shoved the hair out of her eyes and moaned softly, then turned over and closed her eyes again. "Yes."

"Can you come to the telephone? It's for you."

She asked hoarsely, "What time is it anyway?"

"Almost nine."

She frowned; she hadn't slept that long in months. "Okay. Just a minute." She started to ask who it was, but the sound of her father's footsteps had already disappeared down the hall.

She rolled off the edge of the bed and slid her feet into a pair of fluffy slippers. Then, pulling on her robe, she yawned lengthily, her fingertips rubbing the skin under her eyes. God, what a night, she thought. Why was it that when sleep finally came after a sleepness night such as last night had been, it was deepest and most peaceful during those last few minutes before one awakened? It was going to be hard to get going.

But as she made her way down the hallway to the den, she remembered that there really wasn't anything to get going for. The back door clicked shut as she reached the telephone, and she knew it was her father going outside to work on the shed. Looping a lock of hair back behind one ear, Maryanne picked up the receiver and said, "Hello?"

"Hi, Maryanne, it's me. Did I get you out of bed?"

The sound of Sam's voice ricocheted through her body like a bullet. It was totally unexpected, and suddenly she was wide awake, the emotions she had struggled so hard to overcome last night returning now full force.

She answered tightly, "Yes, as a matter of fact, I just woke up." There was a sharpness to her tone and she knew it, but she truly didn't care.

Sam was silent for a moment, but then he said tentatively, "I'm sorry. I can call back later if—"

"What did you want?"

"Well, actually it's something I suppose I could have asked Jonas. He didn't say you were still asleep." The hostility in her tone caught him off guard and he wasn't sure how to deal with it, though in a way he considered it an encouraging sign.

Maryanne said nothing, her silence forcing him to go on. "I wanted to ask what you two are doing on Christmas

254

Day. Melissa is going to be here, and Joe and Lily and I are going to cook up a storm. We'd love to have you over."

Along with Pamela Morgan? Maryanne added silently, cursing herself for the thought. "I don't know. I'll have to ask Dad," she told him.

"Of course."

"I'll tell him to give you a ring. Thanks for asking." Her tone was flat, emotionless, and Sam scrambled mentally for a way to keep her from hanging up. *Not yet,* he thought, *not until I find out for sure if what I think is bothering you really is.*

"Well, like I said, we'd love to have you. Melissa's already asked a couple of times if Jonas was going to be there. She's been boning up on her checkers game."

Enough of the big come-on, Maryanne thought irritably. What was the point of all this? "I'll tell him," she mumbled. It took an extreme effort to remain polite, especially when she didn't feel that way in the least, but she forced herself to do it. However, she had no intention of standing in the chilly den in her nightgown and robe much longer, so she said, "Well, if that's all—"

"Actually, it's not," Sam cut in quickly. "I wanted to thank you for bringing over the documents for your father the other day. They were very important."

"It was no problem," Maryanne said, recalling vividly how long she'd had to stand freezing on his front porch until Pamela finally came to the door.

"I'm sorry I wasn't able to ask you in," Sam apologized, feeling all over again his anger on learning Maryanne had been there; Pamela hadn't told him about it until yesterday. She'd called last night, having suddenly remembered, she claimed, that "some woman" had stopped by the other

255

day to drop off a folder. She'd told Sam where it was and he'd almost chewed her out on the spot, but he'd stopped himself—what good would it have done at that point? He'd assumed Jonas was still looking over the bids; if he'd known they were there in his house, he could have gotten to them a day and a half ago. He'd stayed up late into the night as a result of her careless forgetfulness. Damn, but she was aggravating; he didn't know why in the world he'd decided to give her a second chance and listen to the new proposal she'd worked up for AndLan. He supposed he'd felt sorry for her, and she'd come across so sincerely and had sounded so contrite that he'd agreed to hear her out. But after this he'd given up completely and had let her know right then and there that she was finished.

"I had to get back home anyway," Maryanne was saying, her mind filled with visions of what *had* kept him from coming to the door that day.

"Well, I wish I'd known you were there." He paused, then changed the subject. "Say, how were final exams? Did you make it through all right?"

"Yes, everything turned out very well." She wished he didn't feel the need to continue the chitchat and searched her mind for a handy way to get off the phone.

Sensing her intention to hang up, Sam decided to take the plunge and ask her what he'd *really* called to ask. "Ah . . . I was wondering, what are you doing tonight?"

Maryanne was surprised by the unexpected question and blurted out the first evasive words that came to mind, unconvincing ones, to say the least. "I'm pretty busy, actually. Why do you ask?" Damn it, why in the world had she said *that*?

"I'd like to take you out to dinner," Sam said. "If you can work it in, that is."

Now that's a new one, she thought. *Why ask me for a date now—of all times?* "I'll be pretty busy. Thank you, but I don't think so."

"How about tomorrow?"

She felt her resistance to him weakening. It was simply so good to hear his voice again. She missed him. But then she remembered Pamela—lovely, *barefoot* Pamela. The thought gave her the strength she needed to refuse. She gave a short sigh and said, "There's no point to it, Sam. Look, let's not get into that sort of thing, all right?"

"I don't know what you mean by 'that sort of thing.' All I—"

"Listen, the doorbell's ringing. I'll have Dad call you back about Christmas Day, all right? Good-bye." She hung up abruptly and stared at her hand, which was still grasping the receiver—it was shaking visibly. She hated doing things like that, cutting people off, inventing fake excuses. She hated fake anything. A huge part of her life had been nothing but a fake and she certainly wanted no more of that. And despite her feelings of disappointment in him, she felt bad doing this to Sam. But he'd gotten pretty persistent there, and she didn't want to give him another chance. *Chicken,* a voice badgered at her. So, all right, she was chicken, but she had no intention of getting into a situation that was risky at best. She simply wasn't a fighter in matters of this sort; if Sam still was seeing Pamela, and he had every right in the world to do so, then Maryanne would back off. He either wanted to be with her or he didn't, and she had no desire to help him make up his mind.

The irony of the situation struck her in a sad sort of way—after finally having reached the point where she would have *willingly, happily* accepted Sam's invitation, her decision now was to avoid seeing him altogether. Her hand dropped from the receiver and she brought both palms up to her face, rubbing it wearily. She trudged back to her bedroom and gathered up her around-the-house uniform—a pair of old, soft jeans, a blue woolen pullover, and a pair of thick argyle socks. Then she went into the bathroom, undressed and pulled her hair into a top knot, and stepped into the tub and turned on the shower. She closed her eyes and turned around, her back tingling with the steady pelt of steaming water. It felt wonderful, restorative, and it was easy to let her mind go blank for a few precious moments.

So what *was* she going to do today, she wondered, reaching for the bar of soap. She should have gotten a job to get her through the long days ahead. But it was too late now, and anyway, that really wasn't what she wanted to do. But she did need something, anything, to help her shake off this nagging depression that had settled over her.

She spent an inordinate amount of time in the shower, but it was worth it; she did feel a little better. She got out and dressed, deciding to leave her hair the way it was. On the sloppy side, maybe, but definitely more practical.

The enticing aromas of coffee brewing and bread toasting perked up her appetite, and she began to feel a little more human. Jonas was whistling when she walked into the kitchen.

"Mmmm, toast smells delicious," Maryanne commented, taking two coffee mugs from the cupboard and pouring them each some coffee.

"That's because it is—or will be. Have a seat; I'll have it on the table in a second."

"All right." Maryanne dropped down on the padded cushion of the dinette chair and reached for the morning paper. She glanced at the headlines and cover stories, decided they were much too depressing, and thumbed through until she found the leisure section. It was nice and thick, as it usually was on Saturday morning, filled with all sorts of perky, informative articles about weekend happenings in the area, plus a few routine human-interest stories. She was struck by an idea suddenly and said, "Hmmm. You know . . ."

"What are you mumbling about?" Jonas asked, setting their plates on the table.

"I was just thinking, they ought to write up something about AndLan in this section. You know, something like 'AndLan Enterprises brings welcome development to Nacogdoches.' "

Jonas sat down and pulled his napkin onto his lap, cocking his head to one side in contemplation. "Not a bad idea. Not bad at all," he said as he buttered his toast and applied a low-sugar jam. He offered the jar to Maryanne. "Want some?"

"No, I'll take honey."

"*You* ought to try it, Maryanne. I'll bet you'd be good at it."

"What?"

"The article for the newspaper."

Maryanne laughed lightly and shook her head. "Come on, Dad, I'm not a writer."

"You could give it a try. It would give you something to do over the holidays."

Maryanne's smile faded somewhat and she busied herself with putting honey on her toast. His suggestion was revealing; he'd obviously picked up on her bored, depressed mood, though she'd tried her best to conceal it. "I've got plenty to do, Dad. But maybe you should check it out."

"I agree. I'll bring it up with Sam."

She said nothing to that, but Jonas caught the expression that flitted across her features. He'd hit a sore spot there. He knew her well enough by now to be able to read her moods; she was still upset about something and it had to do with Sam—there was no doubt of that. He wished with all his heart he knew what it was, but was as reluctant as ever to try to sound her out on the subject.

"So what are *you* going to do today?" she asked in a bright tone of voice.

"Well, thought I'd go by Holloway's and see what kind of trees they've got that don't cost an arm and a leg. Want to come along?"

Maryanne thought it over. It would probably do her good to get out in the open for a while, but looking for a Christmas tree was the last thing in the world she felt like doing right now.

"I thought I would stay here and drag down the ornament boxes. Are they still in the same place in the attic?"

"They might be shoved back in a corner since I moved some things around up there. You'll have to look around a little." He took a bite of toast, chewed and swallowed it, then said, "I hope you're planning to do most of the decorating."

Maryanne smiled as she remembered the sight of her father grumbling and griping every Christmas, his large

260

hands hopelessly attempting to sort out the confusion of satin balls, tangled hooks, miniature lights, and ropes of silver and gold tinsel. "I sure am," she said. "I'm not about to let you mess everything up."

"You're not hurtin' my feelings one bit by saying that, believe me. All right, we've got a deal. I get the tree, you get everything else ready. You want to do it tonight?"

"Sure, why not?"

There was no indication in her tone—or so she hoped—of the melancholy that rushed over her just then. It should be a fun thing, trimming the tree—with lots of people and laughter and singing . . . But it wasn't going to be that way and the image of her and Jonas alone, trying to pretend everything was perfectly fine, was depressing and sad. She should be happy, of course, that they were both well and had each other. But that wasn't the way she felt at all. She swallowed the last of her toast, the action requiring an enormous effort for a lump had formed in the back of her throat. She was ashamed of being so childish. She couldn't, she *wouldn't* let him see her like this, so once again the happy face reappeared, and by the time her father got ready and was on his way out the door, Maryanne had managed to convince him—or so she thought—that everything was all right.

She stood at the kitchen window, watching him drive off and desperately fighting back the tears welling up in her eyes. But it was hopeless and the next second they brimmed over her lower lids and streamed down her cheeks. Her shoulders heaved in misery and her chest felt as if someone had carved a huge hole in the middle of it. *Ridiculous,* she chided herself, wiping her cheeks with a dry dish towel. *Get yourself together.*

She drew a deep, shaky breath and let it out slowly, and after a few minutes managed to gain a measure of composure over her runaway emotions. She walked back into the den and stood in the middle of it, hands shoved down into the back pockets of her jeans. Weak—she always felt weak after crying. *Ah, well, so what. Put your mind on something else and you'll feel better in no time.* It was a simple cliché, one her mother had been fond of using, but it had worked often enough to make Maryanne decide to give it a try.

Her gaze came to rest on the area in front of the bay window. It would be the best place for the tree; there was an electrical outlet nearby and it would look pretty from the front of the house. But she'd have to move her father's lounge chair first, which wasn't such an easy job; it weighed a ton. She could wait, she supposed, until he got home to help her, but suddenly she wanted to give it a try. She only managed to move it a few feet, but the physical exertion involved was just what she needed and soon her thoughts were channeled into another, more welcome direction.

When she finally stopped, unable to move it farther, she placed her hands on her lower back and arched her spine. Then she walked into the hallway, pulled the string to release the attic ladder, and flipped on the light switch. She climbed the wooden steps and stepped onto the solid plywood flooring that extended throughout the entire attic. Her gaze scanned the conglomeration of old furniture and dusty boxes crammed close together, searching for the cartons of Christmas decorations. Finally she spotted an open cardboard box with the tip of a giant silver star poking out of one corner. She made her way to it, pushed back her sleeves, and started pulling out the various boxes, bringing them one by one down the wooden stairs. She was in the process of moving the fifth and heaviest box when the doorbell rang.

"Now, who in the . . ." she muttered aloud, tucking back a wisp of hair and inadvertently smudging her cheek with dust. At first she thought her father had forgotten something, but Jonas had his key; he wouldn't need to ring the doorbell.

The mailman, more than likely, with something she had to sign for, she thought. Sighing, she climbed back down the stairs, accidentally catching the side of her jeans on a bottom hinge. But she saw it too late and when she stepped down onto the floor, the denim ripped loudly.

"Damn," she muttered, examining the tear, which would certainly require a patch. The doorbell rang again and she called out in an irritated tone of voice, "Just a *minute*. I'm coming!"

She shook her head in disgust as she unlocked the front door, but when she opened it, she suddenly froze. Her green eyes widened in genuine surprise as she said, "Sam. Wha—"

He was dressed as casually as she was, in jeans and Wellingtons and a tan-and-brown parka. His dark hair was blowing in every direction in the brisk wind. "Can I come in?" His nose and cheeks were bright red and his eyes watery, and Maryanne suddenly drew back to avoid the chilly gust of wind that whipped around the door.

"Dad just left. He won't be back for a while."

But Sam took advantage of the open door and walked right in, saying, "That's all right. I didn't come to see him."

Maryanne frowned, shocked by his uncharacteristic

263

boldness. Still, it was too cold to leave the door open, so she shut it and remained standing next to it, as if she were waiting for him to leave.

"Well, what did you come for?" It was very difficult for her to pretend she was unaffected by his presence. His boots had added a few inches to his already considerable height, and standing there with only her socks on, she felt overwhelmingly small and vulnerable—which only made her frown deepen, a vain attempt to appear annoyed and impatient.

Sam's gaze slowly lingered over the sight of her; to his way of thinking, her disheveled appearance was sexy as hell. He saw her flinch at his look and the reaction was an encouraging one to him. He knew well enough how she could respond to him, and he wasn't about to be taken in by her ruse of indifference. Not now. Unzipping his parka, he said truthfully, "I came to see you."

Maryanne chewed at a corner of her mouth and crossed her arms over her chest. "I see," she said carefully, "but I can't think of anything you could add to what you told me on the phone."

Sam's dark-brown eyes bored into hers and Maryanne felt a quivering inside. "There's plenty I didn't say," he told her slowly. He looked over his shoulder into the den, saw the chair she'd managed to drag halfway across the room, and then spotted the lowered attic ladder farther down the hall.

"What's going on around here?"

Wishing he'd just leave, Maryanne quickly said, "I'm getting the decorations down for the tree. Dad's down at Holloway's looking for one." Something was wrong here, she thought. The quivering sensation hadn't stopped; it had only expanded to a disturbing excitement. She didn't need this, not one bit. Carefully controlling her voice, she asked, "So what is it, Sam? I have a lot to do, as you can see."

He turned back to her. "This is what's keeping you so busy, I take it."

"That's right."

He reached up and pushed a lock of dark hair off his forehead. Then he asked, "Is there any reason we can't sit down for a minute? I want to talk to you, Maryanne."

She opened her mouth to voice some sort of objection, but he cut her off. "And don't tell me you don't want to, or you don't have time. It's important."

She clenched her teeth for a second, then sighed heavily and walked past him into the den. Sitting down on the love seat, she motioned him with one outstretched arm toward the couch. "All right, sit down."

Unhurriedly he took off his parka and placed it on the arm of the couch. Then he sat down. The red-and-black plaid flannel shirt he wore suited him very well, enhancing his rugged, outdoorsy good looks. He pulled at the knees of his jeans, easing them up somewhat over his boots, then leaned forward slightly, resting his elbows on his thighs and linking his hands together loosely.

"Okay. First of all, I want to know why you came by my house the other day."

Maryanne looked at him skeptically. "You know why. I had to drop off some papers for Dad."

"That's all?"

Something in the way he asked the question cut through her defenses and she hesitated, crossed one leg over the other casually, and swung it nervously a few times before giving him a guileless look. "Of course that's all."

"I don't believe you."

She uttered a hollow chuckle and shrugged one shoulder. "Suit yourself. Why are you making such a big deal out of it, anyway?"

"I'm not dating her." He was staring straight at her and Maryanne was clearly taken aback.

She blinked and said, "What?"

"I said I'm not dating her, or seeing her, or whatever you want to call it."

"What, or who, may I ask, are you talking about?"

But he knew she knew, for her face had that same old telltale flush that he recognized so well. "Pamela Morgan."

Her heart did a flip-flop and she struggled for an appropriate response. "Oh . . . her. Well, fine. But I don't know why you feel it necessary to tell me."

"Are you sure about that?" He was betting heavily that she wasn't sure at all. He'd sensed something—how or why, he had no idea—and it was the strongest intuitive feeling he had ever experienced. He was willing to risk everything on the hunch that there *had* been a change in her—a very big one indeed.

Suddenly, Maryanne got up and crossed the room to the bay window, pulling back the curtain to look outside. She turned around abruptly and said, "Look, Sam, you're making a mountain out of a molehill as far as I'm concerned. Whether or not you're dating Pamela is none of my business—or my concern."

His eyes stared directly into hers and there was such an intensity in them that she found it impossible to break the

266

connection. "She was only there on business." he told her firmly.

Maryanne shrugged again and turned her back to him. "Fine."

His voice boomed across the room, causing her to whip around in surprise. "Damn it, Maryanne, let's cut the games! I know something is bothering you, and I've been praying to God it was the fact that you saw another woman at my house, a woman you believed I was still seeing. It bothered you, admit it!"

That did it. Suddenly all the emotion she'd kept so carefully under control unleashed itself. "Yes. All right," she answered curtly, "it bothered me. But only to the extent that I hated to see you get all involved with someone so obviously not your type. Looks like Sissy all over again to me."

"Fortunately, I deserve a little more credit than that." He took a few steps across the room, moving to within a few feet of where she stood, and they looked at each other in silence for a moment.

And suddenly the question just popped out of her mouth. "Well, then, what *was* she doing there?"

"She'd come to show me a proposal. She's wanted to come back ever since I dismissed her from AndLan, and I finally agreed to hear her out. As I said, the visit was strictly business."

Maryanne raised her eyebrows and said, "I didn't know business meetings were conducted without shoes."

Sam frowned and Maryanne said, "That's how she came to the door—no shoes, only socks. You must admit it looked . . . well, rather casual."

"Would you believe me if I told you I didn't even notice? I have no idea why she would have taken her shoes off."

His confused expression was genuine and Maryanne believed him. Suddenly the triviality of what they were saying was almost amusing—all the emotion, all her anger had boiled down to this, a discussion of socks. A sense of profound relief washed over her as the whole situation suddenly became clear. The spark of hope that had burned down to a tiny ember now leaped into a flame of anticipation as it dawned on her what was happening; he was saying the very words she had longed to hear. But it was happening so fast—it couldn't be real.

He closed the space between them and placed his hands on her shoulders, his gaze penetrating her own. "Tell me that I'm right, Maryanne," he said in a low, vibrant voice. Her eyes focused on his muscular neck, and her sudden impulse to place her lips there was almost overwhelming. She shifted her gaze, staring across the room over his shoulder. "Tell me it's time now," he said quietly, his fingers pressing on her shoulders, making her look at him directly.

One corner of her mouth quivered slightly and her green eyes were mirrors of all the suffering, all the past pain that had stood between them for so long. Yet there was something more there, something he had never seen before, and his stomach contracted with hope.

"I . . . I don't know what to say," she said in a small voice.

"Just tell me how you feel, Maryanne. No lies, no defenses or pretenses. Just what *you* really want now." He paused and said, "You know how I feel about you, Maryanne. The same as always. It will never change."

She lowered her head slightly, her gaze traveling down to his chin, then back up to meet his eyes. Something was happening inside her, some wonderful, marvelous feeling that she could not recall having felt before. She stood very still, listening intently to what he was saying.

"I know you've been through a lot, Maryanne, a hell of a lot. But time has passed—not very much, I admit, but enough for me to know I can't go on forever not having you. I love you, and I'd give anything to hear you say those words to me, but I'll understand if you can't. All I want to know is if we can try. I've got to know at least that much."

There was a pleading in his tone that touched her deeply, and she knew then that she couldn't stand the thought of ever hearing it in his voice again.

She brought her hands up to the sides of his neck, sliding them around to caress the back of his neck. And then she nodded and a beautiful smile of happiness spread slowly across her entire face as she said softly, "Yes. I think it is time, Sam. You asked me what I want. Well, I want to be with you, *really* be with you. I'm tired of the games too." She sighed softly. "We're too old for that sort of thing, you know."

His arms slid around her back and he nuzzled his face against the top of her head. "You'll never be too old for me," he muttered thickly, pulling her to him tightly, their bodies responding immediately to the physical contact both had been denied so long.

And then he moved his hands up to hold her head

between his hands as his lips moved down to meet hers. Maryanne's eyes closed as she submitted to the wondrous physical reality, the deep fulfillment of the moment. *That same magic,* a tiny voice whispered in the back of her mind, and deep inside she knew it was true. It was the only magic she had ever known. She kissed him back with all the pent-up fervor she had restrained for so long, communicating as no words ever could her willingness to try once again.

Sam stayed the rest of the afternoon and helped to decorate the tree Jonas brought home. Jonas hid his surprise at seeing Sam and Maryanne sitting in the middle of the den, unpacking the boxes of decorations, but it was a sight for sore eyes to see Maryanne smiling and laughing again.

Maryanne popped some corn and made a pitcher of Jager tea—her specialty, she called it—and it was a full two hours before they had everything done. The den looked beautiful. The Christmas tree glimmered and twinkled, and as the three of them stood appraising their work from the kitchen, Maryanne remarked, "Not bad, huh?"

"Not at all," Jonas agreed, sipping the remainder of his hot rum drink.

"How about going out to dinner with us, Jonas?" Sam proposed.

"Nah, I'm kind of pooped out from all this," Jonas said with a smile. "Anyway, there's a movie on cable I've been waiting for. I think I'll just stick around and watch it."

"Well, all right," Sam said, turning to Maryanne. "Do you want me to come back for you or—?"

"If you don't mind staying a few minutes longer, I'll get ready now."

"Sure. Your father and I have a few things to discuss anyway."

Maryanne started for her bedroom, calling happily over her shoulder, "All right. I won't be too long."

But there was no dinner that night. After Maryanne finished dressing, Sam drove her to his house so that he could shower and dress first. It was early evening, but darkness had descended already and the two of them hurried from the garage into the house.

"Brrr—it's freezing," Maryanne said, her teeth chattering as she waited for Sam to unlock the back door.

"Aw, come on, it's not that bad," Sam teased, shutting the door behind them. "You're just a big baby."

"I am not!" she objected, laughing as he pulled her by the coat toward him. "And don't yank on my coat."

"You are cold, aren't you?" he asked softly.

"Yes, but—"

"Then come here and let me make you warm."

Suddenly he reached around her, placed his arms under her buttocks, and lifted her off her feet, throwing her over his shoulder easily and starting toward the hallway. Maryanne exclaimed in surprise and straightened her back, pounding his head with her fists. "Put me down, you big dummy," she yelled, but he kept on walking, carrying her as easily as a football. "You're going to break your back, Sam, slip a disc, dislocate your shoulder. What— Where are—"

"Will you quit yapping and keep still. Lord, a man can't even be a little chivalrous these days."

271

Maryanne laughed outright as he rounded a corner and headed down a shorter hallway toward his bedroom. "You call this chivalry? Prehistoric brute force is what I—"

Sam reached the bed and hesitated only a second before bending forward and dropping her onto the middle of it. She bounced once and then again as he, too, fell onto the green and beige comforter next to her. Maryanne loved the silliness of the moment and egged him on by pinching and tickling him.

But her tactics only served to make Sam quickly forget the playfulness he'd started. Rolling onto his side, he propped himself up on his elbow and rested his head in the palm of his hand. He looked at her with such tenderness and longing that Maryanne felt something melt within her. She smiled at him, a wistful, sad sort of smile that said all the things she couldn't yet say—that she was sorry for all the wasted months, the lack of trust, the time she had needed to be alone and to find herself again.

But her smile was enough for Sam, and as he said once more, "I love you, Maryanne," he bent his head to hers, touching her mouth with his, slipping his tongue between her lips, and meeting her tongue as it invited him into the depths of her waiting kiss.

And this, the beginning of their second physical union, was everything and more than their first had been. There was no haste now, only loving, tempered restraint as they slowly and tantalizingly rediscovered each other. Finally, Sam rolled out of bed, crossed the room, and turned off the light. Then he returned to the side of the bed and stood there watching Maryanne. Her honey-blond hair glistened with platinum highlights in the moonlight streaming down through the skylight. He began undressing as he stared at her, and watching him, Maryanne experienced a liquid rush of excitement. She sat up, lifted her arms above her head, and removed her sweater, her blouse, and then her bra. Sam knelt beside her, accepting her garments one by one as she removed them, and placing them on the back of a nearby chair. Then he pulled back the comforter and they both slid under it, clinging to one another for warmth against the chill sheets.

They kissed, and as Maryanne felt his turgid manhood against her thigh, she moaned softly, the most beautiful sound in the world to him. Moving her arms from around his neck, Sam placed one on either side of the pillow under her head and with a whispered "Shhh . . ." bid her lie still.

She closed her eyes and felt him moving above her, wanting him so badly she nearly cried out. Slowly, methodically, he traced a trail of hot probing kisses along her smooth skin, his tongue caressing her throat, her breasts, her midriff, and her lower abdomen. When his head dipped even lower, she suddenly couldn't stand it another second. Her hands grasped the back of his neck and she gasped, "Please, Sam . . . don't wait."

He lifted his head, his heart pounding fiercely in response to the passion she had ignited within him. And he did as she bid him, raising himself above her to enter her, groaning in pure ecstasy as her womanly warmth surrounded and engulfed him. He moved within her slowly at first, but her hands kneaded the taut flesh of his buttocks, demanding more of him until he could hold back no longer. His body drove into hers furiously and rapidly, and as she wrapped her legs around him, she cried out, her climax pulsing and spreading through her loins with an intensity that equaled the enormous shudder rippling through him, spilling over into her.

And as they lay spent, the heat of their passion at last sated, Sam felt as if his soul had opened up to welcome hers.

CHAPTER SEVENTEEN

Sam's house was alive with sounds, all of them happy. Traditional Christmas songs played on the stereo system mingled with talking, playfully arguing, and laughing voices. It was the laughter Maryanne loved most, laughter born of genuine mirth and good will.

"Melissa, do you want to help me in the kitchen for a minute, honey?" Lily was standing in the doorway of the library, where Jonas and the young girl were hunched over a table playing yet another game of checkers. Neither of them said a word.

"Well, I guess I know the answer to that already," Lily answered herself, shaking her head and smiling.

Jonas glanced up and told her in a serious tone, "We've got a pretty important game going here."

"I can see that," Lily said, winking as she indicated the dark brown head bent so solemnly, chin resting on his fist, blue eyes narrowed in fierce concentration. "Well, I hope you two wind that up in a few minutes. We're almost ready to eat."

"Just give a holler," Jonas said, turning back to see that he'd just lost his king. "What! Now, how did you do that? Cheatin' behind my back?"

Melissa laughed delightedly and exclaimed, "I did not. You looked away, that's your fault."

Lily chuckled and left for the kitchen. Joe was leaning against the refrigerator with a glass of Scotch on the rocks in one hand, happily watching the goings-on around him.

Lily hustled into the room, clucked her tongue as she saw Joe, and said to Sam and Maryanne, "Look at him, would you? Drinking up all Sam's good liquor and standing around getting in the way."

"I'm directing traffic," Joe said calmly, taking another swig of his drink. "There are so many chefs in here, *somebody* has to supervise things."

Sam and Maryanne chuckled as Lily sent him one of her notorious withering looks. But Joe only stuck out his tongue playfully at his wife and sauntered over to the table.

"Where are the dynamic-duo checker players?" Sam asked Lily, busy carving the ham with an electric knife.

"Still at it. They're about to finish up, Jonas assures me. I told him we were almost ready."

"Good." Sam stopped what he was doing, turned around, and sipped from the spoon Maryanne was holding up to his lips.

"What do you think?" she asked hopefully.

Sam smacked his lips loudly, narrowed his eyes, and then declared in a somber voice, "Very good. You're learning, kiddo, you're learning."

"Oh, go away, Sam. I'm a much better cook than you are any day," Maryanne insisted cheerfully.

Lily placed her hands on her aproned hips and asked her husband, "What's with these Lancasters and Andersons? They're either griping at each other or totally inseparable. I don't understand it."

"I don't either, dear, but don't discourage it. Whatever it is they've got is good for the business."

The mild teasing continued as everyone, except Joe, who continued to nurse his drink happily and "supervise," finished the preparation of the meal that was to be their Christmas feast.

And feast it was! The long dining room table was brimming with an assortment of meats and gravies, vegetables and dressings, and several types of bread. The leftovers would last each family for weeks, Maryanne thought as she sat next to Sam, enjoying every single minute of this wonderful day. How different it was from Thanksgiving, she mused; as nice as that occasion had been, this was a far more intimate and joyful day. It was as though they'd all been close friends forever. But the real reason for her joy was Sam.

The past week had been absolutely wonderful; the melancholy she'd fought so hard to dispel had vanished completely. She and Sam had been seeing one another as many minutes out of the day as possible since that day they had set up the Christmas tree. Dinner had been completely forgotten in their eagerness to consumate their love; and afterward they'd fed their ravenous appetites with a snack of wine and crackers and cheese, each dressed in one of Sam's dressing gowns.

Sam had taken her home afterward and since Jonas was

already in bed, no explanations for her lateness had been necessary. But Sam had shown up at nine o'clock the next morning and Jonas was indeed surprised. Sam explained that he was there to pick up Maryanne and that they were going to meet Melissa at the airport in Houston and would be back later that day. Jonas had waved good-bye to them as they drove off in Sam's car, a smug grin on his face. Love, he thought, what a wonderful thing it was. And it couldn't have happened to two nicer or more deserving people.

Melissa had bounced off the airplane with a smile on her face, jumping up and wrapping her arms around her father's neck. Then she'd quite unabashedly kissed Maryanne. Maryanne had blinked back the film of tears that suddenly rose in her eyes, almost overwhelmed by the rush of emotion that washed over her. Halfway home they'd stopped to eat at a home-style café and Melissa chattered on and on about what school had been like and how she hoped she wouldn't have the same teacher and how glad she was to leave "ugly old Chicago."

"Chicago's not ugly, honey," Sam had told her as they started in on dessert.

"It is too," Melissa insisted with a pout. She looked at him with her big blue eyes and said bluntly, "I wish I didn't have to live there. I wish I could live here with you, Daddy."

Maryanne had seen the pained expression in Sam's eyes and looked away. Her heart went out to him at that moment, and for the first time in a very long while she thought of Elliot. How could it be that he and Sam had once been the best of friends? There had to have been something they shared in common—youth, probably. If it

278

had been anything more, it could only have been superficial, for the two of them were like night and day. She couldn't imagine Elliot capable of loving a child the way Sam loved his daughter, or capable of the hurt Sam felt in being separated from his only child.

They'd talked about it a couple of days later at Sam's house. "Yeah, it's tough," he admitted bluntly. "It's the worst thing about divorce."

"Have you ever thought of trying for total custody?"

"Sure. It's *all* I think about. But it would never work. Sissy would never give her up."

"Melissa doesn't sound happy, though," Maryanne persisted.

Sam sighed. "She's not as bad off as it sounds. It's hard on her, though, having to adjust to a stepfather. I really hate seeing her have to go through all this."

Maryanne felt really sorry for him; as much as she'd wanted children, she could see how relatively uncomplicated her own divorce had been because there had been none involved. "What will you do?" she asked finally.

Sam shrugged. "Keep on going like we have been. There's nothing else to do. I hope, I pray, that time will help. She'll get used to the situation. Maybe Sissy will relent some too. I don't know. We'll just have to wait and see."

"Well, I'm glad she's here for the holidays. That's what Christmas is all about, really. Children."

Sam smiled and kissed the top of her head. "Yeah, and you, too, as far as I'm concerned." His hands slid through her hair and he bent his head to kiss her fervently on the mouth, drawing back to say, "There's only one thing wrong with having Melissa here, though."

"What?"

"It kind of limits our physical activity, you know?"

Maryanne's eyes sparkled. "Want to check into a motel for a couple of hours?" she teased.

"That's not such a bad idea," Sam responded. "Get your coat—let's go."

He made as if to stand up, but Maryanne laughed and tugged at his arm, pulling him back down beside her on the couch. "Come on, Sam. You're forgetting your daughter will be back in a few minutes."

Sam slumped down on the couch, spreading his arm out behind her. "Oh, yeah. Well, we'll just have to wait. You know, I couldn't have hired a better sitter than your father."

Maryanne laughed. "Isn't it the truth? You know, Sam, he's having the time of his life with Melissa."

"I've forgotten—where were they headed today?"

"He took her into Lufkin to see the original Snow White movie. Tomorrow they're going bowling. He's really having a ball."

Sam's expression sobered as he looked steadily at her. "I know a way to make him even happier."

"What's that?"

"You could marry me, you know, and before long he could have another kid to entertain—his own grandchild."

Some of the brightness in her eyes faded and she looked down at her hands. "Oh, Sam . . . I wish . . ."

"You wish what?"

She sighed. "I wish you wouldn't say things like that."

"Why not? I mean it. I want to marry you, Maryanne.

And I think that if you were completely honest with yourself, you would agree it's what you want too."

She plucked gently at the tweed material of her slacks and said, "The timing's not right."

Sam's heart did a little somersault; it wasn't the answer he wanted to hear, but she hadn't refused, either. "What would be the purpose in waiting, Maryanne? We've known each other forever. It's not as though we need years to find out if it's the right thing."

"I know, but . . ."

"But what?"

She looked up at him with a pleading expression. "I can't just abandon everything I've accomplished, Sam. I'm enjoying college. For the first time in my life I've done something for myself, and I don't want to stop when I've just begun."

"Who's saying you'd have to stop? I would never stand in your way, Maryanne. You know that."

She swallowed deeply and glanced away again. She knew Sam, and recognized the vast differences there would be in living with him compared to living with the man she'd chosen before. Yet it was still frightening to face the realities of marrying again, the changes there would be in her life. They were talking marriage here, a very serious matter to her. She didn't look at things the way she had when she was eighteen years old; love was not the cement adhesive that held a commitment together forever, and she told him as much.

Sam looked at her as she said it, his fingers lightly stroking the silky sheen of her hair. Gradually his lips spread into a smile and he asked softly, "Am I to understand by that, Miss Anderson, that you love me?"

281

Her green eyes shimmered as she met his gaze, and then she nodded, almost imperceptibly. "I haven't told you that?"

Sam shook his head and Maryanne smiled gently at him. "Well, I do. I do love you, Sam Lancaster." And with the words came a warmth that spread through her veins, filling her with a peace and contentment that warmed and soothed her soul.

Sam kissed her once more and said softly, "You have no idea how long I've waited to hear you say those words."

Maryanne wrapped her arms around his neck and laid her head against his chest, loving the familiar smell of him, the touch of his body against hers. "I'm sorry it took me so long."

"There's only one thing that will make me even happier," he said gently.

"What if I promise to think about it?"

Sam drew back, grasped her by the shoulders, his brown eyes searching her own. "Do you mean that?"

Maryanne nodded and once more he held her to him, locking her within his protective embrace.

And she did think about it; indeed, she thought of nothing else for the next three days. But by Christmas Day there were no doubts left, no questions to resolve. There was a special glow, a sense of being totally alive that filled her completely. And as they sat around the table after Christmas dinner, she felt the glow expanding to an all-encompassing warmth drawing in these dear, lovely people who had become her family now.

Melissa had opened some of her presents the first thing that morning, but Sam had set the rest aside for the afternoon when everyone was there. The little girl declared herself in charge, and as she bustled about with an authoritative air, distributing the presents among the adults, Maryanne felt a lump rise in her throat. No present could ever measure up to the gift of love she felt radiating from those around her.

The gifts she received were especially meaningful this year, and she was touched most of all by her father's present. He had given her a delicate gold wristwatch, simply inscribed on the back, "I'm here for you." Her own gift to him was less glamorous but he was no less touched by her thoughtfulness when he unwrapped a Black & Decker electric chain saw to replace his old broken one. Jonas was delighted and declared that he was going to give it a try as soon as he got home.

"And you can try it out right here, Jonas," Sam said. "I've been meaning to cut up that pine that blew down last week, but I haven't gotten around to it."

"I'm ready when you are," Jonas said, and everyone laughed.

Maryanne finished opening her presents and was thanking Lily and Joe for theirs when Melissa piped up, "You forgot one!"

"I did?"

"Yeah, it's a little one—right there next to you."

Maryanne picked up a small box wrapped in silver paper and red ribbon and taped to a huge white envelope. Carefully she detached the box and removed the card.

"Read it out loud," Melissa demanded, and suddenly everyone's attention was drawn to Maryanne. She swallowed and looked over at Sam, her eyes suddenly filling with tears.

Then she read it aloud, finding it difficult to do because

283

of the enormous lump in her throat. " 'Whenever you're ready, you can put this on. I know it can happen for us . . . All in good time. Love, Sam.' "

She fumbled with the red ribbon, finally got the box open, and then gasped at the beautiful diamond solitaire that lay on a bed of black velvet. "Oh, Sam," she breathed, her heart swelling with love for him.

Lily got up and came over to look at the ring, oohing and aahing with everyone else. But Maryanne heard none of it. She couldn't take her blurred gaze from Sam. She blinked once and he came back into focus, and she knew right then and there that there could be no other answer.

"I don't think it's necessary to wait any longer, do you?" she asked.

And as Sam shook his head, she removed the ring and slid it onto her finger. Melissa jumped up and down, clapping her hands, and everyone noisily congratulated the two of them.

Sam hardly heard a word and just hoped he was giving the right answers. Finally he walked over to Maryanne and held his hand out to her. She took it gladly and allowed him to help her up. And then Sam kissed her with unabashed passion.

"No doubts?" he asked her sotto voce, and she shook her head, smiling up at him, her green eyes more beautiful than ever.

"None whatsoever, Mr. Lancaster."

Jonas stood watching them from the other side of the room, thinking how lucky they were to have found each other and how grateful he was to see his daughter happy at last. And he thought about Miriam. How she would

284

have loved to see this. But there was no sadness in the thought this time, only a good, proud feeling that he'd handled this one the right way. Granted, he hadn't done much, except be there for her, but maybe that was what it was all about.

LOOK FOR NEXT MONTH'S
CANDLELIGHT ECSTASY SUPREMES ®

CANDLELIGHT
Ecstasy Supreme

Candlelight
Ecstasy Romances™

$1.95 each

At your local bookstore or use this handy coupon for ordering

DELL BOOKS
P.O. BOX 1000, PINE BROOK, N.J. 07058-1000   B194B

Please send me the books I have checked above I am enclosing $_____ (please add 75¢ per copy to cover postage and handling) Send check or money order no cash or C.O.D.s Please allow up to 8 weeks for shipment

Name_____

Address_____

City_____ State/Zip_____